D1527353

This novel is a work of fiction. The characters names, incidents, dialog and plot are products of the author's imagination or are used fictiously. Any resemblance to actual persons, companies or events is purely coincidental.

DEDICATION

To my wife Carolyn and my sons Timothy and Michael for their
unwavering support of anything I attempt.

"High Road delivers a cycling tale with plenty of drama and tension. It's a realistic look at the Tour de France from all angles and explores many of the crazy decisions that need to be made during the toughest cycling race on earth. It brings to life the gritty world of cycling while capturing the essence of the sport that many of us love."

Frankie Andreu, nine-time Tour de France finisher.

ACKNOWLEDGMENTS

This book would not be possible without the bizarre world of professional cycling and the athletes, fans, officials, and hangers-on who drink the Kool-Aid. A special thanks to Henri Desgrange, the impresario who dreamed up the crazy idea of a bicycle race around France back in 1903, an epic event that has come to define the essence, both good and bad, of human character.

Thanks also to John Wilcockson whose great editing skills and lifetime spent as a top cycling journalist added professionalism and authenticity to the manuscript and to David Michaels, John Tesh, and Phil Liggett for introducing me to the world of American television as it struggled in 1983 to interpret the Tour de France to a new American audience.

CONTENTS

Chapter One

Crash

He felt the light first. A warm, flowing sensation that pushed back the darkness and spread a dull pain through his head, his shoulders, and to other areas of his body of which he was only vaguely aware. His mind awoke slowly. He lay on his back, eyes closed, trying to think where he was, why his body felt so detached. Then he heard the voices, unintelligible mumbling from nearby. Finally, he stirred and opened his eyes.

There was a blur, a face pressed closely to his. Slowly it came into focus and he recognized the square jaw and the blond wavy hair hovering over him. A bright light from somewhere behind stabbed at him.

"Otto…Otto…where am I?" He struggled to sit up. A piercing pain shot through his shoulder and chest, instantly dropping him back to the bed. He was vaguely aware of several people rushing toward him. "Oh, *Jesus.*"

Other faces, people he didn't know, stared down at him. Only Otto, smiling broadly, spoke. "Welcome back, *mon ami.* We thought you ate it for sure this time."

He struggled again, gaining some clarity. "Where…where am I? What happened?"

Otto leaned close to his friend, blocking out the rest of the room. He whispered, slowly and deliberately. "You're supposed to say 'put me back on my bike.'"

The humor escaped him. There was only pain. "I can't move. What the fuck happened, Otto?"

"Pierre, my boy, you've been out for a while. Cold-cocked. You missed the turn, asshole…and you landed on a pile of rocks. Of course, that was after you slid twenty yards on the pavement, smashed through the guardrail, and then tumbled, ass over teacups, down a fifty-foot embankment. You're lucky Wester found you in that fog. The only clue to your whereabouts was your bike wrapped around the guardrail. And he only found that after he went back to search for you."

"Otto...I, I don't remember what happened." Peter Dufour closed his eyes, slowly and deliberately searching his mind for clues to connect what Otto said, why he was in so much pain.

"Relax." Otto put a hand gently on his battered friend's shoulder. "You've surprised everybody by just waking up. You'll be fine now."

The panic eased slightly and Peter Dufour, in his aching mind, tried his best to rationally piece together what had happened. It wasn't working too well. Finally, he remembered he was an American bike racer in England, in some big race...the two-week Tour of Britain. And there was fog and cold all around them. They climbed the steep mountain roads and they careened down slippery descents. He was barely in control...had to stay with the mad Pole and that Frenchman. He was pushing too hard. Maybe it was a dream. He wasn't sure.

"You were right there, pal. They couldn't drop you. The rest of us were blown and we knew you'd be coming up with Gervais and Kowalski. If you hadn't missed that fuckin' turn, you would've been home free, probably would've moved into second place if not overall leader." Otto shook his head slowly back and forth. "Shit," he said, "you might've been the first. We were there, we almost did it...."

For a moment, Otto Werner had forgotten that he was there to comfort his friend. The outcome of the race shouldn't matter at a time like this. Otto knew that. But he was absorbed by his sport. Nothing else mattered but to win, to help the team achieve a level of greatness that, until now, had been impossible in the tough European arena of international cycling. And the center of the campaign, the driving force of the team, had been Peter Dufour, the rich kid from Greenwich, Connecticut. He had the passion too. He had been their leader, the rock-steady force that held the team together without having to always be in the spotlight. He had helped Otto to each one of his important victories, setting him up for the sprints, many times risking his own skin to clear Otto's path. And when Peter was about to come into his own, to perhaps win the kind of race that suited his more even-tempered style, Otto was happy to return the favor. But that chance was gone now—off the road in the fog.

2

"How…how long have I been out?" Dufour kept his eyes closed; not sure he wanted to know.

"Nearly a week. Six days."

"Oh, *shit*."

"The guys hung around for a while and then they had to go home. Your parents have been here the whole time. Thank God they had you brought to this hospital. We're somewhere in London and they ran out to eat. They wanted to be here when you woke up."

"Who won the race?" Peter just wanted to hear Otto talk. He had to be dreaming. His body felt heavy and his mind was slow. He needed to think, to comprehend what six days of unconsciousness meant.

"The frog won. Gervais. Sort of. But I nailed the bastard."

"What do you mean, nailed him?" Peter was half listening. His head throbbed unmercifully.

Otto leaned close to his friend's ear and dropped his voice to just above a whisper. "You know those guys were juiced." Peter nodded slightly, not necessarily comprehending what Otto had waited nearly a week to tell him. "Well, after the finish when you were discovered missing, Gervais acted like he thought it was funny—you know, the cowboy lost his horse. Well, I snapped and I threw the fucker up against the wall. And guess what fell out of his jersey?"

This question was too hard. An image of some small vials being dumped into a water bottle came to his mind, then a pill being crushed into a little sandwich. If they used some sort of painkiller, he wanted it right now.

Otto imagined his friend being glued to the story. "That's right. It was a test tube full of clean piss and the chief commissaire, who came over to break up the fight, picked it up. They found enough uppers in his other pocket to send a horse to the moon. Gave him a piss test right then. Next morning the jury DQ'd the bastard. And I heard yesterday that the whole French federation is under review, and they've been ordered to clean house. There'll be suspensions and maybe even a banishment or two."

Dufour closed his eyes again. Everything seemed like a bad dream. He didn't care about the Frenchmen or the race or who won or what dirty games may be going on. He just wanted to get up and walk out of there, to be with his other teammates, to get back on his bike. But the pain, the dull ache, made it hard to make even the smallest move. Then the fear hit.

He summoned all his concentration. "Otto, how bad is it?"

"It's going to take a while to recover."

"For God's sake, what's that supposed to mean?"

Otto again put his hand on his friend's shoulder and looked him in the eyes: "Punctured lung, five broken ribs, both collarbones, shattered left elbow, serious road rash on your ass and your legs...."

"What about this?" Peter struggled to point to his bandaged head. "I wasn't out for a week with a headache."

Otto looked down. "Your skull was split, Peter. Big time. They thought there might have been a tear in the brain. There wasn't, thank God. But they're going to have to put a plate in there. A big one."

"So when can I get back on the bike?"

Otto cleared his throat. He walked to the other side of the small hospital room, now empty except for the two of them, and looked out the window. He turned to his friend, sadly.

"The doctor says never."

***

And so ended Peter Dufour's career as a bike racer. It was hard to take at age 23. But he healed. And he wasn't the type to look back.

Later, much later, when the drive to excel had long been transferred from bike racing to business, he still thought of his aborted athletic career. One that had taken him from the playing fields of his prep school, Choate, to the back roads of France, Belgium, Mexico, and England. Then it had been a rebellious choice. But it had made him strong, and it had made him tough. He was reminded of this every time he passed through airport security and set off the alarm with the steel plate that held his head together.

****

Chapter Two

The Dufour Legacy

Twenty-five years later

Kurt Dufour shifted in the big leather chair and turned his head slightly so he could look out the window facing the water. It was a mid-October afternoon, a warm sunlit day when quickly lengthening afternoon shadows foretold the coming of a chilly fall evening. His eyes followed the slope of the leaf-covered lawn to the top of the stone wall and the short path to the Dufours' small private beach and weatherworn boat dock just below. Beyond that was the calm water of Long Island Sound, a haven for pleasure boats owned by the rich and successful of New York and shoreline Fairfield County, Connecticut. There was only one small sailboat out this late afternoon, tacking its way up the coast toward Westport. Kurt imagined the skipper as some young, well-to-do free spirit who had nothing better to do on a Fall Tuesday than capture one last warm afternoon before the sailing season was over.

Kurt sniffed to himself, sensing the irony in the vision. That could easily be him out there. It *was* him out there—at a more carefree point in time that now seemed very far away.

"Kurt...Kurt...Kurt, dear!" His mother's voice came from a distant room. He decided not to shout an answer; she would find him soon enough.

In a moment Sharon Dufour, an attractive fiftyish woman, entered the study and walked, with the characteristic grace of a former dancer, to where her son was seated. Her life had been shaped by dancing, as a little ballerina in the fifties to a touring professional with the avant-garde Alvin Ailey troupe in the late-sixties. His dad met her when she was performing as a Rockette in New York—a can-can dancer, he said. He fell for her legs first, her smile second.

"Here you are, Kurt." She laid a hand on his shoulder and smiled down at him.

"Your father just called. He said the train is running late. He expects he and Otto won't be here for another half hour."

6

Kurt nodded, sensing that his mother wanted more than silent acknowledgment. He patted her hand, looked up, and smiled. "Thanks," he said. "I'm looking forward to finally meeting Otto Werner."

It was all the invitation Sharon Dufour needed to capture a moment with her son. She sat quickly on the edge of the chair across from Kurt, leaning forward, with her hands clasped in front of her.

"I…I think you'll like him, Kurt. He's one of those genuinely warm and principled characters your father always seems to attract."

"Mom, you're on the soap box." But he did want to meet Otto Werner, the man who, a long time ago, sat at his father's bedside for nearly a week, waiting for the coma to lift.

His mother smiled the quick, knowing smile that had always been part of the special communication she had with her son. He was glad to see it back, along with the twinkle in her eyes.

She clasped her hands tighter together and leaned more toward him. The look told him she had come to some new resolution, that her mind had been largely released from the worry that had plagued her since it all began. She was more radiant than he had seen her in months.

"Kurt, I just want you to know that I feel much better about things now. I think perhaps now we can put this…this whole mess…finally behind us." That was all. She gave a deep, contented sigh then quickly stood. On the way to the door, she called back, "If I don't see you later, I'll catch you in the morning. Good luck."

He made the effort to smile and settled back in the chair, letting her new mood and the words sink in.

Until recently, Kurt Dufour had lived a life many people wish for but few experience. Growing up amid the affluence and propriety of well-heeled Greenwich, Connecticut, he had attended the best schools, learned the correct social skills, and included among his friends the young men and women who came from families with wealth and influence. He had always fit well with this group, a decent student, natural athlete, and a bit of a rabble-rouser.

Now, at nineteen, he was slender and athletic, possessing enough well-bred bearing to seem as if he had stepped out of the pages of *Gentlemen's Quarterly*. And two years at Dartmouth had given him a self-confident yet unpretentious air of natural leadership that few his age possessed. When he smiled, it was with ease and engagement and he had the kind of face and demeanor that naturally attracted people, women in particular. It was this fact that had led him into trouble.

Kurt's eyes scanned the familiar decor of his father's walnut-paneled study. Hundreds of books filled the floor-to-ceiling bookcases, and the open spaces displayed diplomas, richly framed photographs, and various family trinkets. At the end of the room was the massive fieldstone fireplace in front of which he had spent many a cold winter evening. Even the brass lamps and the exquisitely comfortable wing chairs reminded him that, up until that bizarre night last June, his life had been pretty idyllic.

It was a soothing, genteel setting, and it contrasted sharply to the turmoil in Kurt's mind, an inner discomfort that threatened his self-confidence and made him feel that what control he may have had over his life was, at least for now, lost. And even though the whole sordid mess was finally behind him, he didn't like the tempest it had left inside. He was particularly uneasy about the conversation he would soon be having with his father and wondered why Otto Werner, a man he had heard so much about but had never met, was joining them.

While Kurt waited for the two to arrive, he looked for familiar things around the room that would let his mind drift. His eyes rested on a black-and-white photo of a handsome young man in a military uniform. It was a picture of his grandfather, Gilbert Alain Dufour, taken when he was in his early-twenties and just before he had left home to fight on the European front in World War Two. There was a striking resemblance between Kurt and the youth in the picture. But the fifty-year-old photo gave no indication that the young soldier would eventually sire three incredibly successful children and become the founder of one of the nation's most innovative and successful advertising agencies. It was, after all, just a snapshot, a millisecond in time that told nothing of the man's past or future.

Kurt wondered about such things each time he looked at the photos in the study, usually in historical sequence. His father's family photo, taken for Christmas 1967, shuttled him forward a quarter-century. There was Gilbert, the patriarch, now a handsome middle-aged man dressed in a traditional tweed business suit, standing next to Kurt's grandmother, an attractive middle-aged woman, contented looking and obviously proud of the three grown children seated in front of her. Kurt's father, Peter, was on the left, a slender, strong-looking twenty-two-year-old. In the middle was Michelle, then in her last year at Bryn Mawr and a student activist. Beautiful, mildly radical, and the possessor of razor-sharp intelligence. And then there was William, the other intellectual. A recent Yalie who, in this picture wore a Marine captain's uniform, the opposite mind of his sister. He signed up to go to Vietnam to dodge, and eventually catch, real bullets—oddly seeking this as a test of character. What in that picture could have foretold that Aunt Michelle would become the first female ambassador to France or that Uncle William, after a Purple Heart won in the Tet Offensive, would shrewdly acquire four Madison Avenue agencies to secure his father's advertising empire? Or that his dad, Peter, home from globetrotting for that Christmas, would nearly die in an accident and never finish college. Instead, he married a smart can-can dancer and, through some shrewd real estate deals, became the wealthiest of the bunch.

This was a family that had made it. Potentially tragic misfortunes had been survived, and there had never been a question of poor ethical judgment or nagging character flaw. Of late, Kurt had been forced to think a lot about this, of where he fit in. He had decided that his father's family—and his own—were the kind of people who made things happen, who always succeeded in one way or another. He figured that each of them had something burning inside, something that drove them to do things others wouldn't, or couldn't. He knew this because he felt it too.

The discovery had come through sports, for one. He liked to push himself hard, beyond where others seemed willing or capable to go, possessing a desire to win that drove both him and any teams on which he had played to perform beyond expectations. And it had come out in what his mother called his "rebellious stage," a period during adolescence when he had tested the limits of authority, doing stupid things, like driving before he had a license and breaking into the high school—not so much to steal the computer, but more for the challenge it represented. For as long as he could remember, he seemed to come alive when he was on the edge, testing himself between winning and losing, right and wrong. Much more so than most of his peers.

Kurt's gaze settled upon another photo at which he had stared countless times before. It was of his father, Peter Gilbert Dufour, as a young man, standing slender and proud next to his sleek racing bicycle and surrounded by five other youths—one of whom was Otto Werner—also astride their bikes. The photo was taken in front of a café in St. Brieuc, a town in Brittany, France, where Peter Dufour had spent a summer bicycle racing when he was nineteen, four years before the accident. A handwritten caption at the bottom of the photo read: "L'Équipe Stade Bretagne, 1965." This image had always fascinated Kurt. The father, now so successful in business, got his higher education bouncing around in an old Peugeot, and racing bicycles through little villages in northwest France. Then, in 1969, he was almost killed in England practicing this obscure sport, barely understood by Americans in the sixties.

Here, in this room, Kurt had absorbed many of the pieces that combined to form his family history, the legacy that he would somehow carry forward one day. He knew now it wouldn't come from an impeccable Ivy League education, and probably not from being an investment banker—the vague, passionless course that, up until this point, had stretched before him. The silver platter, the red carpet, the privileged lifestyle had come to a crossroads. And now he knew he wanted something else, something different. Something more.

Kurt's mind segued from these disjointed thoughts of family tradition and his own changing realizations to the uncomfortable position in which he now found himself. The prospect of discussing this with his father pained him. The man had influenced him more than anyone else in his life, treating him as a friend and an equal, always. He wanted to be like him, and he wanted to be different at the same time. And for the first time in his life, he had a frustrating, burning desire to change course, most of all to challenge himself in a way that would define who he was.

This had surfaced as a result of what had happened in the last six months. Kurt had lurched out of bounds—badly. His nagging frustration came out of a realization that he was a long way from figuring out why he had gotten into this mess, much less where he was headed. In fact, despite the new forgiveness displayed by his mother a few minutes ago, he questioned if he even cared.

Being nearly convicted of murder was not part of the Dufour tradition.

****

Chapter Three

Mistake

The jury had acquitted him of all charges—but not until after two months of lurid testimony had dragged the Dufour name through the local, and then the national, media. The trial had spun into a tabloid feast, epitomized for Kurt by the one sleazy headline that he was unable to shake from his mind: "Murder Case Derails Dufour Legacy."

It was true. If none of this had happened, Kurt would be back at Dartmouth, still on the same track, despite his increasing disconnection with it. He would be running at the head of Dartmouth's cross-country team, which he loved, and taking his first serious business courses, which he hated. But the trial had dragged on past the start of the school year and, even if he had entered mid-semester, it would be with the label of an accused murderer. It was not the way to continue a college career.

Kurt's mind drifted to the bizarre episode that led to the only real crisis he had faced in his life and, worse, the death of a vivacious young woman.

***

Leslie Conway was beautiful and eager.

She had met him on the beach one warm May evening—Kurt and a few of his buddies home from college for the summer and she, a recent Brown graduate, hanging out with some friends of Kurt's older sister. Leslie had a job in Greenwich for the summer, Kurt was told, before starting graduate school in the fall down in Philadelphia.

Kurt's sister said she was a knockout. Katherine always looked out for her little brother and seemed to enjoy introducing her friends to him. One time she had told Kurt that girls were attracted to him because he stood apart from his peers the way a superstar athlete stands apart from the other players on the bench. She said he had the right posture, a certain self-assurance that was particularly attractive to young, available women. It came with the breeding.

"You have this...this lovable magnetism," she had said with sisterly candor.

"Give me the big build-up for this one," Kurt had joked. He would willingly play it, of course.

It worked. The first time Leslie Conway ended up on the beach at the same time as Kurt and his friends, she sought him out.

"So you're Katherine's little brother" was her way of introducing herself. "I've heard all about you."

"How do you know Katherine?" was his polite response.

"I don't, very well. I've just heard about you. You're supposed to be a real charmer. If your mind's as good as that body, I guess I'd believe it."

Kurt was mildly put off. He didn't like overly forward women, magnetism or no magnetism. He told her so. Nicely, of course. And with a smile to keep her coming.

Leslie was too beautiful to not stir his interest. Her wavy blonde hair fell graciously on her bronzed shoulders, and the skimpy bikini she was wearing revealed a near perfect, athletic body. When she smiled, she did so warmly, never taking her deep blue eyes off his. It made Kurt catch his breath.

"Let's walk up the beach," she said and headed off in the direction of Greenwich Point.

Kurt watched her shapely hips sway seductively away for a few yards before he said anything. The others were wading in the surf, looking for shells, and didn't seem to notice them together.

"You're going the wrong way," he called after her. "It's too rocky up there." Kurt knew the Greenwich shoreline like the back of his hand. About a half-mile from the town beach in the other direction was one of his favorite spots. After walking along a narrow spit and carefully picking your way past some piled rocks, the beach widened out into a gracefully curving cove, protected on either end by sea walls and, toward one end, a charming gray boathouse with white trim and a wood-shingled roof. It was one of many private beaches in this

12

direction. Kurt knew that this one was part of the Gallagher estate and seldom used, particularly in mid-May.

He started out and soon she was beside him. It took them about ten minutes to get to the cove. As Kurt suspected, it was completely empty, with no evidence of anyone having been there recently.

"What a great spot," the girl said after she'd taken a moment to gaze from one end of the cove to the other. She turned to him and he instantly felt his pulse race. "Why did you bring me here?"

"It was your idea to go for a walk," Kurt said lamely. "I just know the nicest beaches."

He was no stranger to the charms of good-looking women—and he knew instinctively what she wanted.

She moved in front of him and placed her hands on his shoulders. She drew him toward her, and he felt her warm full lips press against his. He hesitated for a moment but, when she placed his hands firmly on her buttocks, Kurt's instincts took over.

Nearly a half-hour later, he found himself lying naked next to her on a bed of soft grass under a huge pine tree some hundred yards from the beach. He raised his head and saw the trail of passion—her bikini top on the sand where they first embraced, his shorts and the bottom of her suit on the grass by the boathouse.

The light was fading and he wanted to see her naked body before she had a chance to retrieve her suit. He looked over just as she was getting to her feet. When she saw he was looking, she slowly and purposefully stood up and stretched. Her breasts were full and firm, and her flat stomach and well-shaped hips made Kurt draw in his breath. She was gorgeous. Without displaying the least bit of modesty, she went to find her bikini. Only when she had secured the top did she come back to him.

She leaned over and whispered in his ear: "Meet me here Thursday at seven and we'll do it again." Before he could respond, she turned from him and disappeared on the path back toward the public beach.

Kurt fell back and looked up into the spreading pine tree. He felt satisfied. She liked him and she wanted more. At that bizarre moment, it didn't matter who she was or where she came from; it was almost too good to be true. And he had known her for less than an hour.

**

They started to meet at the Gallagher's private cove regularly. At first Kurt thought she would skip one of their bizarre appointments, never to be seen again. Part of him wanted it that way. Reality that became fantasy. But she seemed more and more enthusiastic about their carnal relationship, devoid of anything more than basic, primal lust. On their third encounter he found her lying naked and spread-eagled on the lawn, waiting for him. On another occasion, he found articles of her clothing leading him to where she was hiding in the boathouse, naked in the shadows, watching his face intently. Hide-and-seek seduction.

On each encounter, the two spoke very little to each other. It was spontaneous, exciting for both of them. From the standpoint of pure, sexual desire, there could be nothing better. But Kurt wondered about her. He wondered why she gave herself so willingly to him, why there was absolutely no reservation from her at all, like no other woman he'd met. In a strange way he felt like he was being used.

"We need to talk about this," he said. "I feel like we're a couple of animals in heat."

"Isn't it great?" She was lying on her back, eyes half-closed, looking up at the twilight sky. "I've always fancied myself as a lioness. You know, dominating the big dumbass king of the jungle." She looked at him, as if this was part joke, part challenge.

Kurt did not want to hear that. The old expression, "Slam, bam, thank you ma'am," popped into his mind. Only "sir" replaced the "ma'am." His raunchier friends would've died to have such a captive playmate. He had certainly liked it so far. But he didn't like being called a dumbass lion.

He thought he should suggest meeting for coffee, maybe in town where there would be less temptation.

"Tomorrow we talk", he said. "Be here at eight…and try to show up with your clothes on." He wasn't ready to abandon this carnal venue just yet.

***

He arrived early. It was a beautiful June evening and Kurt leaned against the boathouse gazing out over the tranquil water. The fading sunlight and warm salt air wrapped around him, creating the thick, sensuous feeling of early summer. As he waited for her, he heard the distant boom of a cannon, signaling the lowering of the flag at the Riverside Yacht Club just down the shoreline, a sound he had always associated with June and the arrival of the sailing season. He vaguely recalled that the Gallaghers were big into sailing and had, years ago, hosted an annual summer kick-off to the season when they returned from the Cayman Islands around this time.

When he looked at his watch it was almost 8:30 and the light was beginning to fade. Maybe she wouldn't show up, he thought. Perhaps a serious conversation was too much for her.

But Kurt didn't believe that. His sister knew she had graduated pre-law and was headed to Penn for law school in the fall. She was the strangest woman he had ever met.

"Hi Kurt."

Startled, he wheeled around to see her standing only a few feet away.

He couldn't believe his eyes. Leslie Conway was dressed in a long formal gown, bare at the shoulders and with an expensive pearl necklace around her throat. Her beautiful blonde hair was pulled back and up, and her lips, a rich crimson, parted in a seductive smile to reveal her perfect white teeth. She was the sexiest, most beautiful woman he had ever seen. Kurt's pulse started to race even more than usual.

"I thought you wanted to talk," she murmured, moving closer.

Kurt snapped himself back. He thought he had detected a slight slur in her words and, when he looked closely at her, he noticed that her eyes were partly closed, and not from another attempt at seduction.

"Yes, I do," he said, trying to sound stern. He fought the desire to kiss the nape of her neck.

15

She leaned against the boathouse and looked up at him. "I'm not a slut," she said softly. "I'm a good girl. I'm everything any man could ever want in a woman. Can't you see that?"

Kurt was stunned. She was not behaving like the self-assured, take-charge lioness he had known carnally. She was obviously drunk or high, or both.

"Look, I know you want to talk," she said, recovering herself. "Let's go sit on the rocks and have a drink." He hadn't noticed that she'd brought a small picnic basket until she reached down for it. Anything to start a conversation, he thought. And, although he rarely drank, the thought of a good belt right now was very appealing.

They had never ventured onto the rocks before, mainly because they were out in the open and in full view of the imposing Gallagher estate at the top of the broad yard. Kurt glanced up at the dark house and remained confident that the Gallaghers and their servants had not yet returned for the summer. Besides, he and Leslie were fully clothed and, anyway, what was the harm in trespass by two young people on such a fine, romantic evening.

When they were comfortably settled on the rocks, Leslie reached into the picnic basket and pulled out a bottle of opened champagne and two glasses. Kurt didn't care for champagne but she obviously had some routine in mind and he didn't want to spoil the moment. She looked intently into his eyes as she handed him his glass.

"Here's to learning the whole story," she said. She smiled and put the glass to her lips.

"Here's to the lioness…." he said, trying at a little humor, "…and to the dumb-ass king of the jungle."

She reacted with a patronizing smile, making him realize that she was a couple of years older and more in control of the situation than he would have liked.

Kurt drank deeply and raised his glass for more. He knew one was supposed to sip champagne genteelly but he figured a nice buzz would help him with this conversation.

She started talking about college, about how much she had enjoyed Brown because it had been her first chance to get away from home—which was somewhere around Philadelphia.

As she talked, Kurt started to feel strange, much more so than a couple of glasses of champagne would cause. He looked at Leslie. She had stopped talking and was fumbling around in her dress. She pulled out a small vial of pills and, before he realized what she was doing, emptied the contents into her mouth. She appeared to offer him a toast with her champagne glass before putting it to her lips.

Kurt's head was swimming and he suddenly felt a wave of nausea sweep over him. He struck at her hand, knocking the glass onto the rocks, then staggered to his feet. He stood over her, trying to reach her mouth with his hands. His instincts were telling him to get the pills before she swallowed them all....

***

T. Bertram Gallagher strode into the darkened house. In just a few minutes, they would all be arriving. The place needed some fresh air from being closed up for months, and he wanted to make sure that they were welcomed by the last sunlight of this beautiful June evening as it washed the marble of the sitting room floor at the back of the mansion.

As soon as he reached the far wall of the sitting room, he flung back the tall curtains to reveal the nine-foot windows that overlooked his private cove on the Sound. But as he reached for the handles to the French doors that opened to the verandah, he stopped short.

There on his favorite rocks, not one hundred yards from the house, was a scene beyond belief. A young man in khakis and T-shirt was trying to shove something in the mouth of a beautiful young woman, dressed in a long white evening gown. As Gallagher watched transfixed, the young man toppled over, striking his head on the rocks. The girl fell limply backward.

With shaking hands, Gallagher reached for the telephone and punched in several numbers.

"Emergency Operator." The answer was immediate.

"Is...is this nine-one-one?" Gallagher kept his eyes on the two still figures lying on the rocks.

"Yes it is. Who's calling please? Do you have an emergency?" The voice was female, firm and efficient.

"This is Bert...uh...T. Bertram Gallagher. Twelve Soundview, Greenwich. There are two young people...a man and a woman...they appear to have been fighting and...uh...well I just came home for the summer and...I'm standing at the back door...."

"Sir. What's the situation? The man and the woman...is anyone hurt?"

He moved to open the French doors so he could get a better look.

"He stuffed something in her mouth," he said. "They're not moving, haven't moved yet."

The operator's voice stopped him from going for a better look.

"Where are you now, Mr. Gallagher?"

"I'm here in the house. In the back. I can see them out there on the rocks. They...neither of them has moved yet." Gallagher's initial shock was turning to outrage. Trespassers. He read the newspapers. Young people today were into all kinds of weird things. Some kind of cult, and on his property....

"Mr. Gallagher, stay right where you are and stay on the phone. We're sending police and an ambulance to Twelve Soundview right away."

Gallagher's eyes narrowed and stayed fixed on the two lifeless forms splayed on the rocks. He lowered his voice and spoke slowly into the phone. "Young couple, illegal trespassers on my beach...looks like a murder, suicide."

****

Chapter Four

The Trial

The memory of the trial and all that led up to it haunted Kurt Dufour. By now, parts of it seemed surreal, especially the fact that he had been the center of it all.

The stares had bothered him the most. Perfect strangers, as well as many he knew, looked at him throughout those agonizing weeks as if he were a sideshow oddity, a creature on display who outwardly looked normal but who did strange things in a dark, private life. Because he was looked at in such a manner by so many, he had often felt guilty—certainly never of murder—but of somehow contributing to the girl's death through the lust they shared. At first it was hard to stay strong, to convince himself that he was not the cause.

Benjamin Storrow's opening defense argument was an articulate presentation of Kurt's innocence, eloquently delivered as the rumpled and bespectacled attorney paced back and forth in front of the jurors:

> *I challenge you, is this young man a murderer? He has no record of any sort. He doesn't drink, he has no history of drug abuse, he doesn't travel with a bad crowd.... As a matter of fact, he's actually quite normal, by anyone's standards.*

> *He's a good student. He works hard at college, and he's a top athlete, has been all his life. His friends and family characterize him as popular and well adjusted.*

> *There is no history of violence or craziness here, ladies and gentlemen—and there's certainly no motive for murder.*

> *Now we aren't denying that he had sex with Leslie Conway...and on more than one occasion. But, ladies and gentlemen, we will prove that this was precipitated by the alluring seduction of a very beautiful...and very mixed up, young woman...a woman who was bent on her own demise....*

Kurt found himself turning this over and over in his mind. For sure, Storrow's description played well in his defense and he knew the importance of conveying the right message in the courtroom. But it only partially fit. In his own mind, Kurt knew the seduction was mutual and the motive for it driven by his needs to test the limits. The unexpected tragedy was her death, seemingly so senseless and something he deeply and profoundly regretted, no matter who she was.

He sat impassively at the defense table, as he was instructed to do by Storrow. It was difficult to sit quietly as the prosecution tried to build its case for murder, initially around the eyewitness testimony of T. Bertram Gallagher, owner of the estate where the girl died.

Kurt knew this man only by reputation, a wealthy and somewhat arrogant retired commodities trader. It was clear that what he saw had rattled him that June evening, and he had drawn his own conclusion. He had no idea who these young trespassers were and why the girl had been—in his view—force-fed a lethal dose of drugs in front of his very eyes.

Although not admissible in court, the public knew from outside the courtroom that Gallagher had his own opinion as to why the autopsy results on the girl and the blood taken from Kurt had revealed barbiturates in both of their systems—three times the amount in hers than his. "Probably an attempted double suicide" is what, the tabloids reported, Gallagher had told friends before the trial. "Who knows what dark secrets these two kids shared?" Adding to the mystery, the autopsy had also revealed fresh scrapes and bruises on the girl's back and thighs even though she was fully clothed at the time of death. They couldn't have come from falling on the rocks.

And then there was Donald Conway, the dead girl's father. He took the witness stand impeccably dressed in a dark business suit: starched, blue-striped shirt with white collar and expensive red silk tie. He had a tanned and rounded face, slicked-back silver hair and a perpetual half-smile that Kurt felt projected a strange combination of arrogance and insecurity. He had the slightly paunchy look of a man in his early-fifties. And he was full of himself.

Kurt listened carefully as the prosecuting attorney, a wily, less-than-pleasing character named Joel Sepperstein, let Conway tell how he was a respected senior partner in a prominent Philadelphia law firm. He painted himself as a loving father who, having lost his wife in a tragic automobile accident when Leslie was only ten, devoted himself to making sure his only offspring wanted for nothing during her upbringing. She had done well at the Baldwin School, an exclusive private girls' academy on Philadelphia's Main Line and, having no brothers and sisters, was constantly doing things and going places with her father. Conway's voice faltered when he told the packed courtroom how proud he was of his daughter the night she was introduced into Philadelphia society at the annual Debutante Ball. "She was radiant, happy, and loved", he said.

But there was something off about this slick Philadelphia lawyer. His portrayal of his relationship with his daughter—her purity and beauty—bordered on worship. Plus, his eyes were shifty, seeming to frequently dart around the packed courtroom and over the jury like maybe not everything was being told.

Storrow, as grand-fatherly and relaxed as he appeared, saw this right away, as, he thought, did the jury. And he instinctively read into it the chance to completely exonerate his client, not just from murder but from moral responsibility as well. In these cases involving prominent families and public opinion, it was nearly as important to preserve good reputations as it was to gain acquittal.

Storrow had been hired by the Dufours, at considerable cost, because he was familiar with crimes of passion and perversity, and because he had achieved brilliant acquittals for celebrities and high-profile individuals accused of rape, incest, and child abuse—often through uncovering bizarre and seemingly unrelated relationships and circumstances. This, of course, made him no stranger to perversity. And by now he could recognize it in a person's eyes and hear it in their speech.

Donald Conway was perverse, and he was hiding something. Storrow told the Dufours this during discovery well before the trial actually started. And so he probed Conway with no sympathy during first cross-examination....

"Where were you, Mr. Conway, on the day of your daughter's death?"

"In my home, in Gladwyne, Pennsylvania." Conway sniffed his reply, affronted that this question would even be asked.

"You were home all day, on a Thursday?" Storrow rocked back on his heels, thumbs inserted in his suspenders and looked at the courtroom ceiling.

"No, of course not. I was at a meeting with a client during the day. I got home around six in the evening."

"And where was this client meeting, Mr. Conway?"

"In New York."

"In Manhattan?"

"Objection!" Sepperstein's high-pitched voice interrupted. "This line of questioning is totally irrelevant, your honor."

Storrow rocked forward slightly, leveling a patient, almost condescending gaze at Sepperstein. He spoke to the judge. "I need to establish some new facts in this case, your honor. This questioning *is* relevant."

"I'm not sure I agree.... On what grounds counselor?"

"Permission to approach the bench, your honor." The judge nodded and Storrow confidently stepped forward. Sepperstein leaped to his feet to join them. After a few minutes of heated exchange, the huddle broke.

"Objection overruled. But please get to the point, counselor." The judge, about Storrow's age, peered over his glasses and made a motion with his hand to keep moving.

Storrow nodded, then turned to face Conway directly.

"Was your New York meeting in Manhattan that Thursday?"

"No, actually, it was in White Plains."

"What time was the meeting and how long did it last, Mr. Conway?"

"About three hours. It was from nine to noon." Conway answered confidently.

"How did you get from your home in Gladwyne to your meeting in White Plains?"

"I drove my car." His half-smile turned into a slight sneer, as if this was too obvious to be asked.

"Given that it's a good three hours' drive from Gladwyne to White Plains, you must've left quite early, about five-thirty or six. Is that a correct assumption, Mr. Conway?" Storrow moved a little closer toward the witness stand.

"Yes, that's correct. I left about five-fifteen, it was just getting light then."

"To your knowledge, did anyone see you leaving at that hour?"

"I don't think so, a neighbor, perhaps." Conway shrugged his shoulders, staying arrogantly detached.

"As an attorney of your stature, I assume you were driven to New York in a chauffeured limousine," Storrow probed.

Conway straightened in the chair and appeared to puff up his chest. "Of course, I have access to the firm's limo whenever I want," he said. "But I happen to have a BMW 850 that I enjoy driving. So I drove myself."

"And after your meeting, Mr. Conway, did you drive straight back to Gladwyne, or did you have other business in the area?"

Conway smiled smugly, as if he had anticipated the question. "No, I had lunch by myself, and I made some phone calls, at the Jockey Club across from the County offices."

"Who were those calls made to?"

He thought for a moment. "My office, one or two clients. That's it."

"And then you drove home?"

Conway nodded. "Yes, I left about two."

"And you got home about six, you said earlier."

"That's right." Conway rolled his eyes in the direction of the jury.

"Can anyone verify when you arrived at home, according to you, at around 6 p.m.?"

"Probably not. I wasn't required to check in with anyone." He smiled and looked around. Somehow, this didn't come off with the humor he had intended.

Storrow moved a little closer and made sure he stood completely out of the jury's sight line to the witness. He spoke in a booming voice, directed at the jury box. "Did you, Mr. Conway, by any chance, make a phone call from that restaurant to your daughter in nearby Greenwich and then go see her?"

Conway's body twitched and quickly, too quickly, he crossed and uncrossed his arms. For an instant, the half-smile disappeared.

"Objection!" Sepperstein jumped to his feet and whined at the judge, "That was a leading question, your honor, the witness already answered that he drove straight home."

"Objection sustained." The judge looked disapprovingly at Storrow.

"No further questions, your honor." Storrow sat down, a grim look of satisfaction on his face. He had planted the seed.

***

One of Kurt Dufour's methods of dealing with the case against him was to participate in the defense. He got close to Storrow and, in a detached sort of way, tried to provide insight into what might have motivated the girl to plan what clearly seemed to be her own death.

But, like everyone else, this young woman confused him. He became more driven than ever to learn who she was and why she had been so obsessed with giving herself to him. He learned more as the trial unfolded.

"Kurt, we have two critical elements for the defense." Storrow said this as he paced back and forth in his temporary office, close to the courthouse in Stamford where the trial was being conducted. It was subleased space, with walls of diplomas from attorneys unknown and bookcases full of case histories that probably hadn't been looked at in years. The background for his own case was a growing stack of cardboard file boxes in the corner, added to each day by various secretaries and associates who gathered the material to support Storrow's arguments.

"Number one, your testimony. I think you can articulate what happened in a way that will build sympathy. Plus, I think you'll stand up well under cross-examination. Sepperstein is a dickhead…the jury will definitely side with you."

"Great, what's number two?" Kurt wasn't afraid to testify; in fact, he wanted to, despite the uncomfortable prospect of describing the sexual liaisons. But he had hoped it would be more than his story against Gallagher's witness of the deed and the circumstantial evidence that was being presented by the coroner, the father, and others.

"Number two, Kurt, is Leslie's roommate at Brown."

"You said she has nothing to say." Kurt's interest was piqued, particularly since the girl, Mary Weingrath, had roomed with Conway for three out of four years of college. Everyone had figured she had to know more about the girl than anyone else. But, to this point, she had refused to reveal anything of consequence about the private life of Leslie Conway.

"I finally got her to agree to testify." Storrow rubbed his hands together. "And she'll slam the lid."

***

After the usual and, in this case, effective character witnesses on behalf of Kurt Dufour were paraded on and off the stand, the real defense case began when the defendant himself was asked to testify.

The way he told the story captivated the courtroom audience. He admitted to lusting for the girl. He was as guilty as she was for not being able, or interested in, controlling himself. But he had no thought of murder, or suicide. He admitted to feeling uncomfortable about this bizarre relationship, about wanting to know more about the girl. And, that night, all he was looking for was some insight, not booze, not pills, not even more sex. Certainly not her very life. As for Gallagher, his observation was flawed, more conjecture than fact. And the bruises on her body, they remained a complete mystery. He never laid a hand on her. His testimony was earnest and believable and it stood up under Sepperstein's unusually nasty cross-examination.

And there was the Dufour family, grim and steadfast in support of one of their own. Kurt's father and mother sat in the front row of the courtroom day after day and, in every chance they had on the witness stand or in terse comments to the hungry press outside, refused to acknowledge that their son could even remotely consider either taking someone's life or knowingly participate in a drug-related suicide. When the tabloid press—quickly enamored by the sleazy aspects of the case—could uncover no skeletons in the Dufour closet, they naturally turned, like everyone else, to the only real mystery in the whole affair: Who was Leslie Conway?

Storrow recognized that this was the crux of the case. Establishing her death wish and why she had been driven to it would cast further doubt on Dufour's guilt, certainly enough for acquittal. But he wanted more—the subsequent removal of as much doubt as possible concerning his client's character and a shift of blame to someone else.

Mary Weingrath sat stoop-shouldered on the witness stand, peering over her glasses at Storrow as he paced back and forth in front of her. Her thin, white hands clutched nervously at a handkerchief in her lap, and she spoke slowly and deliberately. Her voice was so soft that the jammed courtroom remained absolutely silent so as not to miss a word of her testimony.

As it turned out, Mary Weingrath was more like a sister to Leslie Conway than a college roommate. Weingrath had adored and admired the victim, seeing in Conway the vivacious and attractive woman that she could never be. Conway, on the other hand, needed the steadiness and stability that Weingrath personified. In the confines of their dorm room, they shared their deepest secrets.

Storrow drew out of her that Leslie Conway, as her college career neared completion, had become increasingly preoccupied with her own death. She had been drinking more than usual and had started taking sleeping pills in alarmingly heavy doses. She became loose and casual with sexual relationships, as if that kind of intimacy meant little to her. Men came to call for her all the time.

But most of all, Conway had feared starting law school at Penn. She didn't want to live at home, a huge house in Gladwyne, one of the

Main Line's most prestigious communities. And, as Leslie grew more and more distraught, Weingrath finally got her to open up.

Storrow looked out over the courtroom gallery, his hands clasping the lapels of his suit coat. He slowly turned to face the trembling young woman on the witness stand and asked, in a soothing, kindly voice, "Would you please, Mary, tell me why Leslie Conway did not want to live with her father?"

"She...she", Weingrath struggled to get the words out. "She was afraid he would abuse her again."

"What do you mean, abuse her?" Storrow wanted the truth to come out quickly.

"He...she said he made her have sex with him."

"Objection!" came Sepperstein's predictable cry. "I think we're getting away from the facts of the case, here, your honor. I don't see how...."

Storrow interrupted. "I intend to establish the mental state of the deceased, your Honor. Her relationship with her father is crucial to that."

"Overruled." The judge was as interested in the dead woman as everyone else.

Storrow continued. "Did she tell you details of this abusive relationship? Had it been going on for a long time?"

Mary Weingrath wanted to get it out. Her best friend was dead through no fault of the man on trial. It wasn't fair to condemn someone for something she knew he didn't have anything to do with.

"Her father forced her to have intercourse with him starting at age thirteen," she stammered. "She just couldn't take it anymore and...."

Mary Weingrath lost control of her voice. Storrow gave her a few moments to collect herself and then began again, using a different tack.

"Ms. Weingrath, did you receive a phone call on the night Leslie Conway died?"

Weingrath, tightly clutching the handkerchief to her lowered chin, nodded and uttered, almost imperceptibly, "Yes."

"Had she seen her father that afternoon?" Storrow spoke in a low, soothing voice.

"Yes."

"What did she say happened?"

Weingrath bent over her handkerchief and started sobbing.

"Mary, please tell the court what she said happened." Even Sepperstein was riveted to the girl on the stand.

"He...he beat her...and, and..." her voice was shaking with emotion, "...and he tried to rape her!" Weingrath was unable to continue. Her shoulders shook and she took shallow, sobbing breaths into her handkerchief. The gallery and the jury sat in stunned disbelief and then erupted into a buzz of outrage.

A scuffle ensued at the back of the gallery. Donald Conway, still in a dark business suit, had leaped to his feet and was pushing toward the bench, punching his finger at Kurt Dufour. "Bastard!" he shouted. "You *fucking* bastard!"

Two courtroom guards rushed to subdue him. But Conway was strong, and he pushed forward, trying to get to Kurt at the defense table. "I'm not on trial here—*you* killed her! *I* was the one who loved her—to you, she was just a plaything!"

The guards had reached Conway and now pinned his arms behind him. They started to drag him back toward the exit door. Conway continued shouting as they struggled to control him. "She was a good girl, she was no slut! You...you fucking bastard, you'll never get away with this!" The courtroom erupted into pandemonium. The judge repeatedly banged his gavel on the bench and shouted for order....

Conway was dragged right in front of Kurt and, for a moment, their faces were only a few feet apart. Strands of Conway's silver hair fell wildly out of place and there were traces of dried spittle in the corners of his mouth, now twisted into a hideous smile. Kurt instinctively recoiled and, with eyes locked in a communication of souls, felt a chill flash through him. The arrogance was gone, replaced by a burning, uncontrolled hatred.

At that moment, he knew he had not seen the last of Donald Conway.

****

Chapter Five

Reunion

"Next stop, Stamford!" The conductor smiled at the balding, middle-aged man seated below him and pointed to the ticket stub wedged above the seat. "This is your stop, sir."

It was getting toward evening and the four-hour train ride from Boston had passed quickly. Otto Werner folded the manila file folder labeled "Kurt Dufour" and stuffed it into his battered briefcase. He removed his reading glasses and, after fumbling a bit, carefully returned them to the breast pocket of his rumpled sport coat. He had to think twice about where he put his glasses because he dressed in suits and sport coats only occasionally. Otto's normal attire was a jacket or sweat top like the ones he wore in the team car when following his cyclists, or "players" as he called them, as they pedaled over the mountains and cobblestone roads of Europe. But it was October, and Otto annually accepted the fact that this was the time of year that he had to start making the rounds to his professional cycling team's corporate sponsors and his players' agents, lining up funding for next year and tying up deals that he'd been negotiating since the summer and didn't break the budget. He accepted the fact that business meetings required a different uniform.

Otto looked forward to seeing his old friend, Peter Dufour. It had been three decades since they had raced bicycles together in France, Holland, and Mexico. And twenty-six years since Otto had left his friend's hospital bedside in London, ending what had been one of the best periods in Otto's life.

Although they had exchanged Christmas cards nearly every year, their lives had become very different, and Otto wondered how much Peter had really changed. He knew his Connecticut friend and long-ago teammate had fully recovered from the crash and had emerged from the genteel poverty of their late-sixties amateur cycling days to become a very successful real estate developer. His home was selected—Peter had written this under the picture of it in one of his Christmas cards—because it resembled the French manor houses they had pedaled by in Brittany thirty years earlier. Otto knew it was on Connecticut's so-called Gold Coast and probably worth millions. Coming from a working-class German neighborhood outside of

Milwaukee, he was somewhat in awe of the material wealth Peter Dufour had amassed.

But there was concern for his wealthy friend as well. Otto had followed the bizarre case against Peter's son in the papers. Why the hell would a talented young kid like Kurt Dufour get mixed up in such a sleazy affair, particularly when he had caring, concerned parents like Peter and Sharon Dufour? Otto had trouble figuring out things like this. His explanation always came back to the times in which they lived. Too many choices. Too much permissiveness. Otto thought of the talented young players on his professional cycling team. Even though they were not paid outrageous amounts of money to race their bicycles, many of them had become prima donnas. None of them had displayed the character that Peter had. Money corrupts, fame corrupts, he thought.

The train lurched to a stop, shaking Otto from his reverie. When his eyes scanned the well-lit passenger-pick-up area beyond the platform, he quickly recognized his tall, still slender, former teammate standing next to a black Mercedes sedan. Peter didn't see him at first, giving Otto a chance to mentally note any changes brought on by the quarter-century that had separated them. Otto was amazed that there were surprisingly few. Only the deeper creases around the mouth and the thinner, graying hair. Age and prosperity had been good to him, Otto thought. He had always had the bearing of a leader but now, with the deeper lines of experience, Otto thought his friend looked like royalty—the King of Belgium, or something. He wanted to sneak up and greet him with a clever line. But since all he could think of was "Money must be a good preservative," he instead shouted, *"Eh, Pierre, ici, mon ami!"* and threw clenched fists above his head like he used to do whenever he crossed the finish line first.

When Peter Dufour automatically responded in kind and moved quickly toward the platform, Otto Werner guessed that, whatever this man had done in life, he had done so with the same character he had possessed as a lad in France thirty years ago. Peter had been a great teammate. Although he had the ability to win races, and occasionally did, he was respected more for his levelheaded approach to racing, his ability to understand the subtle tactics of cycling, and sacrifice his own chances if it meant victory for someone else on the team. He was tenacious and never gave up or gave in without a fight. Peter had been born a leader and, Otto mused, probably would have been a great pro had it not been for the accident. No wonder he had been so successful.

The two hugged then held each other at arm's length. Otto, on the stocky side to begin with, had expanded his girth and lost most of his blond, wavy hair. His ruddy complexion, benevolent wrinkles, and bushy mustache had him well on his way to looking like Santa Claus.

"Otto, you look fat and prosperous in your old age." Time had not changed Peter's good-natured teasing.

"And I can see you have missed all the good Belgian beer and French pastries I have had the fortune to consume," Otto shot back, clapping his taller, leaner friend on the shoulder.

The two were glad to see each other again and, as they started away from the station in Peter's plush Mercedes, recalled the several summers of their youth spent together rattling from race to race in a battered old Peugeot, two zany young Americans determined to conquer France by bicycle. And they talked about the crash and the awful week Otto had spent at Peter's bedside wondering if he would ever come out of the coma.

"Kurt is waiting for us at the house," said Peter, finally getting down to the real purpose of Otto's visit. It was a short ride to Greenwich and Peter wanted to make sure they had a chance to talk. "He's had a rough time, and I'm not really sure what's going on inside his head. I hope you've given more thought to the idea."

Otto nodded. When Peter had first suggested that his son be added to Otto's pro cycling team for a year, Otto had considered the idea totally preposterous and a sign that his old teammate must have suffered brain damage after all. But Peter, in typical analytical fashion, had presented his plan in such a way that it started to seem plausible to Otto. Peter had pointed out in a long phone conversation right after the trial that Kurt grew up loving to ride a bike with his dad and even did some racing in his early teens. He had natural style and power, and he was quick to absorb his dad's pointers about riding in a pack and using his head as effectively as his legs. One summer they went around to a dozen junior-age-group races in New England, and Kurt won five of them. But the boy was also a talented cross-country runner, and the high school coach lobbied hard to keep him away from bike racing where a bad accident and the wrong kind of muscle development would hold him back. Strangely, Peter sided with the coach and pointed out to his son that school sports were better for him than falling into the vagabond life of an itinerant bike racer, perhaps ending with a split skull, or worse. Sharon, of course, agreed. But the choice was left up to Kurt and, even though he loved cycling, he opted to stick with his school buddies on the cross-country team. Peter felt it was the correct decision, but it nagged at him that it might not have been the right one. Privately, he thought his son would've turned out differently if he'd been encouraged to follow his passion instead of suppress it. Maybe this was the chance to make it right.

Otto was aware of all this. If he hadn't known Peter, he would have rejected this as a father's wishful thinking and dismissed the whole idea without a second thought. And he had been concerned that Peter may be pushing this to satisfy his own aborted dreams. But there was more than a father's wishes here. Peter had asked that some physiological tests be done on Kurt as a member of Dartmouth's cross-country team be sent to Otto by the team's physician.

"I have to tell you, Peter, I had thought you had gone crazy with this idea." Otto struggled to find the right words. "You know, running the team, I see a lot of fathers who act like assholes. They think their sons can all be the world champion. They don't know that it takes a lot more than winning a few American bike races or showing a flash of brilliance once in a while...."

Peter interrupted. "Come on Otto, I know what it takes. I'm the first one to admit that Kurt is totally unproved. But look at the tests. You're the one who told me how scientific the sport has become. I wouldn't have pushed this thing at all if you hadn't told me how unusual he is."

Peter guided the Mercedes into the right lane to exit. Otto looked out the window and saw the sign for Greenwich. He tugged nervously at his mustache and tried not to succumb to his friend's persuasion, even though he wanted desperately for the scheme to work. Otto, more than Peter, knew that Kurt Dufour was blessed with a physiology that few mortals possessed. One in a million, was the consensus of the team doctors and Dartmouth sports medicine experts after they had reviewed the traditional stationary bicycle tests now performed routinely on college and professional athletes. Ever since the early-seventies, when the former East Germans began producing superior athletes through a combination of testing for innate physiological ability and scientific training, it had become essential to determine an athlete's physical potential before encouraging a life devoted to the intense training and competition it took to be successful. Otto knew this to be a fact of life. No amount of training or desire could compensate for someone who didn't have the basic physical equipment.

But Otto also knew that all the physical talent in the world was worth nothing if the athlete didn't have the mental toughness to fight to the top. He'd seen it too many times. He'd handled dozens of world-beaters over the years only to be disappointed when they fell short of expectations: too much money too soon, the temptation of performance-enhancing drugs, overly pushy parents, a screwed-up view of their own importance, problems with wives and girlfriends.... The list went on and on.

Otto looked over at Peter. He desperately needed a superstar to revitalize his team. Maybe Peter's kid would be it.

"I've never seen a nineteen-year-old with a VO_2 max over 80 who isn't already on the circuit," Otto said matter-of-factly.

He ticked off the stats, as much for his own ears again as for Peter's: "Five-eleven, one-fifty-five pounds, five percent body fat—we can get that down a point or two—minimal lactate production, evidence of exceptional pulmonary membranes, exceptionally low resting pulse, excellent recovery rate, good fast twitch/slow twitch ratio...."

He paused. "Pierre, you and Sharon produced a real racehorse. I just hope he's got the balls."

****

Chapter Six

Requiem

Kurt Dufour had been waiting in the study for nearly an hour. It was now almost dark and he wondered why his father was so late. Finally he heard the sound of the Mercedes come to a stop on the gravel driveway out front, and a moment later the front door of the house opened and closed with its familiar solid thud.

He could hear his father talking to another man. Kurt heard a low whistle from the stranger and a comment he couldn't understand. He was on his feet by the time the two men entered the room.

The stranger entered first, followed quickly by Kurt's father. They converged in front of the fireplace where Kurt stood, back to the window and off to one side.

"Kurt, meet my old cycling friend, Otto Werner. We go back thirty years."

Kurt shook Otto's outstretched hand firmly and looked him straight in the eye, as he had been taught. He could see the resemblance, time rounded and thinned on top, to the youth in several of his dad's old racing photos. Kurt instantly liked him.

"Pleased to meet you, Mr. Werner, my Dad's told me…."

Otto interrupted, "It's Otto, son. And it's nice to get a firm handshake from a youngster for a change, not like those wimpy Frenchmen."

Peter jumped in. "Have a seat, Otto." He motioned for his guest to sit in one of the big leather wing chairs next to the fireplace. "Can I get you a beer, or a glass of wine, or something?"

"I'll take a Trappist. And if you don't have that, I'll have a Pilsner Urquell or a Chimay." He winked at Kurt as he eased into the big wing chair. "Bring me whatever you have, Pierre, and make it fast. And bring something for the lad here, he looks a little parched."

Peter chuckled and disappeared to get the drinks, leaving Kurt and Otto alone seated across from each other on either side of the stone fireplace.

It was dark outside but the table lamps were on, giving the room a comfortable, cozy glow.

As soon as Peter was out of the room, Otto leaned toward Kurt. "I'll leave it up to your old man to tell you why I'm here," he said in a more serious tone. "But I want you to know that I know the whole story. Pretty shitty business, if you ask me. You gotta put it behind you and make it work for you. If I can help, I will, because there's never been a better friend to me than your dad."

With that, Otto settled back and, with a contented sigh, let himself be absorbed into the softness of the chair.

***

It took nearly an hour for Peter and Otto to present their plan to Kurt, the father's methodical, rational presentation punctuated by Otto's occasional witticisms and rambling anecdotes.

Kurt was completely blindsided and, at first, incredulous that these men were suggesting that he start a new life as a professional cyclist. Suspend his studies at Dartmouth. End a top-level intercollegiate running career. Head into the complete unknown with no track record and little experience from which to draw.

But his father was not pushing; he never did. Kurt knew it would be his own choice. Getting mixed up with this woman and dragged through an ugly murder trial had unwittingly put his life under harsh examination. Innocence of the killing couldn't help that, a fact that they both recognized. Take some time to regroup, his father suggested. Focus on something strong enough to overcome the temptation and perhaps provide the clarity to see the consequences of your actions before they cause trouble. Then the father talked about something they had rarely discussed. He brought up the issue of character, of making judgments that were morally and ethically sound. And just to bring it to the nineteen-year-old level, he said, "It's important to get your brain to run your life, not your dick."

And then he came full circle. He reminded Kurt that his early, aborted success as a cyclist had been stifled more by pressure from others than a lack of the boy's desire. Perhaps he had learned the wrong lesson in doing more what others expected of him than what he wanted in his heart. "I've always felt that a little spark left you with that decision," he said.

It was true. As an adolescent, Kurt had lived and breathed cycling for more than a year. The fire within him had burned with it. His walls were covered with the great champions of the Tour de France. Bernard Hinault and Greg LeMond raced over his headboard, Laurent Fignon grimaced by the window, and Sean Kelly rode, battered and bloody, on the wall next to his desk. He had dreamed of riding the Tour de France someday. But that dream came crashing down with his heroes' posters the day he made the decision, at age 15, to focus on running and Dartmouth, neither of which ever fueled the same fire again.

Kurt had come to accept that his year as a cyclist had been adolescent fantasy. He was practically a grown man now and he was faced with adult issues, like living with that woman's death which, like it or not, implicated him. If he bought into this crazy scheme, would he be running away or getting a shot at changing his life for the better?

He thought of the track he had been on. Finish at Dartmouth, then business school. With luck, land a job with one of the big investment firms in New York, maybe live in the city or take the train in every day so he could work long hours handling other people's money. Then what? Prestige and a bigger salary? The thought of someday making vice-president had somehow lost the vague attraction it may once have had.

The trial made him think hard about his life. Investment banking, his presumed destiny, really depressed him now. Sometime, a while back, he had switched to automatic pilot and the plan just kept rolling along. He had felt the need to shake free. Maybe this was the way. And he was desperate to escape—to some different world where he could start his life over and where the trial and the memory of Leslie Conway, and the hatred shown by her father, could be left behind. He felt something stirring inside, a welling desire to grab this and run hard.

By now it was well past nightfall. A fire had been lit and its glow flickered across the bookcases and now shadowy photos. The brass lamps added a diffused yellow glow to the sitting area in front of the fireplace. The two men had fallen silent and all three gazed into the fire as if the answer to the questions with which they struggled would somehow be revealed in the glowing embers. Kurt turned his gaze from the fire to study his father's face. The flickering light deepened the creases, and the angle of his jaw seemed more chiseled than usual. It was a ruggedly handsome face, carved by wisdom and kindness, and, to the son, conveyed a strength and character that he had always admired and, in many ways, leaned on.

Peter looked at his son and smiled faintly. "It sounds crazy, doesn't it, Kurt? But at least you have the choice. You'll only be young once and you'll never get this kind of choice again…maybe you need a new focus for a while."

Otto shifted his weight in the big wing chair, spilling part of his third glass of beer. He had dozed off and suddenly caught himself. He put his glass down and leaned forward to bring himself back into the conversation, turning to Kurt so he could look directly into his eyes. The Santa Claus was gone, and Kurt could see that the old pro was dead serious: "Don't get the idea that this is the gravy train, kid. I don't put up with any bullshit, and I don't want anyone on my team who feels sorry for himself. You'll have to work your ass off and learn fast. But I'll tell you this…. If you give me a hundred twenty percent, I'll turn you into the best goddam racehorse your old man has ever seen."

After a lingering moment, Otto's eyes seemed to glaze over. He let out a belch and turned to find his beer glass.

***

Kurt had arranged to meet Mark Rawlins right after he had talked with his father and Otto. It was now nine o'clock and, as he headed the car toward town, he wondered if his best friend and Dartmouth teammate would still be at the bar. Kurt hadn't been there since before the trial, and he didn't want to have to deal with any stares from the locals who would undoubtedly recognize him from the stories and photos that had recently saturated the media. The only attention he wanted was from the one kindred spirit he had known all his life.

Rawlins, two years older than Kurt and recently graduated, knew the serious, as well as the reckless, side to Kurt. He was a crazy bastard too. And he was smart. No commuter trains for him. In another three weeks, Rawlins would be in Costa Rica, chasing a raven-haired au pair whose old man needed someone to bring his exotic hardwoods into the U.S. Why not?

38

He had helped Kurt maintain his sanity throughout the last several months by meeting him at dawn nearly every morning so they could run their favorite ten-mile route without much notice. Ironically, the two had become as lean and as fit as they had been at peak season last year at Dartmouth.

"You're not going to believe this," Kurt said as he slipped into the booth Rawlins had wisely secured near the back of Tumbledowns, a favorite hangout on the Post Road in Cos Cob. For a Tuesday night, the place was crowded and noisy, enough so that no one seemed to notice his entry.

Rawlins' semi-drunk eyes got wider and narrowed, and got wider again as his friend laid out the bizarre plan that had been presented to him back at the house.

Kurt told him everything: He would be a rookie on one of the world's top pro teams with a starting salary of fifty thousand dollars, and a chance to split several hundred thousand more in prize money if he progressed and did his job. He would be measured for bikes right away, train on his own for two months until the team assembled in December on the West Coast, and then hit the circuit beginning in the South of France just after the first of the year. He would be an *équipier*, a team member working for the more experienced riders on the team until, perhaps, he showed enough talent to move up the ladder. If he did okay the first season, he may get a renewed contract, and maybe, in a few years, a shot to ride the Tour de France. If he screwed up, got injured, or couldn't take it, he'd be back at Dartmouth the following year.

Rawlins had sat transfixed throughout the entire story, the familiar shit-ass grin slowly spreading across his face. "I like it," he said.

"So what do you think I should do?" Kurt's eyes met Rawlins' with an intensity that wanted a straight answer, knowing deep down what it would be. Reassurance from the one who understood was all he sought.

Without blinking or lowering his gaze, Rawlins slowly drained the entire contents of his sixteen-ounce beer mug and slammed the empty glass on the table. With a deliberate move of his right hand, he wiped the foam from his chin and leaned forward until his face was only a few inches from Kurt's.

"I say you better fuckin' go for it, and kick some French ass, my friend!"

"Somehow, I thought you'd say that," Kurt said as a broad smile spread over his face. The two stood up and clasped hands over the table. "I'll write you from wherever," he said and then disappeared.

Rawlins sat back down just as another beer was placed in front of him, and an attractive brunette slid into the booth just occupied by Kurt.

"Wasn't that the poor guy who was accused of killing that whacko last summer?" the girl asked.

Rawlins, now pretty much in the bag, acknowledged that indeed it was. He also recognized the girl to be Jennifer Scott, one of the new freshmen from Greenwich he had met at a Dartmouth orientation party not too long ago. When he met her, he had thought her to be a nice package for Kurt, if he ever showed any interest in women again.

"What in heaven's name will he do now?" she asked.

Rawlins leaned back so he could get a better look at this attractive young intruder and decided against saying what the beer wanted him to say.

"He'll be back in the headlines," Rawlins said, only half kidding. "And you can meet him in Paris just about the time you graduate."

****

Chapter Seven

Baptism

Three days after Otto left, the bike arrived. It came with Manuel Ramos, a neatly dressed Mexican who knew more about racing bikes than anyone on the planet—according to Otto, anyway.

He stood at the front door in an expensive deerskin coat over pressed blue jeans and politely introduced himself with a toothy white-and-gold smile, cowboy hat held casually to his chest. His face had character. It was tanned and crinkled by the sun, and his dark eyes were clear and sharp, indicating to Kurt intelligence bred in faraway places. Kurt welcomed him and wasted no time showing him out to the carriage house where his van could be parked and unloaded indoors. Interesting man, Kurt thought. The first of many, no doubt.

Ramos was left alone to unpack after the long drive from Milwaukee. He could have flown in with his tools, the bikes, and parts but he had chosen instead to drive. It was better that way because he could bring most of his shop with him. It was okay with Otto because this was a slack month, in between closing out one season and gearing up for the next.

Besides, Ramos liked driving around the country to visit the guys on the team. He got to see friends along the way, and it gave him a chance to get to know the riders he would be servicing during the hectic season, without the pressure. He couldn't explain it but he felt that part of his job was to know everything about each rider, what he expected from the mechanic, and the kind of equipment each rider got excited about. It was important to know if the rider was neat or sloppy, if he understood about how things worked, or he just wanted to hurtle down the road. Some guys cared a lot about how their equipment went together, some didn't give a shit. Ramos didn't pass judgment; he just wanted to know.

This kid, Kurt Dufour, was bound to be different. All Otto said on the phone was: "He's got a jet engine and not a goddam clue about what kind of bike to ride. Oh, and he lives in a big mansion."

41

Otto was right about the mansion. Ramos had driven slowly along the shore road looking for the stone pillars with the weathered brass lanterns that marked the entrance to the driveway. It went back a long ways, a hundred-year-old cobblestone lane that swept into a graceful circle when it reached the front of the house. The mansion was huge, a long and high expanse of fieldstone, gabled and turreted, with a manicured lawn that sloped gently back to the sea. Across the cobbled circle was the smaller but equally impressive carriage house, once no doubt home to butlers and chauffeurs. Ramos had seen houses like this before. But they were in France and Belgium, lived in by the team owners or, in one case, by France's top rider, Jacques Poulain, only a few years older than Dufour and already a multimillionaire. Poulain's formative years had been focused on one thing—to become France's next great Tour de France champion—and, by age twenty-two, he had won his first. The mansion *he* lived in had been bought by his victories, not by rich parents.

The upstairs of the carriage house was where Ramos was to sleep. It, alone, was bigger than the family *casa* in Mexicali, once home to him and all thirteen of his brothers and sisters. Ramos had certainly been in these kinds of digs, but never were they the homes of *novicios*. He pushed from his mind the conventional wisdom that the best bike riders came from hardship. He would find out.

Ramos busied himself with getting his things ready. This evening he would get to know Kurt Dufour during the fitting. First, he would take dozens of measurements—leg length, arms, feet, torso, shoulders— everything Ramos would need in order to have Kurt's first real bike designed, like a fine suit of clothes, to fit him and him alone. After that, he would set him up on the loaner bike and tell him how to ride it.

The *muchacho* appeared for his fitting wearing a running suit and carrying two beers. He handed one to Ramos and smiled, a little nervously.

"*Gracias, señor*. But I will save *la cerveza* until we finish. First, I must fit you to *el biciclo*. The one you will use until we can get your own built." Ramos disappeared around the side of the van and proudly reappeared wheeling a sleek racing bike, or part of one, anyway.

"Where's the seat and the handlebars?" Kurt asked. He was trying to look excited, but his eye couldn't yet appreciate something that wasn't the complete package. Years ago, in his adolescent season of bike racing, he had liked the clean, classic look of Italian handcrafted racing bikes, and he had cherished the white Bottecchia his father had helped him pick out at the local racing shop. This bike was blue.

Ramos lifted the partly assembled machine into the mechanic's stand he had set up next to the van. From a dresser-like drawer built into the inner side of the vehicle, he pulled out three different saddles and laid them on the floor of the van for Kurt's inspection. "Escoge, *choose*," he said.

"Which one?"

"Which do you like?"

"What am I looking for?"

"Ligero, agradable. *One that is light and fits your ass*."

Kurt looked at the saddles, back and forth. He smiled and turned to Ramos. "Am I going to sit on it or stick it up there?"

The dark eyes twinkled. "Of course, that is up to you, *muchacho*." They both laughed.

"Look, Manuel, I'm just starting this thing and I imagine I'm going to be pretty sore at first. You're the pro, choose the best one to start on."

"First, everyone calls me Ramos. Second, you are soft there. We give you one that is a little more wide and a little more soft, so…." They laughed again as he set one aside and quickly replaced the others in the drawer. Ramos was pleased. The *muchacho* was willing to trust him and did not have the need to pretend he knew it all like so many of them. It would be easy for Ramos to help. For sure they would get along—if the kid lasted.

They chatted easily throughout the two-hour fitting, mostly questions from Kurt and answers from Ramos. As they talked, Ramos stretched his tape measure over various parts of Kurt's body, pausing after each measurement to fill in a space on a piece of paper upon which was the outline of a blank human form, identified at the top of the page as Kurt's. How appropriate, Kurt thought: Blankman.

Ramos explained that copies of the completed body form would be sent to the team's clothing supplier, Lycramax, for fabrication of his team clothing, and to Fabio Bassini, the legendary Italian frame builder who custom-made the team's racing bikes.

The loaner bike on the stand took shape simultaneously with the measurements that marched around the blank man on the paper. First, leg measurements and the saddle. Then torso and arm measurements. Then, from another part of the van, a handlebar stem. A shoulder measurement, a pair of handlebars. Another piece of paper came out, this one a blank outline of a bicycle with no wheels. Ramos filled in measurements on this page, too. Slowly, the blank man and the blank bike became defined by scribbled measurements, no doubt understood only by a small cadre of specialists who knew how to place a man on a bicycle in the most efficient way possible.

"Takes two or three years," Ramos explained, "to find the best *posición* for you. How you pedal, how the back bends. Maybe Otto will want you to go to the lab and the aero tunnel." He waved his hand, as if to dismiss the thought. "Ah, I forget, you are so…so *falto de experiencia*. Perhaps later."

The moment came for Kurt to mount the bike. First, he had to select a pair of shoes that fit, the new step-in binding type that Kurt had only read about. Then he was told to put on a pair of Lycra racing shorts, both of which came from other drawers in the van. Ramos had placed the bike in some sort of stand so Kurt could sit and pedal in this new gear while Ramos measured some more and analyzed his position.

"I'm leaning way over."

"That is correct. We want you to cut through the air like the knife."

"But I feel like I have to reach so far to the 'bars."

Ramos had noticed the old white Bottecchia hanging in the back of the garage when he first came in. He pointed to it. "You are used to the dog bike. Sit up and beg. I can see it is too short for you from here. Trust Ramos. He will start you right."

Although he didn't show it, Ramos was amazed by this young pro. Kurt Dufour knew nothing beyond an adolescent fascination with the sport, so strange for one picked to ride on America's best team of professional cyclists. To be sure, he was lean and fit. But his legs lacked even the hint of quadriceps development that the most basic of training on the bike would create. On the stand, he pedaled smoothly enough, but his upper body was tense and his arms stiff. The overall picture was one of mild discomfort, an awkwardness that would not be expected even from the newest of *corredores*. Even so, Ramos knew Otto had his reasons for bringing the kid on. It was up to him to make sure Kurt adapted to the bike right away. In a few short months, he would be thrown into the team. It would not be an easy landing.

Ramos was finished. Kurt had a top bike to ride, extra wheels, and enough cycling clothing for the cold weather to come. It would take him through November and December and until the new gear arrived in the New Year. Kurt's mission was to get used to the equipment and build a base of fitness on the bike until the early-season training camp opened in mid-January. In California, where it was warm.

"Otto will give you the schedule for training," Ramos said. "You must do everything he says. In two months, you must become part of *la bici*. We will meet again in California, at the camp."

It was getting late. The two popped the beers and chatted a little longer. Ramos would leave before dawn the next morning, and Kurt would do his first training ride. The start of a new life.

Kurt thought about this as he walked slowly back to the house. He liked Ramos. The man conveyed a passion for his work that Kurt had rarely seen in anyone. He had learned that Ramos, the youngest of fourteen had grown up scavenging old bike parts in Mexicali, a dusty desert town just south of the California border. He got so he could put the pieces together and sell for a few pesos something that actually rolled. According to Ramos, it would also feed his brothers and sisters for a week. And each year, when the Tour of Baja would come through his village, little Ramos would hang around the racing team mechanics from places like Argentina, Colombia, Cuba, and the United States. From that to being the top mechanic on Otto Werner's team, paid well, and taken all over the world—and no doubt sending many more pesos back to Mexicali. Amazing.

Kurt reached the phone in the house on the third ring.

"Hi. I'm looking for the future world champion." The voice and the tone were unmistakably Otto's.

"Hold on, please. He's in the garage drinking cerveza."

There was a chuckle from the other end. "Just like your old man," Otto said.

They chatted briefly about Ramos's visit and confirmed that Kurt was ready to get started.

"Listen, Kurt." The tone changed into what Kurt was beginning to recognize as Otto's business voice. "I'm faxing you the training schedule tonight. In case the weather turns real bad, I'm shipping out a turbo trainer for your basement. You've got a lot of work to do before camp, son. No sittin' around."

Kurt felt the blood rush to his cheeks. He didn't like anyone hinting that he was lazy, and he didn't want to feel like he was being ordered around, even if he was on the lowest rung of the ladder.

The heat subsided and he spoke calmly, "Listen, Otto. Work never bothered me. I told you I'd make the commitment to this. Just keep sending guys like Ramos to teach me what I need to know. We'll all find out soon enough if I can cut it." In his mind, Kurt had already doubled whatever was coming on that fax.

"Okay, okay." Otto's tone changed again. Kurt could almost see his smile on the other end. "We're in this together, kid. I stuck my neck out figuring you *would* work your young Dufour ass off. Look, I'm here to give you advice, not to dictate your life. The guys on the team, though…well…."

Kurt cut him off. "Yeah, I know. They'll want to see what the rookie's made of. Like I said, I made the commitment. I plan to be ready to take their best shots."

Otto cleared his throat. "Just…just do what's on the schedule. Nobody expects miracles. The best thing you can do is come to camp with some miles in your legs; you'll learn more if you're fit. For now, just get used to the bike. Stay in the low gears. We'll talk every Monday. Now please tell Ramos to get his ass back to Milwaukee."

Otto hung up. Kurt replaced the phone and headed for the front door, the carriage house, and Ramos. He wanted to thank him and make sure

46

he had left enough warm clothes. Tomorrow was Day One, and it was expected to be cold and wet.

***

The next day had indeed been cold and wet. And so had many more as fall turned to winter and Kurt Dufour rode the bicycle to catch up. At first it was neither easy nor fun, the seemingly endless days of pedaling in the cold by himself, getting used to a fast bike and a hard saddle. There were long days when he wanted to turn around and, particularly in the beginning, when he didn't even want to get out of bed, so tired was his body and so sore were his legs. But he had been a runner, a good one, and he knew the pain. He forced himself to keep going, to power through the rough patches, and ignore the awful weather.

Gradually, this bizarre new routine became a period of cleansing, an escape from an old life that had ended abruptly with the death of Leslie Conway. For a welcome time now, he had lived in anonymity, clad from head to toe in the Lycra disguise of an unknown professional cyclist. That awful summer was past with certain finality. His future summers would be entirely different. He looked forward to them with anticipation and a nagging apprehension.

During the day, every day, he had ridden the blue Bassini that Ramos had given him. And for the first time in his life, Kurt Dufour had become a planner. He wrote down goals, and he followed schedules. He had taken Otto's weekly faxes on how far to ride, what to eat, and how to monitor his body, and he had turned them into charts and graphs on his laptop computer. He played with it now, noting that the 4,537 miles he had ridden in the last ninety days was 1,537 more than Otto had expected. He had come to enjoy those long rides along the shoreline, the hilly treks to Danbury, Easton, and Bethel. An average of 54 miles a day, a good percentage of it in cold, rain, and even snow. He had not missed one day since Ramos came with the bike. Even on the coldest and most miserable ones he rode at least twenty miles, making up for the short days with five to six hours in the saddle when the temperature topped 40 degrees Fahrenheit. No one else on the team would even be near that. But then they had put in a 20,000-mile season last summer while he was screwing on the beach. He had to play catch up if he was going to do this right.

At night, he had read everything he could. No academics anymore—books and magazines on cycling, the history of the sport, the techniques and advice of the great champions of Europe. As he had been during his one adolescent season, he was inspired by lyrical descriptions of cyclists and curious about how the sport was really played, about the inside of the game he would soon enter. One passage stuck in his mind, written three decades earlier by Robert Daley of the *New York Times*. He wondered if it still applied:

> *Even those who do not crash suffer intensely. From saddle sores, from colic, from the side effects of drugs which all racers take when so near exhaustion that they cannot continue without a stimulant…. It is a grim, grueling business, but each year hundreds of young hopefuls clamor for a place on one team or another….*

Two and a half months passed and Kurt Dufour was finally on the plane to California. The cold winter was behind him. Greenwich was behind him. And he felt ready. He hoped he was, anyway. At least, he would soon find out.

Near the end of the long flight to San Diego he again bent over his laptop and clicked open the file labeled "Vital Statistics," where he had carefully and meticulously entered the way his body had adapted to the new training regimen. His resting pulse had been low to begin with but, for the last twenty-seven mornings, it had never been above forty. Aerobic capacity, recovery rate: both improved. The weight chart showed he had actually gained two pounds since he started riding, all of it seemingly added to his thighs. There was a satisfying tightness there and he had noticed that his pants legs didn't hang so freely anymore.

He didn't dwell on these things, nor did he particularly want to share them with Otto or anyone else. It was more part of a recent and curious self-examination, objective facts and statistics that were there to tell him that his life was changing. He shook his head and shut down his computer. It was high time he met some teammates.

***

"So you're the new guy, Otto's guinea pig. Welcome to the zoo." Paul Spencer offered his hand and the others chuckled in the background.

Here it comes, Kurt thought. He extended his hand and looked Spencer directly in the eye, noting the frizzy shoulder length hair and small diamond earring. "So when do the animals exercise?" he said, smiling. "I'd like to tag along." He ignored the guinea pig reference but filed it away.

Another face stepped forward, older and kinder looking than Spencer's. "Hi. I'm Paul Brock, unofficial tour guide. Tomorrow's our annual shakedown cruise. Tecate to Mexicali over the Rumorosa. Then we party down at Ramos's family Cantina, all the *frijoles* you can eat, and the last *cerveza* for months. Think you're up for it?" His expression was somewhere between challenge and concern. At least Kurt felt he could talk to this guy even if he was confused by the next day's agenda.

Brock took him by the arm and steered him through the door, away from the others and out a few steps to the curb. They stood at the front entrance of the Borrego Motor Lodge in Poway, California, home of the official pre-season training camp for Team GTI, Kurt Dufour's new employer.

"Did you mean we're riding south of the border tomorrow?"

"Yeah. Makes Ramos real happy. The bikes will be here in a few minutes. Otto's doing the last airport run to pick up the rest of the guys. I hear Steele's comin' in too, just for the afternoon." Obviously, Brock liked the role of tour guide. Self-appointed Kurt figured.

"Who's Steele?" Kurt hadn't seen the name on the team roster.

"Boss man. *Capo dei capi*. Grant Steele the second, CEO, chairman, president, all those things, of GTI—you know, the guy who pays your salary. He loves bikes and he likes his name out there. He even won a national championship once, about twenty years ago." Brock leaned close to Kurt's ear and looked around in mock secrecy and whispered, "But that means fuck all, next to the fact that GTI is the nineteenth largest privately held company in the U.S., and Steele owns it all."

Something clicked in Kurt's mind. The Grant in *Grant Titanium Industries*. So that's why Otto said the multibillion-dollar company was so committed to sponsoring the team. But the name Steele had never been mentioned, nor, for that matter, the connection. Kurt answered his own next question.

49

"I guess *Steele Titanium Industries* just doesn't sound right."

"Hey, I'm the tour guide," Brock said. "But that's a pretty good guess. I bet you can figure out what the bikes are made of too." Brock motioned to the big blue truck that was pulling in, a huge red and white *Grant Titanium Industries* billboard plastered on the side. "Here they are."

Within a few minutes, the rest of the team appeared, including Otto and his load from the airport. As they got out of the van, Otto waved and Kurt recognized the team's heavy hitters from pictures he had seen in the magazines: Jeff Martin, team leader; Claude Berclaz, the young climbing sensation; and Mickey Spain, the tough Canadian who, for three days last summer, led the Tour de France as a member of another team.

Otto collected them and herded them over to meet the rookie. Kurt felt a chill race up his spine. Holy shit, what to say to these guys. Instinctively though, he waded in, determined to be the first to extend a hand.

"Hi Jeff, I'm Kurt Dufour, the new guy." He went right for Martin, the leader and a recent world championship medalist.

Martin showed no hesitation. "Otto told us. Welcome aboard." The response was polite, if not friendly, the handshake strong and confident. And it was the same from Spain and Berclaz. Obviously, Otto had their respect and he'd done a good sales job. But for at least the fifth time today, Kurt wondered what he was doing here, in the company of such cycling legends.

For the next couple of hours, the new titanium Bassinis were handed out and adjusted, appointment style, by Ramos and a couple of assistants in a special meeting room that had been set aside in the hotel to store the team's equipment, enough to stock a good sized bike shop. There were nineteen bicycles to be done, Kurt's last. When his turn finally came, Ramos seemed genuinely happy to see him.

"Do we really ride to Mexicali tomorrow?" Kurt still hadn't figured this out and knew he could eventually get the story out of Ramos.

"*Si, muchacho.*" Ramos's gold teeth sparkled. "It is the best day of the year for me. All the new *bici* and all the *muchachos*, we all come to the Ramos *Cantina* and we take the photos. *Fantástico!*"

"But how do we get there?"

"Over *La Rumorosa.*"

"On our bikes?"

"*Si, muchacho.* About six hours."

"From here?"

"No, no." Ramos shook his finger back and forth, smiling. "From Tijuana. The truck takes *los bicicli* to Tijuana and you go by the cars. Then you make the nice ride, Tijuana to Mexicali, over *La Rumorosa.*"

"So, how is your ass?" Ramos had the diagrams in front of him and wanted to finish up. Kurt's new titanium Bassini was in the stand.

"Tougher and tighter, for sure. But it looks like there are a lot of those around here." Kurt had met most all his new teammates by now. Counting himself, nine Americans, two each from Australia, Great Britain, and Canada and one each from Mexico, Colombia, France, and Germany. They seemed a likable bunch. A little aloof around him but then he was the only one without any real roots in the sport. He knew he would have to earn their respect. Maybe tomorrow on *La Rumorosa*, although he wondered about this apparently legendary climb.

He turned his attention to the new bike. It had clean lines and the latest Campagnolo components. He ran his hand over the saddle, noting that it was thinner and lighter looking than the one Ramos had first given him. It was a beautiful blue machine. "Can't get one in white, eh?" he joked.

Ramos shook his head, smiling. "You like to be *diferente*," he muttered, as much to himself as to Kurt.

It only took a few minutes to fine tune the bike, working with the diagrams, and a tape measure. Ramos took it from the stand and turned it over to him, along with a travel bag stuffed with clothes. Everything was color-coordinated in the blue, red, and white team colors. And everywhere was stenciled *GTI* or *Lycramax* or *Bassini* or some other name of a lesser team sponsor or supplier of everything from cars to energy bars. Obviously Otto had been busy last fall.

Before Kurt left the room, Ramos pulled him aside and opened a second door that must have led back to another part of the hotel. Otto Werner and two others entered, men that Kurt did not recognize.

Otto, smiling, eagerly made the introductions.

"Kurt, this is Grant Steele, owner and CEO of Grant Titanium Industries and Tomas Kobzolinski, our new coach and assistant director, from the Czech Republic. Call him Tomi K, he knows his shit."

Tomi K smiled and gave a quick nod. He had a jagged scar that ran from somewhere in his thinning hair to the corner of his right eye. "Glad…finally meet you. Heard much good tings about yurr pulse and lungs. We now make you go…veddy fast." A Czech magician, just what Kurt needed. He liked the heavy Slavic accent, the clipped words, and the rolled r's.

He turned to Grant Steele, whose eyes had not wavered from Kurt since entering the room. Kurt guessed he was in his early-forties, tall with a little gray around the temples. It looked like he kept himself in good shape. Probably kept a bike in his Learjet.

"Welcome to the team, Kurt." His grip was firm, his eyes sharp, and he wore the well-tailored slacks and sport coat of a person who appreciated quality. Kurt sensed why this guy ran the company.

"I know this is all new to you but my guess is that you'll figure it out. Otto's usually right." He smiled easily and clapped Otto on the shoulder. It looked like he was about ready to leave.

"Excuse me, Mr. Steele." Otto, Tomi K, and Ramos all turned in Kurt's direction. Steele waited while the rookie cleared his throat. "I heard you used to race, that you won a national championship." Kurt thought he saw a slight flush wash over Steele's face.

"I...uh...rode a lot when I was a kid," he answered, obviously pleased that he was asked but not used to talking about himself as a cyclist. "But I stopped when I was about your age, maybe a few years older."

"So why did you quit?" The others leaned closer, watching Steele. It was unusual for a player, a rookie at that, to ask such a question of the big boss.

He smiled, a little tentatively, as if he wasn't quite sure how to answer. "Well...that's a question I often asked myself. But I...my father wanted me to take over the family business so I had to make a choice." He shrugged his shoulders. "So now I sponsor the team."

"Well, thanks for giving me a shot," Kurt said. He paused for a moment. "Any advice you could give the rookie?"

Steele thought, carefully. It was clear that Otto's players rarely came to him for counsel and he wanted it to be good...no "tear 'em apart" bullshit speeches from this guy.

He looked intently at Kurt. "At the risk of sounding trite, I guess the most important thing I could say to you is...set your standards high. And don't compromise them, particularly when you run into lowlifes who try to pull you down." He hesitated for a moment, looked at Otto, Tomi K, Ramos, and then back to Kurt. "And pay attention to these guys. You have a lot to learn. They'll help steer you through the bullshit." His look said they were all willing to take the chance.

They shook hands and Steele motioned for Otto to walk out with him.

Kurt wondered why Steele and the others who knew cycling so well— Otto, his father, Ramos—all seemed so concerned about his ability to handle whatever was coming. They didn't seem to realize that he was prepared, mentally at least, to play this game. How tough could it be, he thought. As bad as the death of a girl? Being accused of murder, seeing doubt in the eyes of the people closest to you? For chrissake, it was just a sport.

Kurt watched Grant Steele II, his benefactor, follow Otto out of the room. Little did he know then that he would never see the man again.

****

Chapter Eight

La Rumorosa

It was a beautiful day in the arid high country around Poway above San Diego. Some January days, like this one, were as near perfect as days could be. The early-morning chill burned off rapidly, leaving the promise of warm, sun-drenched hours filled with the sensual fragrance of eucalyptus, manzanita, and pine. And the sky was a deep, cloudless blue splashed over endless low hills and high mountains, a natural playground between the Pacific Ocean and Mojave Desert.

This was where the young men on bicycles came for a short time each year to ride like boys, pedaling along quiet roads throughout the endless days, sometimes at a slow ramble, and sometimes at an energetic pace that fanned their pedals like the blurred paddles of a windmill. But what play these weeks offered was only part of the story. It was spring training, and the miles pedaled, the exercises done, and the measurements taken were all part of the critical foundation of a long, hard racing season that would take each one to his limit of physical and mental stamina. Some bowed out after one or two seasons. Some came back year after year, over time becoming tough, and hard, and realistic. Realistic about who they were and who they could become in a sport that had no place for weakness and only a small opening for winners.

And in this hardest of sports, winners are created from the remains of fallen and battered men, from bodies and minds that push aside pain, and from roads and conditions that twist steel and sear lungs. And from a fire. A fire deep within the soul that cannot accept defeat that is fueled, for undefined reason, by whatever is thrown in the road. When such a winner comes along, the others eventually must step aside, moving to another, smaller team or staying on to become *équipiers* or *domestiques*. They will earn their salaries by helping to fan the winner's fire, by understanding that the quarterback gets the glory and the lineman opens the holes. This is a lesson that needs to be learned by every rider, for none steps directly to the podium.

For Team GTI, spring training started with the annual rite south of the border, dubbed by Otto several seasons ago simply as the Rumorosa Cruise. It was mostly in honor of Manuel Ramos who, in all the glory of a made-good native son, got to show off his *ciclistas* and *bicicletas* to his aging papa, and hundreds of family and friends, most of whom regarded this day as their annual look at the world outside Mexicali. A world that only Ramos knew and one that must be special because from there came the pesos that bought their *Cantina*.

Kurt Dufour was impatient. The two-by-two column of his teammates formed nine tight ranks in front of him. He watched their backs and their shoulders gently sway to the rhythm of easy spinning. They were poking along, he thought. They talked and they told jokes. Only he, as number nineteen and with no one riding next to him, had to suffer the slow pace in silence. Tomi K, Otto, and a big guy with a red bandanna on his head and cameras around his neck, the team photographer Kurt guessed, rode sleepily in the team car behind. The equipment truck and extra vehicles had deposited them just east of Tijuana and were already long gone to Mexicali.

Kurt had bought a road map last night and finally found out from Brock that La Rumorosa was the long climb over the Sierra de Juarez, the high spine of mountains that stretched south from the California border and, in the northern part of Mexico, separated the fertile coastal region from the lower, drier Mexican Mojave. It was explained that they would pedal easily the whole way—about fifty miles across the coastal plain to the foot of the mountains, twelve miles up the Rumorosa, and forty-some miles from the summit down to the desert and across to Mexicali. With all the miles he had been riding, a piece of cake, Kurt thought.

They had been pedaling easily for two hours now. It had given Kurt time to think. He felt good, his legs felt strong, and the warm, dry air had cleared away the memory of the weeks and months he had spent pounding through the raw Connecticut winter. The new bike felt comfortable under him, his pedals spun smoothly and effortlessly, far more so than during those first few weeks. He was in the best physical condition of his life, and he was frustrated at being the new guy, the fresh-faced rookie who arrived at camp with no reputation other than that of Otto's weird experiment, the rehab case. He knew they saw it that way.

There was a line in the sand he had to cross, and not by being courteous, and humble, and brown-nosed. Up to this point, he had been polite and nice to everyone. But now Kurt Dufour, with fire burning inside, wanted to kick some ass.

The road out of Tecate rose gradually, still about twenty miles from the base of La Rumorosa. Dufour pulled out from behind, clicked into a bigger gear, and moved along the outside line of riders. He looked straight ahead as he passed each of the nine ranks, sensing that the heads turned in wonderment at the new guy picking up the pace. There were a couple of catcalls and, from Spencer, something unintelligible—and, then, "Whoa…watch out…there he goes!" But no one chased, and soon Kurt was several hundred yards out front, by himself. Way ahead he could see the mountains, their tops obscured by heavy clouds.

It was where he wanted to be. Alone and pedaling hard, eating up the road, and feeling the power of his newly strengthened legs drive him forward. The small odometer on his handlebars said he was cruising at a steady 26 miles per hour. At this pace, the lazy group behind would fall farther and farther back. He knew he could ride hard like this for the next seventy miles, all the way to Mexicali. Even the Rumorosa didn't scare him. He didn't care about the ground rules—an easy cruise, Otto said. For Kurt, this was a *race*. He would prove that he could go the distance, that he'd come to camp better prepared than all of them. He would get to Mexicali first.

The road started to climb, gradually at first. And then came the clouds and a heavy mist. Up and up, no sign of the team or anyone behind. Kurt powered on, still feeling good. He was on the lower slopes of the mountain, lush green farmland shrouded in mist. A farmer in rubber boots and straw hat paused to watch the lone cyclist pedal by.
Like the scarecrow in the "Wizard of Oz" he pointed up toward the clouds, where the road disappeared. "*La Rumorosa!*" he shouted. The dog by his side emitted a long, baleful howl.

The road got steeper and it started to rain, lightly at first, and then a steady downpour. And it got colder. Kurt wondered about his teammates behind. Did they stop somewhere and wait out the rain, or did they keep going? Just when his hands and his toes were starting to feel uncomfortably cold, he saw headlights coming from behind. In a moment the team car was beside him, Otto leaning out the passenger window. He wasn't smiling.

"Pull over," he commanded.

"But I want to keep going, I feel good." Show no weakness.

56

"Pull the fuck over, you dipshit!"

The heavy photographer was leaning out the back window, flashing shots rapid fire. "This is great stuff," he said. "Look at the snot running off his nose!"

Kurt pulled to the side of the road. Otto jumped out with a handful of clothes. Thick cotton gloves, long tights, a long-sleeved top, and toe warmers to put over his shoes. And a wool cap with ear flaps.

"Put these on, quickly, and keep going." Otto helped and Ramos jumped out to hold the bike. The photographer clicked away. "Whoa…Titanium Man," he said.

"Where are they?"

"They're where they're supposed to be, you dumb shit. Way down the mountain, riding easy. Nice and toasty." Otto wrenched the jersey over Kurt's head. They were nose to nose. "Now, you want to be the hero. Get back on your bike and bust your ass over the mountain and across the desert. Throw the clothes on the side of the road when you start getting hot. And eat this." He jammed some sort of mushy energy bar into Kurt's mouth. Ramos had already put two full plastic bottles in the cages on the bike. They pushed him off into the chilling rain, up La Rumorosa. The car sped ahead and then turned around in the road. Ramos was driving, and his gold teeth flashed at Kurt as they passed on the way back down. An outstretched thumbs-up drew back into the car. And then they were gone.

The rain turned to sleet and the road got steeper. Kurt pushed back second thoughts. The confrontation with Otto furthered his resolve, and he was warmer now. He pressed on, wondering how far he was from the summit.

There were no hills in Connecticut that came near the Rumorosa. This was a true mountain pass where, in January even this far south, rain, sleet, and sometimes snow marked increasing elevation changes. Kurt Dufour, alone, rode through it all. By the time he reached the summit, his bike and his body were covered with an icy crust and, with teeth chattering and legs weakening, he began the fourteen-mile, twisting plunge to the desert floor. As he dropped out of the clouds, the weather changed dramatically. Warm winds blew up from the desert, some of them so strong that he was almost blown off his bike. He descended as fast as he could—speed rarely below fifty miles per hour—and tried desperately to keep his now fragile-feeling rail of titanium under control around the tight switchbacks and against the buffeting winds. On one long straight stretch, he got his first view of the desert below and the solitary line of asphalt that lay across it. And way off, the only hint of civilization he could see: Mexicali.

It was hot by the time he got down to the desert. Brutally hot. He stopped briefly to shed the clothes Otto had brought. With a touch of sick humor, he laid them out on the side of the road as if they were still on. He stretched the left arm out, pointing it in the direction of Mexicali.

He climbed back on the bike. The road was hot and lifeless, stretching as far as he could see, undulating over the sand toward the finish. He was not so energetic now. His legs were heavy and he felt a general weakness start to spread over him. And a growing hunger from the pit of his stomach. But there was no sign of anyone behind. He decided to try to keep his odometer pegged at twenty-two miles per hour. Maybe he could still hold them off.

Gradually, he began to lose his sense of time and distance. It seemed like he had been pedaling across the desert forever, and then, shimmering on the side of the road, a sign: "Mexicali 10." Ten miles? Ten kilometers? His mind wrestled with this problem for quite some time. Trucks passed him and a few cars. A guy in a pick-up eased alongside. "How 'bout a ride boy?" the cowboy shouted. "Y'all look lower than a snake's belly, boy." Kurt shook his head and barely looked up. His tongue was too dry to speak. He stared down at the odometer: 21.5…22.0…21.5.

Kurt had no sense of what was coming from behind. If he had the energy to look over his shoulder, back over the undulating black band toward the mountains he had crossed, he would have seen a tight, fast-moving string of eighteen cyclists eating up the gap he had so long struggled to create.

From somewhere inside his head, he thought he heard the sound of a car horn. Honking…relentlessly, right behind him. He mustered the energy to weakly wave the car around. His dry lips and tongue tried to form the words: "Pass me…asshole."

A face suddenly appeared next to him. He felt cool water splashing all over him, over his hot, uncovered head. Otto Werner was there again. Or was it Ramos? Kurt was blind with fatigue, and hunger, and emptiness.

It was Otto. He grinned, shaking his head. "Four miles to go you dumb rookie. Stay to the right when they go by."

The car disappeared somewhere off to the side. And suddenly Kurt sensed motion on his left, his right, bicycles blowing by at tremendous speed. And shouting. "*Hop on!*" was all he understood.

"Hop on *what*?" he thought. He raised his head and watched the blue snake disappear over the next rise. Gone. "What the hell was that? A mirage." He shook his head and looked down: 18.5...19.0...18.5.

The next thing he felt was a hand in the middle of his back. It must've been there for a while because his bike was moving and he was barely pedaling. He had the sensation of chewing, something soft and moist. And then liquid, in his mouth, down his back, all over his head. The fog that had owned his mind started to drift away. He looked to his left into a hard, angular face. There was a smile there, and intelligent, kind eyes that were searching for something in his.

"'Ey mate...anybody home?" Patterson, the Australian. He pedaled close and strongly alongside. It was his hand on Kurt's back, pushing.

"Are you the first one to catch me?" Kurt croaked.

"Fuck me! You've gone bloody daft on us now, mate. What d'ya think that was that just went by?" Patterson was chuckling, still pushing.

"A mirage. You see them sometimes in the desert." Kurt was beginning to realize what happened. "Oh shit," he added.

"That was no mirage, mate. That was the bloody fuckin' freight train, that was."

"Oh shit."

What a fool, he thought. They were playing with him. And here he thought he could beat them to Mexicali. He tried to pedal harder, hoping that Patterson would stop pushing. It didn't work; his legs felt locked up.

"Toughest bloody rookie *I've* ever seen." Patterson's push changed to a few pats and then back to a push. "Usually, we catch 'em halfway up the Rumorosa." When Kurt turned to him, he was looking straight ahead.

***

Kurt would never forget that long day over La Rumorosa or that night at the Ramos *Cantina* in Mexicali. The big baptism was over, the line was crossed, and the *cerveza* flowed freely.

They laughed and they joked, mostly at the expense of the *neo-pro,* the greenest of the green, who, despite his lack of knowledge of the sport's subtleties, had the balls to go it alone until he had pushed himself beyond all reason. The guys liked that. And Ramos's Mexican friends frequently passed by for a close look at the *gringo* who knew how to suffer because Ramos told them, in passionate Spanish, how important that was in his world of *el ciclismo.*

Kurt Dufour had recovered quickly that evening, cured by plenty of Mexican food, and high energy concoctions whipped up by Tomi K. He was glad he was with this bizarre team of cyclists, people who appreciated honest effort, even if his had been naïve and ill-timed. He knew he would learn from this, that it was just the beginning.

The evening ended with Otto, Tomi K, John Patterson, Kurt, and four shots of cognac for each of them, a Tomi K tradition, it was explained.

"*Here's to La Rumorosaaah!*" Otto bellowed, slamming his first empty shot glass on the table.

"*Herre is to man who climb Rum...Rum...Rumoza like goat. Better to haff to pull back...than kick in ass.*" Tomi K smiled through bloodshot eyes, and tossed down his second shot.

"*Here's...here's to being th...thmart.*" Dufour missed his mouth and the cognac dribbled down his chin.

60

Patterson stood up, swaying dangerously. With his left hand, he raised his last full shot glass to the spinning ceiling. He placed his right hand on his heart and looked heavenward.

" 'Ere mates... 'ere's to the Tour and the bloody yellow jersey. And 'ere's to the sweat on me balls that says we can have Comtec and Jacques Poulain before I throw in the friggin' towel!"

They all tossed down their last shots. For the players, the last ones for many months. And then, with Ramos and the rest of their teammates, they staggered from the *Cantina* into the cool desert night.

****

Chapter Nine

The Frenchman

Five Years Later

Jacques Poulain deftly swung his racing bicycle around at the sign for Chalon-sur-Saône and chuckled to himself as André, obviously daydreaming, failed to react quickly enough, piloting his small motorcycle through the intersection and then to a screeching stop. Over his shoulder, Poulain could see André struggling to turn the motorbike around and kick-start it back to life.

The famous French cyclist had steadily punched his bicycle through a headwind for the first half of today's two-hundred-kilometer training ride, only occasionally tucking in behind André's motorcycle for a little relief. He smiled to himself. Less than three hours back to Bourg-en-Bresse, all with a tailwind. With two, nearly imperceptible presses of his right thumb, the bike leaped into a higher gear. Poulain felt his thighs tighten as he applied more force to the pedals, powerfully increasing the speed of his *vélo*. Even on the faster motorbike, it would take André several kilometers to catch up.

Poulain settled into the comfortable and powerful cadence that had been the envy of the European cycling world for a decade. Like a golfer with a great swing, he elevated the seemingly simple act of making pedals go around into an effortless flow of movement. His legs synchronized like pistons, their rapid-fire whirl in complete contrast to his relaxed and motionless upper body. The man and his bicycle flew down the road as one, adding kilometer after kilometer to the distance bank he had been building since adolescence. Jean-Marie Lavec had told him way back then that kilometers were an investment in his future and, to be *un vrai champion,* his account must be bigger than that of any of his competitors.

That was all young Jacques had needed to hear because he loved to ride his bicycle more than anything else. During the countless hours he had spent pedaling over the hills and valleys of his native Burgundy, he had often thought of Lavec's advice. The old man, a winner of the Tour de France on the dusty roads of long ago, would no doubt be proud of him now because Poulain's kilometer bank had made him richer and nearly as famous as any other Frenchman in history.

From Poulain's absolute love of *le vélo* had sprung his insatiable need to win races. Lavec had filled his head full of the dreams of champions—superhuman exploits over high Alpine passes...crushing power on the cobblestones...headlines in all the world's newspapers...absolute glory as a Frenchman winning his country's contribution to the world's legendary sports events: *la plus grande course de cyclisme, Le Tour de France.*

Poulain had become *l'Homme Choisi,* the Chosen One. In five starts, he had won the Tour five times, equaling the records of only three men in the nearly one-hundred-year history of the Tour. In five years, he had restored pride to his people, a nation fearful of losing its identity through the Common Market and Euro Disney. In five years, he had stopped Italians, Belgians, Spaniards, and Americans from stealing his country's national treasure, *le maillot jaune*—the yellow jersey—awarded only to the one who leads the race and eventually wins...

It had been an hour since the turnaround at Chalon-sur-Saône, and Poulain maintained a steady fifty kilometer-per-hour pace with André patiently waiting for instructions a few meters behind. Halfway to Bourg-en Bresse, Poulain drew a small mobile phone from his jersey pocket and motioned for André to pull his motorcycle alongside so he could hand it to him.

"Tell them to be ready at Mâcon. I'm feeling very good and I don't want anything in the way." André nodded and shouted orders into the phone, his head turned sideways so his helmet at least partially blocked interference from the wind.

Twenty minutes later, they had recrossed the Saône and started heading east on the N79 toward Vonnas. Just after the bridge, Poulain spotted the bright yellow Peugeot with his spare bike on top and the additional two escort motorcycles Andre had called for. As he approached, the vehicles accelerated into his lane with the two motorcycles staying a hundred meters ahead. The Peugeot, driven by *directeur sportif* Guy Leguerre, pulled alongside and close enough to Poulain so that the cyclist could hold onto the door and lean into the window.

"You are ahead of schedule, *mon ami*," Leguerre shouted above the sound of the wind and the car.

"So what do you expect from the winner of *six* Tours de France? You must get me back quickly for my massage and my interview with *Katrine*." Poulain shouted back even though his head was almost in the window and his face only a few centimeters from Leguerre's. Leguerre could see traces of spittle at the corners of his mouth, and smell four hours of sweat on the body of France's greatest cyclist.

Leguerre nodded, motioned for Poulain to go ahead, and then quickly reached for the button to raise his window. As they had done countless times before, the three motorcycles and following team car formed a cocoon around Poulain, protecting him from other vehicles and cyclists traveling on the same road. A couple of *gendarmes* would join them at Vandeins for the last few kilometers into Bourg-en-Bresse, and, with a little luck, they would sail through the intersections, stopping enough traffic and drawing enough cheering onlookers to keep Poulain in a jovial mood. This was essential, Leguerre knew, if his superstar were to remain in the right frame of mind for the remaining week before the start of his sixth Tour de France.

"Of course, you think he will win again." The question, phrased as a statement in textbook French, came from the young female reporter accompanying Leguerre. They both looked through the windshield at the twin metronomes that were Poulain's calves.

"Bien sûr, il n'y a pas aucune doute." *Of course, there's not the slightest doubt.* Leguerre had given this response hundreds, perhaps thousands, of times in the last five years. Right now, he did not feel comfortable being stuck in the car with this reporter "from the outside," and the less he had to say, the better. It was never a problem to spend an hour or a whole day with a cycling journalist who knew what to ask and when to ask it. But it made Leguerre nervous that the young woman had never seen *Le Tour*, and that she was assigned to gather background information for Katherine Anderson, an American with one of the big TV networks. It made him even more nervous to think that Poulain had agreed to spend the better part of several days with two attractive female journalists on the eve of the most important race of his career.

"Isn't there anyone who could possibly beat him?" The young woman was probing for a story but she didn't quite know how to get past the surface.

Leguerre looked over at her. She was an attractive young woman with dark, shoulder-length hair, an athletic body, and intelligent brown eyes—and obviously full of energy for what had to be her first big assignment. He wanted to help her do a good job, partly because it seemed so important to her, and partly because she reminded him of his own daughter. He was torn between giving her something to write about and preserving her naïveté. For the time being, he decided to stay near the surface.

"It is unlikely that anyone will beat Jacques again this year. He has the good form and a very strong team. Plus, he has the drive to be the first of any man in history to win six. The only possible problem I can see is if he gets caught in a crash or gets sick."

The reporter was looking for something more. "I've heard that many of the other racers don't like him, and they will try extra hard to stop him."

Leguerre smiled, as if he'd heard this before. "Ah, but what can they do?" He motioned toward Poulain on the road in front, now on a steady uphill stretch. The champion had scarcely slowed, his powerful legs still driving the bike with a pounding rhythm that had not been affected in the least by nearly five hours in the saddle.

"Just look at him. He has the strength, the power, and the will of a superhuman. And he is surrounded by all these people who take care of him…big businessmen, trainers, coaches, drivers…teammates who are paid many, many francs to make sure he wins. Look at us. Five people and two gendarmes who have met him on the road with six vehicles to make sure he has a good ride today…that he doesn't have to slow for a traffic light or be inconvenienced by anyone. Poulain owns the public, and he owns the *peloton.* That is why he will win again…no matter who would like to stop him."

That seemed to be enough for the young reporter for now. She dropped her notepad on the seat between them and settled back for a while, content, it seemed, to watch a little of the French countryside roll by her window.

65

Leguerre casually glanced down at her notepad, and then, more deliberately, focused on something he noticed she had scribbled in the margin. Framed in a penciled square he could read the question: *Pourquoi pas Kurt Dufour?*

Leguerre looked from the page to his passenger. She was watching him now, a broad smile on her face.

"Well, you saw the question," she said. "Don't you think he has any chance at all?"

Leguerre wasn't laughing. So this was the main reason for the American network to press so hard for time with Poulain. They wanted to promote a ridiculous rivalry between this upstart American and the great French champion. Leguerre had agreed to the interview time based solely on the network's intention to do a "lifestyle" piece on Poulain. He should have known that Katherine Anderson would be trying to create something sensational around Kurt Dufour's transformation from an accused killer to a Tour de France contender.

Leguerre softened. Don't dignify the concept, he thought.

"Ridiculous," he said with an unconvincing smile. "Totally ridiculous. Dufour has talent, *oui*. But he is unproved in the Tour. He has been racing only five seasons, and he did not grow up on *le vélo* as all the real champions have done. Do not upset Jacques with this talk now."

Leguerre himself was upset. He knew that the one issue that enraged his champion was the increasing talk of this rivalry. It all stemmed from last month's Giro d'Italia, in which Kurt Dufour suddenly emerged as a possible contender. The telling moment was in the time trial, one man against the clock, on the penultimate day. In this épreuve de verité—*the race of truth*—Dufour had managed to record a time within a few seconds of Poulain over thirty-five kilometers, the closest anyone had come to the legend in some four years. Even though Poulain took the overall victory, Dufour grabbed the headlines, and finally gave the sportswriters something to talk about and, in most cases, hope for.

In his innermost thoughts, Leguerre knew that the sport needed a shakeup. Poulain's dominance of the Tour had been great for France in the beginning, but his growing inability to accept any kind of shortcoming and his arrogance in victory had made him highly vulnerable as his country's premier sports icon. He demanded edification. At any time, day or night, he expected his every wish to be granted, regardless of whom it affected or how much it cost. His agents had demanded, and got, an annual salary of 10 million francs from Jérôme Garnier, one of France's wealthiest businessmen and the backer of *l'équipe Comtec*.

But for Garnier and his Comtec Internationale corporation, their investment in sponsoring the world's top cycling team paid off handsomely—so long as Poulain kept winning the Tour. And Garnier's advertising and communications people saw to it that the expenditure was justified by presenting elaborate charts and graphs showing television audience figures, massive readership numbers, and big sales gains that all somehow indicated a twenty-fold return on its sponsorship investment. In any case, Garnier did what he wanted with Comtec's money. He was the majority shareholder, and he made sure there was no opposition to his way of running the company. The millions he invested in his sporting ventures each year did not really have to be justified to anyone.

Guy Leguerre's investment in Poulain had also been great, in a much different way. He had made a career out of steering Poulain to the top, feeding his ego when it needed feeding, taking care of his every need, so all he had to do was ride his bike and win races. He had even wrestled Poulain from his parents when he saw that their influence might have interfered in his cycling career. Just before Jean-Marie Lavec had died, he and Leguerre had conspired to pull Poulain from his last year of school, telling the parents that he would return after one season with the national amateur team. At the end of that season, Poulain turned eighteen and was able to sign his own pro contract, no matter what his parents wanted him to do. It was Leguerre who drew up the contract and handed Poulain the pen.

Over the past year, Leguerre had begun to regret much of this. He cringed when Poulain referred to him in the press as "mon vrai père." *my true father.* He regretted spending his daughter's youth making this kid into a champion instead of being a real father to her. Tour number six, he promised himself, would be the last.

But for now, as he pulled into the lot of the Comtec headquarters at Bourg-en-Bresse with the pretty young reporter, it was business as usual.

***

Within a few minutes Leguerre had parked the car and ushered her through the security gate. They entered the protected south side of the ultramodern building into an area that appeared more like a lavish country club than a business office. The side entrance to Comtec Internationale's corporate headquarters was for Jérôme Garnier's sports-related businesses—his monthly magazine, *L'Équipe Sportif*, and the operations offices of his soccer, ice hockey, and cycling teams. Here, his champion athletes and the people who administered to them could feel at home. The more formal front entrance, with its circular drive and ring of international flags, was reserved for Comtec's real businessmen, bright young executives from all over the world who bought and sold the building blocks of Garnier's global empire, now a ten-billion-dollar industry founded on developing and marketing leading-edge pharmaceuticals that generated huge profits.

Poulain's bike was resting against the wall just inside the gate. The champion himself was already sitting near the pool surrounded by the team doctor, his *soigneur*, and masseuse, each determined to be the quickest to begin their respective checkups and therapies.

When Poulain saw his *directeur sportif* he called out, "Guy, Guy! How did I look? If I feel like this next week, they must give me *le maillot* without starting." He was obviously quite pleased with himself, and he rattled on a little louder when he saw the woman walking behind Leguerre. "Did you see the look on that old man's face when he jammed on the brakes? *Merde*, I thought he was going through the windshield!"

Leguerre forced a smile and a thumbs-up sign, hoping that this and his purposeful stride to the building would avoid the need to stop and chat. He should have known that Poulain was more interested in the young reporter. But it was just as well for now, he thought; there was a lot to do and not much time in which to do it.

****

Chapter Ten

Preparation

Guy Leguerre, as principal organizer of Comtec's ten-man Tour de France team, was used to living with stress, particularly during the final week leading to the Tour's start. But this year was the worst. Poulain's arrogance was getting on everyone's nerves, Garnier was putting extraordinary pressure on Leguerre to make sure his man won, and now this distraction about some American pretender, fueled, no less, by a couple of good-looking female reporters.

He had a half-dozen cars to be readied, twenty new bikes to be fitted and checked, new uniforms to be issued, accommodations to be reviewed, and several platoons of egos to soothe. His lieutenants were good all right, but the three-week march around France destroyed all but the toughest and best-organized squads. He knew this well. There must not be even the slightest weakness at the start.

These thoughts were uppermost in Leguerre's mind when he made the turn from the hall into his office and bumped awkwardly into a woman he had never seen before but instantly recognized. He recoiled in surprise and knocked into his cluttered desk, sending a pile of papers scattering to the floor, while at the same time noticing that there was another stranger in his office: a man with a TV camera on his shoulder. As he bent over to pick up the mess of papers, Leguerre was aware of a bright light suddenly flooding the room.

Impossible he thought. He purposely lingered over the spilled papers to give himself a moment to think. No reporters had been authorized to be in his office. What a nervy crew.

He slowly straightened up to face Katherine Anderson's question: "Is Poulain afraid of Dufour?"

Leguerre was too seasoned, too smart, to get sucked in by such a cheap trick. A huge smile spread over his face and he looked directly into the camera, making sure he was about ten centimeters from the lens. He cocked his head as he responded: "Shit, fuck, piss, cock, cunt...sont les seuls mots que je connais en anglais...excusez-moi, madame." *[These] are the only words I know in English.*

69

"All right, all right, turn it off." The cameraman lowered his camera and switched off the lights. Anderson, without apology, leaned against the desk, crossed her arms and stared at the floor. After an uncomfortable pause, she shook her head and raised her face to Leguerre.

Katherine Anderson's blonde good looks had a hard edge to them, and her smile was too perfect. So this is the legendary American TV journalist—all business, Leguerre thought. She extended her hand to him, more as an acknowledgment of the standoff than an introduction.

Leguerre took her hand, bringing it gently to his lips. "I am quite charmed, madame," he said in perfect, sarcastic English.

"A gentleman with your charm couldn't possibly know the meaning of all those English words you said to the camera." Her smile was a poor attempt at being friendly.

"*Mais, oui.* Of course I only use words like that when someone enters my office without my permission and without making a reasonable introduction. In any case, I have not agreed to be interviewed, and I am about ready to send you and your little sister out there back to your hotel. Maybe you can spend some time with us after *Le Tour.*" Leguerre plucked one of the papers from the clutter on his desk and pretended to read it. There was a long silence.

Finally, Katherine Anderson leaned back on the desk, brushed a wayward strand of blonde hair from her face, looked intently at Leguerre, and said, "Listen, I apologize if I put you on the spot. But we did have an appointment to spend part of this afternoon with Poulain, and you're the guy who manages him. I thought we could get a word with you first."

"Then try asking. It sounds like the rules are changing. I thought you were supposed to be doing a profile on a great champion, not a sensationalism piece on a pretend rivalry...."

At that moment, they were interrupted by a commotion in the hall. Poulain, trailed by his doctor and masseuse, burst into the room. The young reporter, obviously wounded, trailed behind them.

"Merde, merde, merde!" Poulain exclaimed, gesturing wildly. "Je ne me connais pas ce Dufour!" *I don't know this Dufour!* To me, he is nothing and I do not wish to discuss this so-called challenge. He can meet me in the Alps like the rest of them. Guy, cancel the interview!"

Poulain left by a side door with all but the reporter in tow. The soigneur slammed the door behind them, leaving Leguerre alone with Anderson, her cameraman, and the young assistant. Leguerre looked at Anderson and shrugged his shoulders.

"Perhaps I can call you in the morning and we can start over," Anderson said. For the first time, she looked a little sheepish, but certainly not defeated.

"J'en doute, *I doubt it....*" Leguerre replied. "Our champion is not happy and I have much to do, much to do."

***

"Jenny, get New York on the line, we have to find out when the Americans are arriving. I want a different focus for the opening." Katherine Anderson drummed her fingers nervously on the linen-covered table as she scanned her production schedule. She hadn't touched the croissants but there were already three lipstick-stained cigarette butts crushed in the ashtray and a nearly empty carafe of coffee at her elbow.

"Today's Monday. Remember, the NBA final was yesterday...."

Jennifer Scott reminded her boss that there would be no production staff on duty to call the day after the final NBA championship telecast, and the American team wasn't due to arrive from Switzerland until Thursday. They both knew that coverage of the Tour de France was well below the priority given to basketball and much of the help they would've gotten from New York on a more important assignment just wasn't available to them. It would be a few days yet even until the second skeleton unit arrived with their line producer, director and interpreter. And the decision had already been made to get their opening material from Poulain's camp.

"Goddam French bicycle race," Anderson muttered. "These frogs are a real pain in the ass." She took a long drag on yet another cigarette and looked out the window of the hotel café, obviously wishing she were somewhere other than Lyon. Although she was in her late-thirties and still attractive enough, Katherine Anderson's glory days with the network were behind her. Fifteen years ago, she was a rising star, a fresh young reporter with a shot at an anchor position. Back then, on-camera talent was pampered, even sheltered. When network money had flowed freely, all the talent had to do was step in front of the camera, look pretty, and read the cue cards.

But to be good these days, an on-camera reporter had to do much more. Having to come up with quality material, write her own voice-overs, and sit through overnight edits never quite suited Katherine Anderson. She knew the business well enough, but her own material had rarely gone beyond second-rate, and the hard edges to her personality had barred her from ever reaching the anchor's desk. To the relief of her bosses, she had become one of a handful of second-stringers who settled for providing the network with their sensationalized, behind-the-scenes stories for both the news and sports departments. Often pre-empted and seldom of substance, Anderson's work had fallen into the someone-has-to-do-it category.

So here she was in Lyon, France, charged with wringing a Franco-American rivalry out of two professional bicycle racers during a three-week bicycle race that, to most Americans, had as much relevance as a cricket tournament in the West Indies.

Anderson shook her head, took a last long drag of her cigarette, and then crushed it into the small pile of butts she had already made.

"So now what do we do, miss cub reporter?" The smoke from her question curled toward Scott who, as politely as possible, leaned back in her chair to avoid being engulfed. "Neither of us scored real big with the frogs, and our tease is supposed to be uplinked the day after tomorrow. We've got to get something fresh on Poulain, and Leguerre won't even speak to me on the phone. Goddam frogs."

Jennifer Scott was the antithesis of Katherine Anderson. Recently out of college, this was her first field assignment with the network, and she had accepted it with youthful eagerness. To her, being a production assistant on the network's coverage of the Tour de France, however insignificant it may turn out to be, was a glorious shot at the big time. The fact that they were pretty much on their own in France meant she would have greater opportunity to make a significant contribution to the production. Direct the crew, do some interviews. Things like that.

With that in mind, she pulled a rumpled piece of paper from her pocket and spread it on the table.

"We can get past Leguerre", she said. "Poulain, before he got angry, gave me his private number. I think I can get in to see him."

Anderson shook her head and chuckled. "He wants in your shorts, honey. Don't count on getting near him with a camera."

"We'll see", Scott replied. "I'll go make the call."

***

Within twenty minutes it was all set. They'd have the interview, and they would make the satellite in time. Jennifer Scott breathed a sigh of relief, glad that she was able to turn Poulain around without having to make any promises.

She was a precocious twenty-two-year-old, a recent Dartmouth grad with girl-next-door good looks and a disarming smile that was sometimes misinterpreted by the men she met. Even though Greenwich, Connecticut, was not exactly a cauldron of diversity, she had used the opportunity it provided to get around a bit. She was not happy with everything she had seen.

It was not that she was a feminist, it was just that she was beginning to see people, some men in particular, for what they were, and that her own life had been more a reaction to others than a commitment to herself. She was beginning to figure out how to meld the two. When it came to Jacques Poulain, she felt, instinctively, that a little pandering to his ego would get her what they needed. The risk, of course, was one of misinterpretation.

Guy Leguerre was altogether different. She thought he was someone who could be reached on a more human level, without the raging hormones and the big ego. Jennifer had enjoyed riding with him in the car, following Poulain like a daughter with her father. She was disappointed to hear how Katherine, in her usual, insensitive manner had blown that avenue. Some people just don't get it, she thought.

She was curious about Kurt Dufour. It was ironic that she had ended up in the same place as he, five years after they had both taken separate paths out of Greenwich. It was a strange story, this guy who was all over the news for allegedly murdering some debutante, now about to break into the big time for pedaling his bicycle fast. And she was going to be the one to help tell the world. It scared her a little. At least she was following him because of an assignment, not passion. It was the one part of the story she hoped Katherine Anderson, with her background of sleaze reporting, would warm to.

The table had been cleared by the time Jennifer got back to the dining room. All that remained was Katherine and her ashtray full of crushed, lipstick-stained butts.

"All set!" Jennifer cried cheerily.

"What a wonderful little tart you must be," The half-smile said this was some sort of compliment.

Scott smiled her best Greenwich smile through a new cloud of Anderson's blue smoke. "We have a couple of hours so, if you don't mind, I think I'll go out for some postcards."

Anderson rolled her eyes. "Oh, what fun," she said. "There's the cutest little card shop down the block. I think I'll just stay here and suck on more tobacco." She smiled brightly, making Scott laugh for once. Sick, but funny.

It was clear and warm on the little cobbled street outside their hotel. Jennifer walked slowly, suddenly caught up in the romance of being in France, alone for once, on her own and heading into an exciting television assignment.

For the first time in years she felt no pressure to call him. She even decided against a postcard. Free at last. He, no doubt, was still at the apartment in Hanover for the summer session at Dartmouth College. Maybe by now he had found another young coed to lure with his good looks and his sharp professor's intellect. If he wanted two years from the next one, he'd have to sober up a bit, maybe even give up his stupid softball team for the summer. There were concerts on the Green every Tuesday night. He could impress her with those, play the Renaissance man until his ball and bat leaped out of the closet at him. God, he looked silly in that royal blue softball cap and shirt with "Co-op" on the back. She wondered how he must've reacted when he got home to find everything gone but his books and his softball gear, laid out neatly on the bed she no longer had the stomach to share.

It had not been easy to leave him, the first man to whom she'd been seriously attracted. But she discovered his charm didn't stop with her. It hurt. And the hurt, and catching him in the act, finally gave her the courage to break it off, eased, of course, by graduation and the new career. Thank goodness for brothers with vans, she thought.

She stopped in front of the card shop window. There was a poster of Jacques Poulain, leaning casually against his bike, wearing the unmistakable *maillot jaune*. He was tan and handsome, and his broad smile emitted a white cloud in which was written, "Juillet en France...suivez Le Tour chaque jour dans L'Équipe Sportif! *July in France... follow the Tour every day in L'Equipe Sportif!* She sensed an irony here: same type of man, different uniform, bigger league. Much bigger thighs.

She knew, she hoped, that there were better men out there. Perhaps someday she would find one. From across the street, a lean young man in a black beret whistled to her and waved. Not today. Jennifer Scott was in no hurry at all. All she wanted now was to learn television, to get this job done better than anyone expected.

She went into the shop to find a postcard for her mother.

****

Chapter Eleven

Le Départ

From behind, the two-by-two column of pro bike racers looked like they were connected, a serpentine band clad in blue, red, and white that hugged the edge of the curving road. They rolled along at a good clip, ten pairs of bronzed legs spinning effortlessly through the glorious French countryside.

It was the last training ride before the start of the Tour de France for America's entry, and Team GTI was in unusually good spirits. There was a sense of readiness, a heady feeling that the epic challenges they would face over the next three weeks could be met with nonchalance. Because on this bright sunny day, the new bikes sparkled, the uniforms were fresh, and everyone was healthy. Dismissed, at least until tomorrow, was the pain of the inevitable crashes, the lung-searing alpine ascents, the broken bikes, crumpled cars, and painful saddle sores. Today was every team member's rare moment to drink the champagne afforded only to the elite of professional athletes, the ones who would start the Tour de France. Besides, the focus, and the pressure, was on Comtec and Jacques Poulain, along with a half-dozen other European squads that were ranked higher than the Americans.

Tucked in the middle of the American formation was the young man who had galvanized the squad and given it real hope where there had been little. Kurt Dufour sat comfortably in the saddle, shoulder to shoulder with John Patterson, the Australian who had helped him through his first Rumorosa Cruise five years ago. Kurt knew him now as the toughest and most experienced man on the team. As pros generally do, they chatted easily as they rode, mostly about the final rosters of the squads they would be facing, and the likely strategies that would unfold.

"I reckon old Poulain's a bit more vulnerable this year, mate." Patterson was always ready to exploit the slightest weakness in a competitor, particularly the Frenchman who, in Patterson's mind, had been at the top of the podium entirely too long. Patterson had also recognized Dufour's talent in its rawest form, and he had taken him under his wing from the very beginning on the desert road to Mexicali. Now it was time to push Dufour to his true potential.

"Ya know, Duff, if you can hurt him a little in the Alps, he could crack. He looked a bit strained on the telly the other night, and we ain't even started yet."

"What did he say?" Dufour had heard about the interview from others and knew that Patterson had probably seen it just before he left the States.

"Some sheila was chattin' 'im up, makin' 'im feel good about hisself. Then when she mentioned your name 'e ended the interview real quick. I reckon the frog's scared shitless."

"That'll be the day," Dufour said, ending the conversation. Since he had joined the team, it had been drummed into him that Poulain was invincible. Virtually every pro on the circuit had accepted the fact that, in the Tour anyway, they would be fighting for second, so good was Poulain and his squad of highly paid attendants. In fact, Comtec was known for recruiting talented young riders and grooming them to support the Frenchman, partly to intimidate the competition and partly to keep would-be challengers from knocking him off. Dufour chuckled to himself when he recalled Otto Werner's explanation of this: "Comtec would rather have the boys in the tent pissin' out than have 'em outside the tent pissin' in."

The fact that GTI was outside the tent never made much difference to Comtec until just recently. But Dufour's steady, relatively rapid rise, and GTI's development as a team to support him, had not gone unnoticed. Discounting a rookie year of painful mistakes, some of them marked by loss of skin, Dufour had shown an instant ability to go the distance and do whatever was asked of him by the team. Each year, he had made steady improvement and had managed to avoid the major pitfalls of his profession—bad crashes, bad health, and use of drugs to enhance performance. He possessed a natural pedaling style, a devastating ability to time trial, and an iron determination to prove his worth. If anything, he expected too much from himself and had a hard time accepting the fact that the world of professional cycling dealt cruel blows to the uninitiated. But he had learned, over time, to conserve his energy, play the wheels, ride smart, and keep himself out of trouble. When Jeff Martin, GTI's adequate team leader retired from the international circuit two years ago, Dufour easily moved into the team's number-one spot.

At twenty-four, this was the first year he had been allowed to go the three-week distance at the major tours of both Italy and France. Otto Werner had resisted the pressure to run him sooner, despite the fact that his physical maturity was closer to a twenty-eight-year-old than his own age. But with a fifth-place overall finish in the Tour of Italy only four weeks ago, followed by complete recovery and even signs of reaching a higher plateau of fitness, it was clear now that Werner's decision had been the right one.

"I told you, *mon ami*, that you had a racehorse there." Otto Werner's seat was further in recline than most team drivers would prefer, but then Otto drove best when his ample belly was unencumbered and he could leave his right arm free to gesture to his passenger. Only on hair-raising descents did he tilt the seat forward and grasp the wheel with both hands. He had never put on a seatbelt, and he had never had a serious accident.

"You're right. And he seems to have the balls too." Peter Dufour, who had come to France for a few days to see the start of the Tour, was suddenly caught up in the impact of the moment. His son was not only about to start the biggest bike race in the world, he would do so as a serious contender after only five years on the circuit.

Otto smiled. "He reminds me of you, Pierre. But he's a little more pigheaded. And quite often his balls are bigger than his brains."

"Yeah, but isn't that what it takes sometimes? I think I analyzed things too much when I rode. I remember having to train my mind to listen to my balls once in a while."

"No worries for Kurt on that score," Otto said. They both chuckled at the double meaning. The issue of the dead girl had long since sorted itself out. For them, anyway.

And the gamble had paid off handsomely for Otto. There was no question that Kurt Dufour had superstar potential. In the last three seasons, he had won all the top pro events in the U.S., four World Cup races in Europe, the twelve-day Tour of Switzerland, stages in the major tours of Italy and Spain, and a silver medal in the world professional road championship. His good results and aggressive style made him popular with the press, both at home and abroad. And before Grant Steele was killed in a plane crash four years ago, he had signed a contract for GTI to sponsor the team for ten more years, so long as it stayed ranked in the world's top twenty. It guaranteed Otto an annual base budget of eight million dollars, enough, for the moment anyway, to stay competitive and occasionally add new talent. And the big payoff—acceptance into the Tour de France with at least an underdog's shot at victory—was now finally at hand.

In Otto Werner's opinion, Kurt Dufour was ready, despite open skepticism from some of cycling's old guard. Still too young, they said. Not seasoned enough to withstand two major tours in one season, they wrote. To all of this, Otto just shrugged. The time is never perfect. If he starts now, it is possible to compile one of the best records the sport has ever seen.

Besides, Otto, Tomi K and the new team physician, Dr. Richard Oberman, had carefully monitored the lad's vital signs, everything from blood-cell count to hormone levels to maximum output, recovery rates, and more. The results continued to confirm that Kurt Dufour was, indeed, a rare physical specimen.

"The final team looks good, Otto." Peter Dufour had been carefully scrutinizing the GTI squad as it rolled effortlessly in front of them.

"They earned it," Otto replied. "Tough sumbitches, every one of 'em. And they all want to ride for our boy. I'm looking for Patterson and Spain to keep 'em in line. They've got the experience and they can take the pressure. Berclaz, for sure, and I hope Chicilla and Michaels will help cover us in the mountains...."

Otto went through the ten-man squad, one by one, telling his old friend of their strengths and weaknesses. Gone was Brock—he talked too much—and Spencer, the druggie. Two good sprinters had been added, Geoff Hoban from England and the German, Hans Vokel. And there were others, a couple of rookies and some from other teams. Otto predicted how each would react under different circumstances, who might crack, and who was likely to rise above. Collectively, they were Otto Werner's dream team, the results of a five-year building program with Kurt Dufour at the center. It was true, they were still unproved in the Tour but Otto had worked, and planned, and stretched to leave as little as possible to chance. He had brought Ramos and two other mechanics, and, three years ago, he had hired Piet Van Brugen, his old Belgian friend and the best soigneur in the business. Tomi K, the Czech wizard, was still Otto's most able assistant and the coach who related best to the new guys.

And, of course, there was Dr. Oberman, one of only four full-time team physicians on this year's Tour. His job, as a trained exercise physiologist and sports medicine specialist, was to keep his riders healthy under grossly abnormal physical challenges. Sometimes, administration of treatment tempted the crossing of ethical boundaries, the use of artificial aids to keep imperfect bodies from collapsing under the unnatural strain of racing one's heart out for twenty-one consecutive days. Two years earlier, a drug scandal had ripped through the sport, nearly ending the Tour and forcing a cleanup that seemed pervasive, if not totally effective, in driving the practice further underground. The published list of banned substances was redefined, and daily drug testing designed to keep riders, doctors, and soigneurs honest became as stringent as in any sport. Plus, each rider now had to submit to a health exam four times a year just to establish a normal range of blood count and vital signs that, if significantly altered, would indicate the use of hard-to-detect illegal substances. Dr. Oberman spoke vehemently against any kind of drug use. Werner trusted him to keep his boys clean and legal, regardless of what the other teams might be doing.

Finally, Peter Dufour turned to his old friend in the driver's seat and asked pointedly, "Do we really have a shot at Poulain?"

Otto shifted in his seat. Without taking his eyes off the column of cyclists in front of him, he replied in his most matter-of-fact tone: "If we could put Kurt against the Frenchman one-on-one, I think right now your boy could break his legs. But these Comtec guys have built up a mafia. Their team is so strong and they've survived the pressure cooker for so long…it goes beyond the bike. Don't forget that we're in France and that Poulain is a Frenchman and he *has* to win one more. Kurt's a fresh face—and a welcome one at that—but our fight will also be against the system…the Tour organization, the press, a ruthless corporation that has its hand in the pockets of the sport…."

For the first time during the long conversation, Otto turned away from the windshield to look squarely at his friend. "They won't send him on a straight road, Peter. With that bastard Garnier pulling the strings, I think you recognize that."

Peter Dufour nodded, as if this wisdom was to be seriously considered. "I recall that you mentioned this before."

Otto squirmed. He wasn't sure if this was the right time to seriously address the subject. Peter hadn't been on the inside of the sport for twenty-five years like he had. But every time the two started to talk about the dark side of the sport, aspects that could affect his son, Peter never showed any real concern.

"The sport has changed since *we* raced, Peter."

"I thought you were the one who told me it had been cleaned up." Peter recalled Otto's attempt, when the big scandal hit two years ago, to convince Sharon that their son would be part of a new, more respectable sport. "Hey, you don't have to tell me there's still dirty laundry around." Peter seemed unconcerned.

Otto went on, "The stakes are much higher now. Top riders are few and the sponsors keep driving up the prices. And wherever there's big money, there's big egos." He shrugged as if accepting the inevitable. "Everything's for sale. Performance can still be bought."

"So, Garnier's got a big ego, and he likes to throw his money around."

"Yep. And he doesn't like to lose."

"So we knock him down a peg. The Alps don't care about his methods." Peter leaned back and looked out the window at the peaceful farmland rolling by. He really didn't want to launch Otto on a long, insider's story about the dirt, and the sleaze, and the gossip surrounding Jérôme Garnier and what was going on behind the scenes. His son was here on his own merits, and Peter was convinced that the talent and courage he had developed would slay what evil dragons might be out there.

Otto smiled and shook his head. "You haven't changed, Pierre."

***

It is easy to cast aside worries at the host city of the first day of the Tour de France. The carnival atmosphere, the throngs of holidaymakers, the army of international media, all have a way of drawing in even the most jaded observer. The electricity in the air is felt most strongly right at the starting line, where, traditionally, each individual entrant is introduced by blasting down a ramp to churn through a narrow lane of spectators for a few kilometers. It is called the prologue, a solo race against the clock that establishes the first daily ranking for the leaderboard.

This is the first chance to see who looks to be a contender because, short and seemingly inconsequential as it is, the prologue time trial is always a preliminary indication of who will occupy the top spots in Paris some three weeks off. For the *équipiers,* the servants of each team's designated heavy hitters, the prologue is generally ridden with determined demeanor and a little less than full pressure on the pedals. But, for the team leaders, this first test is deadly serious and to be ridden flat out.

The entire city of Angers and half of Europe, it seemed, was on hand to watch Jacques Poulain lay down his first wheel tracks of this year's Tour and to analyze the first powerful pedal strokes that could propel him to his sixth consecutive victory. He didn't disappoint.

Starting last of the two hundred elite racers, an honor reserved for the defending champion, Poulain deftly negotiated the twisting course at a speed approaching fifty-two kilometers per hour, a clear ten seconds faster than the second-placed rider, Uri Valeslov of Russia. The next dozen finishers, including Kurt Dufour in ninth, all finished within seven seconds of each other.

***

That evening, after the adrenaline-pumping excitement of his first day of the Tour, Kurt Dufour lay in his hotel room, shared with John Patterson, and thought of what lay ahead.

Although he had become somewhat used to it over the last couple of years, the crush of the media and the shouted questions he had experienced as soon as he hit the finish line had been unnerving. Since the trial five years ago, he had not experienced the uncomfortable feeling of being hounded as a prime suspect, this time to knock off one of the world's most invincible sports champions.

"You did bloody well, mate." Patterson entered the room, threw his duffel bag on the next bed, and sank into the only comfortable chair in the room. Dressed in shorts, his lean, thirty-five-year-old body showed the signs of a dozen years on the pro circuit. Like the others in the sport, there was not an ounce of fat on him and his deep brown legs, shaved smooth like a girl's, rippled and bulged with an unnatural excess of sinewy muscle and ugly scar tissue. "That course was trickier than suits ya, old boy. I'm amazed ya slipped through them corners as fast as ya did."

Dufour recalled the sharp knock on his right thigh when he cut too close to one of the steel crowd-control barriers on the next-to-last turn. He decided not to mention it to his roommate. Sometimes, Patterson made too big a deal out of such inconsequential things.

"Where'd you finish, John?" Kurt asked out of genuine interest.

"Twenty seconds out, 'round thirtieth, I reckon. Not bad for this old warhorse."

Patterson suddenly stood up and reached for his bag. "I almost forgot, mate…. I saw a sheila down in the lobby who says she wants to talk to ya. Says she's a reporter for some American TV network and she comes from the town where ya grew up. 'Ere's 'er card."

Kurt didn't recognize the name. "So what does she want to talk about? Bizarre suicides or Jacques Poulain?" He had become somewhat callused to both subjects of late.

"You, I reckon. She's a looker, and I think she was the one who did the interview with the frog I saw last week. She says she'll be down in the lobby around eight, if ya want to talk to her."

Something stirred in Kurt. For the last five years, he had done his best to wipe out his past life as a college student and the trying months he had spent at home in Greenwich during the trial. His friendship with Patterson and his other teammates, the entertaining hours he spent with Otto Werner, and the rough, challenging world of high-speed bicycles had all helped him shape a new life, one that he had come to enjoy. The few times he had been back to see his family had been brief and he had lost contact with old friends like Mark Rawlins and some of his closer schoolmates. With the exception of occasional visits by his father at one race or another, Kurt's teammates had become his family. He had willingly accepted invitations to spend most holidays and vacation time with them, some of whom had wives, young children, and extended families that welcomed him without any regard for his past.

Now that Kurt had truly arrived as a top cyclist, and was the leader of his team, a quiet confidence had settled over him. His new life had the kind of purpose he had wished for five years ago, and now he had become determined to win the Tour de France at least once, no matter what it took. He saw Poulain as a talented, nearly unbeatable cyclist to be sure, but he resented what the Frenchman had become. Rarely had the two spoken for more than a few moments, and then only when they had been thrown together during a press conference or at some post-race function. And never once had Poulain shown that he cared about anyone or anything but himself. Although Kurt realized that it was wrong to race just to defeat a specific opponent, Poulain was the kind of person who fueled the extra impetus to win.

Kurt wondered about the reporter downstairs. His contact with women had been limited to several friendships he had developed along the way, mostly through teammates. He had had a few liaisons, but he had carefully avoided ones initiated by longing gazes and come-on stares of the groupies who followed the teams everywhere. A more serious relationship, with someone to whom he could commit, had been willingly put on hold until sometime in the distant future. Maybe after he started winning the Tour. But for now, he thought, it wouldn't hurt just to meet her.

***

At eight o'clock, the lobby of the small hotel in Angers was nearly empty. The racers in the three teams headquartered there for the night were up in their rooms, taking massage, watching TV, or resting up for the real racing that would start tomorrow. The only sign, at this hour, that the Tour was in town was the solitary labor of the Belgian team mechanic out on the sidewalk, washing down the last of the ten sleek bikes, nine of which were neatly stacked together in front of the café window. He had given a few local children each a team cycling cap, ensuring their riveted attention, as he put the final polish on a machine that would carry its rider across windswept Brittany tomorrow.

By habit, Dufour paused at the foot of the stairs so he could adjust to the dimness of the lobby and determine if there was anyone there to avoid. Two men sat at the bar, drinking tall glasses of beer, their heads partially engulfed in the blue smoke of cheap cigarettes. Dufour recognized them as the soigneurs from the two other teams staying at the hotel.

The rest of the place was empty except for the solitary female figure sitting alone at the opposite end of the room. Kurt could not see her face but was glad she had found a secluded corner where, should anyone enter, they would not be readily noticed.

As Kurt approached, the woman quickly got to her feet and extended her hand, the light washing softly over her face. In an instant, he took her in. She was younger than Kurt expected, a head shorter, slender athletic body, and quite attractive. Her dark, shoulder-length hair was pulled back from her face, and she was dressed with a casual simplicity that Kurt rarely saw on the types of women that hung around the bike races. She greeted him with a warm smile, although he sensed she felt a bit nervous at being there.

"Jennifer Scott," she said as he felt the warmth of her hand briefly in his. "I'm pleased to finally meet you." They settled into the two facing chairs, Kurt with his back to the room. He noticed a nearly empty glass of white wine on the small table between them. She had been waiting for a while.

"My roommate says you're from Greenwich. So what brings you from there to the Tour de France?" Kurt wanted to hear her story first, a technique he had learned early in dealing with reporters.

"I'm here with an American network to cover the Tour. It's actually my first overseas assignment." She paused. "Would you like something to drink?" The bartender had materialized at his elbow.

Kurt turned to the waiter, "De l'eau minérale, s'il vous plait." *Mineral water, please.*

"Un autre verre de vin, monsieur." *Another glass of wine.* Her French was softer and flowed better.

"So you know a little French," he said with a smile. "Maybe we should just pretend we grew up in Angers and never heard of Greenwich, Connecticut."

The comment had its desired effect. Jennifer Scott smiled and relaxed into her chair.

"I haven't been back there for a while," she said. "Since taking this job, I've been traveling a lot."

"I know the feeling."

The bartender returned quickly with their drinks. Kurt waited for her to speak, noticing that the pause seemed to make her uneasy. He wondered just how much she knew about his past.

"I'm with an American crew to cover the whole race...."

"You kind of told me that. It should be quite an experience."

"Well, I'm sure it will be." She seemed to be searching for the right words. "I...you.... Obviously, you will be the focal point of our story now that you seem to have a chance at doing well...."

Kurt stopped her. "Are you the one who interviewed Poulain last week? Patterson told me he saw the show."

At the mention of Poulain, a noticeable change came over the young woman. "Yeah, I finally got an interview with him. He doesn't seem to care much for you."

"He doesn't even know me." Kurt secretly enjoyed the fact that the mere mention of his name seemed to upset the Frenchman. The guy must be really scared.

"Well, my boss, Katherine Anderson, was sent over here to cover this event because of the big rivalry brewing between you two. It'll be quite a story if you win and, frankly, it's the only reason why they decided to cover the Tour again at all. The ratings barely move the needle unless we have an American in contention."

"Maybe this rivalry isn't all it's cracked up to be. Most people think Poulain is unbeatable. He's pretty damn good, you know."

"Do *you* think he's unbeatable? I know *he* thinks he is." Scott watched Kurt closely for his reaction.

He thought for a moment. "All I can do—or anyone else for that matter—is try. And I don't give in easily." Kurt wanted to change the subject. "So why haven't we met yet, if you're here to cover the Americans?"

"We're just gathering background material now. We were at the prologue today and we interviewed Otto Werner. Our first show aired in the U.S. about the time you guys arrived, and it featured your friend, you know, the unbeatable defending champion. Next week, the network is scheduled for an hour show reviewing the first full week." She smiled. "So watch out, we'll be after you a lot in the next few days."

The two chatted on about her work. She explained how her boss, Katherine Anderson, knew little about the sport and really didn't care to get into it, leaving Jennifer and the crew to figure out the story angles, gather most of the information, and occasionally do some interviews, so long as their airtime was minimal. Anderson would step in to do the "stand-ups" with Jeff Martin, GTI's former team leader, as the expert analyst. He was to arrive in a few days, just in time to put the first week's show to bed.

"So what's Poulain like?" Kurt wanted to see if he could gather some intelligence that might provide a clue to any weakness that could be exploited.

Scott again reacted noticeably. But now, feeling more at ease with Kurt, she was ready to open up a bit more.

She eyed Kurt carefully before she spoke, not quite sure how far she should stray from her reporter's role, and how he would interpret friendliness.

"He seemed quite gracious and willing to talk all about his cycling career...and all the little things he knows about the sport and the people in it...."

"Arrogant egotist." Kurt didn't believe in sugar coatings.

A faint smile crossed her lips. "He wanted to know all about where I was going to be during the race, and he said he could arrange to have me ride with the race director, or in his own team car, if I wanted."

"Certified lecher."

"And, most importantly...." She turned more serious. "He told me that he knew how to control everyone in the race, including you."

"Oh, how's that?" Kurt was really beginning to dislike this guy.

"Well, he didn't reveal any game plans, if that's what you're thinking. I just got the sense that he wouldn't hesitate to do anything, including playing dirty, if anyone got in his way. The guy gave me the creeps."

Kurt thought for a moment. Although he was relatively new to the sport, he had learned a lot about the unsavory side of big-time pro bike racing. The big-dollar teams dominated the big events and, backed by financial war chests, didn't hesitate to make deals to ensure they stayed on top. Usually, the directeur sportif called the shots, using his budget to attract the best talent he could afford but also keeping a little in reserve to occasionally "buy" the results he needed to keep his team sponsors happy. It was a shadowy game, open only to those who chose to play it and usually without the knowledge of the sponsors, and often without the riders knowing themselves. Until this point, GTI hadn't been strong enough to be of much concern to the so-called "combinations" that surreptitiously formed and dissolved throughout the long season, and Kurt knew, from talking to Otto, that he and his players would have no part of it. Kurt also knew that Comtec had become particularly brazen about its dominant role in this game and, through an enormous ego like Poulain's, came dangerously close to opening up a scandal, particularly when the Frenchman alluded to his ability to control other riders and teams when speaking to unseasoned reporters like Jennifer Scott.

This was not the time, nor the place, nor the circumstance to get into a discussion about this with the pretty American reporter. Besides, Kurt had learned to take stage racing one day at a time. He preferred not to speculate or worry about what could or might happen. All he wanted to do was ride his best over the long, difficult road ahead of him.

He looked at her for a moment and decided against alluding to what he was feeling.

"It's time for me to get to bed," Kurt said. I enjoyed meeting you." He extended his hand and moved to get up.

Jennifer Scott took his hand and held it for an instant. She felt strangely flush. "I…I really hope you do well, Kurt." She lowered her eyes and continued, "You know…coming from Greenwich and all…I heard a lot about you, and I know what you must've gone through to get here. I hope we can talk more, you know, off the record, during this thing." She stopped herself. She hadn't wanted to say that.

Kurt smiled and stood up slowly. He felt unusually comfortable and relaxed with this girl. "I would like that," he said. He reached down and gently shook her hand.

With that, Kurt turned and went up the stairs. Jennifer Scott, alone, lingered for a moment to finish her glass of wine. As she gazed out the window at the narrow street in front of the hotel, the young reporter felt an odd combination of excitement and concern for what lay ahead. But for the moment all was quiet. She slipped out the door and headed down the empty street, the turmoil and intrigue of the Tour de France submerged in her thoughts of the man she just met.

****

Chapter Twelve

L'Alpe d'Huez

The fateful die had been cast on the lower switchbacks that took the road up and up and up for eight unrelenting and lung-searing miles to the infamous ski station of L'Alpe d'Huez. Never had this popular finishing ascent of a Tour de France stage been so jammed with spectators come to see and, in some cases, run frenzied alongside, the sinewy pedalers who churned and bobbed their way to the summit on this hot and cloudless day in July.

The word had passed from the valley below and, before that—from the Cols de Montgenèvre, du Galibier, du Télégraphe, and de la Croix de Fer, the major high alpine passes the racers had traversed so far today—that a young American named Kurt Dufour was challenging the supremacy of France's two-wheeled icon, Jacques Poulain. The truth would be told on these final switchbacks and, whether as one of the hundreds of thousands at roadside or as one of the millions in front of television sets around the world, the outcome was awaited with a degree of suspense and speculation that had been absent from *Le Tour* for many years.

To appreciate the magnitude of this moment was to appreciate everything that is the Tour de France. This was the sixteenth consecutive day of the twenty-two-day annual whirl around Gaul, *La Grande Boucle* ("The Big Loop"), which each year takes a different route but always fills the month of July with daily stories of heroics and tragedies, eagerly consumed by a world of passionate followers who know there is much more to the epic daily struggles than the mere result of who crosses the finish line first. For this is a sport of subtle tactics, a sort of chess on wheels, whose variables include an extreme amount of brawn as well as a certain type of brain.

The only near constants in the annual route, planned each year by technical experts who pretty nearly understand the limits of men on bicycles, are the finish in Paris, a few strategically placed individual time trials and as many mountain passes in the Pyrenees and Alps as it takes to keep the race interesting—without allowing the few with superior talents to completely pulverize the rest. Daily distances are set according to terrain, the regulations of the sport, and the amount of money offered to the organizers by towns that want to be on the route because of the economic windfall and worldwide notoriety they momentarily achieve for being so. It has been the same, more or less, since the Tour began as a publicity stunt for a sporting paper called *L'Auto* in 1903.

It didn't take long, in those early days of the sport, to discover that a man traveling fast on a bicycle creates a draft or "slipstream" for the man who follows closely behind. Consequently, tactics evolved and teams were formed that learned to exploit the concept of "sitting in," to save energy over the long haul and the fast road. Only when the road climbs unmercifully, or when one man has to go alone against time, do the purest talents of the cyclists emerge—hence the ones who lead the teams are the ones who climb and time trial the best, leaving the rest (the domestiques) to spend their days sheltering their leaders until their true talents are called upon.

And so it was this day on the climb to L'Alpe d'Huez. The stage had started in Sestriere, an alpine resort town just over the Italian border. It was the third of four days in the Alps this year and, because of the four major passes the racers traversed along the two-hundred-kilometer route, it was considered the *étape reine* (the "queen stage"), the hardest and most critical day in the Tour. One hundred forty-eight of the original two hundred starters remained in the race, the dropouts mostly resulting from crashes, sickness, and fatigue. There had been one disqualification for doping, Fons Hoynbeck, a Belgian in the Stella Pilsner squad, who was caught with a plastic bladder of untainted urine sewn cleverly into his shorts—an old trick that hadn't been seen in years—and then sent home in shame for being the only one foolish enough to get caught.

As expected, Comtec had Poulain in yellow, the team seemingly in control as the Tour entered its final week. Since the prologue, Poulain had surrendered the lead momentarily along the route, winking to the press that these were mere pretenders he would crush in the mountains, first in the individual time trial to the top of the Puy-de-Dôme mountain, and then in the four tough Alpine stages to follow. His strategy, by now pretty obvious, was to wear the *maillot jaune* all the way through the Alps and during the entire final week, culminating with a romp in the next-to-last day's time trial in Dijon to seal his sixth Tour victory. So far, the strategy was working, but not quite as flawlessly as Poulain would have wished.

There is a time in every great athlete's career when his reign of dominance is not so certain, when the inevitable challengers rise to a new level and demand to share the glory. It is during these moments that the character of both the challenged and the challenger emerges and, in the eyes of those who see sport as a metaphor for life, human ambition, at its most noble and its most vile, is revealed.

Kurt Dufour, in the role of noble challenger, had shadowed Jacques Poulain with tenacity worthy of the most determined underdog. In second place overall, having conceded only one minute and thirty-seven seconds to Poulain, Dufour's refusal to give in across the north and west of France, through the Pyrenees and in the straight-up time trial to the Puy de Dome summit, had energized his own GTI squad and others in the peloton as well. With each day, as Dufour and his loyal *équipiers* met or matched everything Poulain and Comtec could serve up, interest in the Tour reached a new level, and Poulain became increasingly more agitated and sharp with the press. Last night, with as close to genuine bravado as he could muster, Poulain had promised the press that he would bury Dufour on the way to L'Alpe d'Huez.

But as the road turned up toward that ski resort, Dufour remained shoulder to shoulder with Poulain within a leading group of eight that had been together since the cruel summit of the Croix de Fer. Finally, they had closed in on the Colombian climbing sensation, Luis Alcarta, a tiny dark-skinned man whose spindly legs and courageous heart had kept him far ahead over each of the passes today. It wasn't until the last, long, rapid downhill to the valley of the Romanche that the bigger, stronger contenders representing four of the top teams had put their shoulders into the chase and now captured Alcarta, making nine together in the lead. Somewhere, scattered over the mountains and valleys, behind were the rest of the racers in little clumps or alone, each trying to conserve whatever was left to get them up the final tortuous climb without losing too much time to the leaders or, worse, fall so far behind that they would be eliminated from the rest of the race.

None of these also-rans mattered anymore. The majority were riding in the so-called laughing group, the ever-expanding pack of dropped riders that pedaled just hard enough to make the time cut that would allow them to continue the next day, and once again sacrifice themselves to keep their team leaders in contention.

The most important officials' cars, the helicopters, and the motorcycles carrying photographers and TV cameramen with heavy equipment and microwave transmitters, were all clustered above, behind, and beside the front group of nine as they made the final turn off the valley highway and headed up the climb. In front of them, just far enough away to prevent illegal draft, was the main race director's car carrying the man himself, a silver-haired gentleman standing erect through the sunroof, a king facing backward, symbolically shifting the importance from his lofty position to the cyclists who followed in his wake. In front of this official was a brace of the four-dozen motorcycle-mounted *Garde Républicaine* officers, placed there to clear a path through the throngs of spectators so the riders could pass without interference. Nearly an hour before, a gaggle of odd-shaped and funny-sounding advertising vehicles had entertained and pummeled the crowd with candies, trinkets, and cheap cloth caps—so now many of the fans at roadside chewed happily and looked silly.

The leaders were climbing steadily now. Kurt Dufour rode shoulder to shoulder with Poulain and firmly on the wheel of his only surviving teammate, Claude Berclaz, GTI's climbing expert from Idaho via Switzerland. Over six hours ago, at the start in Sestriere, Otto Werner had given Berclaz the instruction to stick with Kurt all day and, if they started the final climb together, to set the hardest pace possible, believing surely that Poulain would crack before Dufour. But Comtec had two of its best, Langlois and Vanest, there as well, and Kurt could be sure that their only role was to do what they could to prevent Poulain from slipping or to launch him into an attack, depending upon how they and their leader felt.

The rest of the *équipiers*, and the stars of most the other teams, had been the victims of the cruel attrition of this day in the High Alps. John Patterson, no mountain expert but Dufour's most loyal and dedicated teammate, succumbed to the pressure on the upper slopes of the Galibier—but only after he had worked hard, bringing Kurt food and drink and organizing the team's effort to pace him back to the leaders after a flat tire outside of Briançon. In varying degrees, they had all done their work or paid their price, most of them riding in with the laughing group and leaving the day's ultimate outcome to the nine who remained in the lead.

Despite the relentless all-day pressure of agonizing climbs and tortuous descents, Dufour remained clear-headed, and, even though he felt a general tiredness throughout his body, he was in a state where his legs, his lungs, and his heart synchronized as if driven by a mechanical force outside of his being. He knew this to mean that his mind still had control and that he was still capable of directing his body to push harder, depending upon the state of the others. He was able to tell how they felt by their eyes, their shoulders, and their pedal strokes as the strain of the climb intensified.

Alcarta would be gone soon. His shoulders had started to roll and the growing white residue of sweat and saliva around his nose and mouth likely meant that he hadn't had the strength to lift his *bidon* to his lips in many kilometers. Poulain's men were hurting too. Langlois's eyes had glazed over and his right knee had developed a funny little in-and-out tic with each pedal stroke. This had only appeared when Berclaz had started to force the pace. Vanest had dropped a few lengths back, as had Koopman, the Dutchman, making it definite that they too could not match Berclaz's surge. Only Chimello, the Italian lying fourth overall, and Poulain seemed unaffected for the moment.

They labored past the "10 kilometers to go" sign, now rounding steep switchbacks every few hundred meters. The crowds were thicker as the lead group climbed higher, cheering and screaming at their heroes, and parting only as they were forced to by the lead motorcycles and desperate arm-flailing officials in the cars ahead. To the riders, it was a dull, constant roar, punctuated only by a recognizable flag or shouted name, or sometimes by a single man running alongside until the pace or a motorcycle forced him to dive into the mass of people on one side or the other.

Dufour, still riding on Berclaz's wheel, glanced peripherally at Chimello's face, now scarcely a meter to his left. The lanky Italian, shoulders bobbing slightly to the rhythm of his turning pedals, gazed straight ahead. A large drop of sweat formed on his beak-like nose, then dropped off, only to be immediately replaced by another. His thin, black hair was soaked with sweat and plastered flat to his head and, when he turned to look at Kurt, his sunken eyes spoke of impending capitulation. "*Andiamo!*" The word was spoken as Chimello motioned with his head for Kurt to push up the road and then, with a flick of his head to the right, the Italian rolled his eyes toward Poulain.

Dufour, numbed by the roar from the walls of spectators and his own growing fatigue, had enough presence of mind to think of setting his own expression when he turned deliberately to face Poulain. The

Frenchman knew the trick as well, and Kurt stared into the wickedly smiling face of a man who was pretending to be in control. But the smile was too forced, the teeth too clenched, and the eyes too glazed to cover the fact that the five-time Tour winner and defending champion was coming completely and totally apart.

Kurt glanced ahead and noticed that they were approaching another switchback, where the road would get even steeper. Suddenly, through the relentless pain and the cumulative deadening effect of seven hours in the saddle, something deep within Kurt's instinctive mind told him that this was the moment.

He shouted forward: "*Allez, Claude, allez, allez!*"

Berclaz instinctively raised himself out of the saddle and threw his weight forward, driving the speed up another notch. Dufour was ready for this, matching the acceleration of his teammate with every bit of energy he had. Within a few pedal strokes, Chimello had faded badly and Poulain had lost a crucial bike length.

Berclaz, with Dufour seemingly attached to his wheel, knew that this was the time for him to do his job, without question and without hesitation. The finish line had no relevance to him; it was only a matter of getting his man as far ahead of Poulain as possible, even if it meant his own total collapse before reaching the summit.

The steepest, early slopes of the climb, on a road cut into the rocky mountainside, now gave way to a less-severe stretch through more open terrain—today, a giant natural amphitheater completely jammed with thousands of spectators and holidaymakers, many of whom had staked their roadside spots days before. As the motorcycle cavalcade and the lead officials' cars forged slowly into view, followed closely by the two laboring Team GTI cyclists, a deafening roar, mingled with clanging cowbells and short intense blasts from air horns, filled the crisp alpine air. In moments, a second roar went up because there, a dozen lengths behind, emerged a struggling Poulain, his usual flawless style given way to an uncharacteristic chopping at the pedals and drooping head.

On the less-steep section, Berclaz knew the speed had to increase for Poulain to be truly left behind, but, when he tried to move into a higher gear, his legs would not respond and he looked back to Dufour, shaking his head. For a moment, they pedaled side by side and Berclaz gave the young American his last words of encouragement: "Poulain's cooked, give everything to the finish…."

Dufour knew this moment might come, and, without any hesitation or rational weighing of the effort or the toll it would take, he surged forward. In order to become leader of the Tour de France, he had to pull more than a minute and a half out of Poulain by the finish line at the summit, now less than five kilometers away.

As he rode away from Berclaz and into the narrowing sea of faces that chanted his name, Kurt was only vaguely aware of the motorcycles running interference for him, the horns and the helicopters, the camera in his face, and the hoarse shouts of Otto Werner somewhere in the team car behind. His mind automatically piloted his struggling body forward, forward toward the top, and the goal that now was a combination of programmed response and instinctual desire. His eyes saw the road and the motorcycles and the people in front of him, but his mind scrambled these visual messages into confused and random images of people he knew and places he'd been. Strangers' faces, pressed toward his, became his mother, his father, Leslie Conway, Jennifer Scott, and others who seemed familiar, all screaming at him and desperately motioning him to keep coming. He fixed his gaze on the motorcycle helmet traveling a few meters ahead, only to see it transform into the leering face of Jacques Poulain, gradually becoming surrounded by a narrowing tunnel of darkness.

He felt a soaking splash of cold water thrown into his face from somewhere at the side of the road, enough to revive him slightly and push back the closing walls of the dark tunnel, if only for a few moments. From deep within his confused mind, he knew that the agony had to be nearly over…that the line across the road must somehow be reached before he could stop pedaling, and while the enemy behind him was struggling the same as him. With all his willpower, he forced his legs around, now in a jerking, bobbing cadence that kept him moving as fast as possible—faster, anyway, than the beaten man who suffered through a worse agony behind.

***

"Jenny, find Wayne and get your asses over there—we've gotta get in his face before they cart him off! And where the hell's Anderson and Martin? They've got to do the close right at the finish line!"

96

The shouted words from producer Arnie Campbell from Paris filled Jennifer Scott's headset in L'Alpe d'Huez. They were like a slap in the face that forced her, tears running down her cheeks, to look up from the TV monitor and try to figure out how, in a sea of hysterical male reporters and cameramen about to rush the street below, she was going to get the crew assembled and make it to Kurt Dufour right after he crossed the finish line.

For the last twenty minutes, she and hundreds of other international broadcast journalists, reporters, and play-by-play analysts had jammed three tiers of TV monitors and broadcast positions in the media area right above the finish line. They were being fed the dramatic images from the final switchbacks just below, the full-screen faces of two men, first one, then the other, as they struggled upward through the sea of hysterical fans. The cutaways were aerial shots from the chopper high above, showing, with excellent perspective, the time and distance between Dufour, who strained and lunged to increase his lead, and Poulain, in the sweat-soaked *maillot jaune*, flailing his spent mind and body to try and limit the damage.

This was the epic confrontation that created the meat of legendary sports reporting, and the need to capture it, blow by blow, was the one thought running through every journalist's mind. Could Dufour, the young American challenger, pull one minute and thirty-eight seconds out of the greatest living cyclist to take the yellow jersey? It would be less than five minutes now until the struggling cyclist would be in the village and rounding the final turn leading up to the jammed finishing straight. And every photographer and interviewer would want to reach him first.

Jennifer Scott, by now the arms and legs of the American TV crew, tore her mind from the image of Kurt Dufour's dramatic and intense suffering and the personal emotion it evoked in her. She threw down her headset and pushed her way to the edge of the platform, shouting over the din into her walkie-talkie for Wayne, the cameraman, to meet her just past the finish line. She nimbly sprung over a metal retaining fence to reach the landing by the only exit steps, successfully leapfrogging ahead of the lumbering photojournalists and reporters who were jostling and pushing each other to squeeze from the second and third tiers to the street.

Wayne confirmed in her ear that he was on his way. Jennifer ran a few yards through the camp of TV trailers and yanked open the door of the network's RV, looking for Jeff Martin and Katherine Anderson, whom she would somehow have to get through the swelling mass to Wayne and, hopefully, Dufour, so they could get a decent shot and, with luck, some kind of dramatic finish coverage.

"Oh, for chrissake...." Scott blurted the words without thinking. There, pressed together in a passionate embrace against the wall of the trailer was the ex-bike racer and the TV journalist, completely oblivious to the commotion outside. They parted quickly as Jennifer stumbled through the door.

Martin spun away and moved off toward the back of the trailer. Katherine Anderson, the TV journalist who specialized in sensational stories, attempted to quickly button her blouse.

"For chrissake!" Scott repeated, this time losing her patience. "Get yourselves together and get out there, we've got less than five minutes to catch the whole friggin' thing!"

"So what's going on?" Anderson's blank expression conveyed the fact that her mind was far from the Tour de France and more on Jeff Martin, the ex-racer and her new, interesting, broadcast partner. Only when he guffawed from the back did she realize that the diversion was over and she had closed her buttons unevenly, leaving a gap big enough to expose her left breast to the young woman who worked for her.

"Campbell called from Paris. You two have to do a stand-up, *right now!*"

"But Jenny, what the hell's the story?" Anderson was looking down to make sure she properly closed the buttons this time, trying, unconvincingly, to regain some semblance of superiority.

"Dufour dropped Poulain. They're both riding in the twilight zone, and Dufour gets the jersey if the frog finishes more than one-thirty-eight behind. Find Wayne by the Perrier sign just past the finish, I'll try to get Dufour there." She paused, knowing she momentarily had the upper hand. "You can screw around later." With that, Scott was out the door running back toward the thickening crowd of journalists.

Martin, realizing the full impact of Scott's mission and his role in it, leaped out the door, returning instantly to grab Anderson by the arm and pull her out with him, sending her open compact clattering to the ground.

"Goddam bike race," she muttered as she let herself be dragged between the trailers toward the Perrier sign.

In two weeks of jammed finish lines, Jennifer Scott had learned how to get to the front of the surging pack of journalists, each of them intent on reaching the winner first. Her small size, slender athletic figure, and batting eyelashes had gained her some burly friends among the veterans in the press corps, and she knew if she could spot Claude and Giles, both would let her zip underneath them to the front rank. Besides, the day she got them an exclusive with Dufour and Otto Werner meant that they were forever in her debt.

The blue-peaked caps of the gendarmes were visible above the heads of the media, and the blasts of their shrill whistles told Scott that order was still somewhat preserved and Dufour had not yet crossed the finish line. She scrambled into the crowd, pushing her way forward until she saw Claude's broad back, tapped him on the shoulder and, as soon as she saw his characteristic wink of recognition, dove to the ground and forward between his legs and those of Giles standing another pace in front. She surfaced in the front rank, looking between the shoulders of the human chain of gendarmes, the only obstruction between her and the finish line only fifty meters down the gently sloping street. She felt the reassuring pressure of Giles's large hand on her right shoulder and knew, without looking back, that he was flashing his broad, gapped-tooth grin.

From this spot, she had a good view of the cleared roadway all the way down to the "200 meters to go" sign and the final turn the riders would round before coming toward her to the finish. Rigid steel barricades, clad in brightly colored sponsor billboards, held back the huge crowd on both sides of the road, and a giant TV screen mounted high above the roadway transmitted the live images from the motorcycles filming the leaders to the multitudes at the finish, in the press area, and around the world. The scene on the road in front of her was one of frenzied anticipation. Important officials and photographers were jumping from the lead motorcycles and cars as the vehicles were frantically waved into a turnout chute in time to clear the road for the riders.

Almost instantly, the figure of a lone cyclist swung wide around the turn and into the makeshift alpine stadium, followed closely by a pair of motorcycles and a couple of two following cars, one with GTI's team director, Otto Werner, shouting and waving wildly from the sunroof. A deafening roar arose as Kurt Dufour, mouth open wide, lunged, and struggled up the road toward the finish. He veered dangerously close to the roadside barricades and then agonizingly straightened his path and even increased his speed slightly toward the approaching finish line.

Without knowing it, he was headed straight toward Jennifer Scott. She, and every journalist and photographer behind and around her, surged and strained against the weakening arms and shrill whistles of the chain of gendarmes that was struggling to hold back the tide. Just as the line seemed ready to break, Scott saw the plump, middle-aged form of Otto Werner, somehow escaped from his car and sprinting along the barricades, looking for the most direct path that would get him around the gendarmes and to Dufour as soon as he hit the line. She saw her ally and had no choice now but to take her accustomed path. In an instant, she dropped to all fours and forced her way through the legs of the gendarme in front of her. The poor man's balance was upset and the hoard behind broke through, sweeping him and the rest of the collapsed blue line hopelessly aside.

She had broken free and had gained the critical step ahead of the rest, reaching Dufour, along with Werner from the side and two flailing gendarmes, barely a meter beyond the finish line. As the human tide swirled around them, the exhausted winner, his eyes closed and chest heaving, slumped against her, unaware of where he was and the significance of what had just happened....

***

Just over a minute and a half later, Jérôme Garnier, sitting next to Guy Leguerre in the air-conditioned comfort of Comtec's bright yellow Peugeot team sedan, pounded his thick fist on the dashboard with a steady beat that matched the agonizingly slow pedal revolutions of his fallen hero just ahead. In a few seconds, the *maillot jaune* would be swallowed by the uncontrolled mob waiting at the finish, and Garnier wanted no part of it. He didn't care to give excuses or come up with explanations.

"Why must I suffer with this fool, Guy?" The measured tone of Garnier's deep voice was disconcerting to Leguerre. It didn't help that, for the last six kilometers, their car had been thumped and spat upon by thousands of ungrateful, unforgiving fans. "How can Poulain, the great Poulain, be so humiliated by this young upstart? Haven't we bought the best talent? Haven't we taken care of those fools?"

Leguerre, sensing the need to get Garnier away from this scene, wheeled into the pull-out chute and maneuvered around the haphazardly parked motorcycles and abandoned official cars to Comtec's reserved parking area well behind the TV trucks and finish-line commotion.

For the first time in hours, he turned and faced his boss. "The kid is good, monsieur Garnier. He's one of the best young *coureurs* I've seen in my lifetime."

Garnier reached for his door handle and returned the look. His steely blue eyes bore into Leguerre's and left no doubt as to his intent. "Then invite him for dinner with me tomorrow night à mon petit château *at my little castle.* And make sure that moron, Otto Werner, is off cleaning bikes."

****

Chapter Thirteen

Le Maillot Jaune

Kurt Dufour opened his eyes to the bright morning sun streaming through his hotel room window. A cool breeze, fresh from a recent alpine shower, carried the scent of pine trees into the cluttered room, momentarily obscuring the pungent aroma of flowers, hot coffee, and dried-sweat Lycra.

The young athlete, lying on his back and clad only in a pair of white boxer shorts, was in no hurry to wake up. John Patterson, always the early riser, sat with a silver pot of coffee at the little table under the other window across the room, intently reading one of a dozen newspapers that lay piled on the floor. Kurt blinked as the pleasant realization came to him: today was a rest day, and the yellow jersey he had struggled so hard for was draped over the closet door.

"Finally decided to open your eyes, eh, Duff?" Patterson was always chipper in the morning, a trait that Dufour had come to appreciate, more or less, during the daily grind of the Tour de France.

"Listen to this, mate." Patterson continued, knowing that Kurt would need a few minutes before he was ready to say anything intelligent. "*L'Équipe* says you're *le nouveau homme choisi*. I guess that makes Poulain *l'homme non pas choisi*." He chuckled at his own butchered French, scooped up one of the folded papers from the floor, and threw it onto Kurt's bare chest.

"Read about yourself, old boy. I've got 'em in French, German, Spanish, Italian, Dutch, and English. You're a real bloody fuckin' hero, now. And it's about time that arrogant frog finally took it in the shorts." Patterson said this good-naturedly, knowing full well that the effort he, Berclaz, and the others had put in on the road to L'Alpe d'Huez had been in total support of their young leader and fully appreciated by him.

Kurt raised up on his elbow, noting to himself that his entire body felt stiff and his legs were unusually sore. He unfolded the *Gazzetta dello Sport* and spread it flat on the bed where he could absorb the effect of the full-page photo of himself collapsing at the finish line, emblazoned at the top with the huge, single-word headline: *"Campionissimo!"*

"Holy shit...," he muttered to himself, "this is unbelievable." He fell back on the bed as the whole long day flooded back to him. The seemingly endless effort up the final mountain, collapsing at the top, and being revived by Otto Warner and the doctor, the stifling crush of reporters, and then the timing board overhead indicating that he had finished one-fifty-two ahead of Poulain and now led the Tour by a mere fourteen seconds....

Somehow, he had managed to speak right after the finish line and his inane words, repeated over and over in a dozen languages were there for him to reread forever: *"I didn't give a damn about Poulain.... All I wanted to do was get to the finish before I died."*

"Christ, they could've picked a more intelligent quote."

"I got news for ya, mate, that was the most intelligent thing ya said. Ya weren't exactly the smart-ass college boy, what with all that grime, and sweat, and snot running down your face. At least Otto and the sheila wiped ya down before you went on the telly."

Kurt recalled being swept along in the crushing frenzy of reporters and photographers to a spot where Jeff Martin and Katherine Anderson asked him a few questions for their camera and then to the awards stand to get the jersey, and then to the drug control trailer, and then to his hotel where he was finally united with Otto and all his teammates. He also recalled that, through that entire confusing ordeal and up to the entrance to the hotel, Jennifer Scott had been at his side. He wanted to call her.

Sensing what was on Kurt's mind, Patterson said, "Ya know that little girl worked her ass off yesterday. And then she took a chopper back to Paris where they spent all night doing the show. Martin said it's supposed to air today in the U.S."

Dufour wondered to himself if that meant she would be back on the mountain this evening, ready to resume coverage with the start the next morning. He hoped he would have a chance to talk to her. Since their first meeting in Angers at the start of the Tour, they had seen each other frequently, mostly because her assignment was to cover him and his team. But after the cameras shut down and the notes had been taken, she would often linger to talk with him by herself, and he had increasingly looked forward to their conversations. Somehow, their moments together made it easier for him to hang tough, to keep his mind focused on the big prize rather than the daily pressures he faced as a marked man, leader of the team and, now, leader of the race. And, just as importantly, he was happy to encourage her as well, to be someone she could lean on through the difficulties she had in dealing with her boss's lunacy and the big ego personalities of the TV culture. They clicked well together, two determined young people with talent and drive who had jobs to do in an environment they had to fight hard to control.

"Open up, fellas, it's time to get rollin'." Otto Werner's unmistakable voice was followed by his portly body bursting through the door as if they were behind schedule. Kurt knew that Otto always acted this way in the morning regardless of how much time they had. It was partly because he reveled in rallying the troops and partly because he didn't know how to do anything slowly. The more commotion he could stir, the more importance he could convey for the mission of the moment.

"Relax, Otto. I'm on vacation." Kurt, like the rest of the surviving *Tourmen*, viewed a rare day without racing like a major holiday. Even though they would pedal easily for three hours that afternoon, the intense routine of a daily stage was absent, and the few hours of respite this represented reached such a level of importance to their minds and bodies that most of them would be completely refreshed and recovered by the next day. They would have to be, for there was still one more long stage in the Alps and a week of racing left.

"Okay, okay, you've earned a little vacation." Otto Werner pulled the *maillot jaune* off the closet door and threw it playfully in Dufour's face. "But when you put this on tomorrow, the vacation's over. And don't read too many newspapers; you might start believing all that bullshit."

"What bullshit...that now I'm a different man because I wear the jersey, or that I'm suddenly the new Poulain? If I've learned anything, it's that I'll never let myself be like him."

Otto sat down on the end of the bed and looked earnestly at Kurt. "No. I mean don't believe that Poulain's finished. There's no question that he took his first real beating yesterday...."

Patterson interrupted, "I'd say 'e more nearly died, and that ego of 'is got shot out his asshole just about the time ol' Duff 'ere crossed the line."

Warner waved away the comment and the chuckles that followed. "This is no game for Poulain or Comtec. Ego or no ego, he'll be recovered all right, and fourteen seconds is nothing. You guys all rode above and beyond, and I'm proud of everybody left on this team. But now's not the time to take it easy. You know it's still a long ways to Paris, and defending the jersey's a lot harder than getting it."

With that, Otto Werner stood up and moved toward the door. He looked back and spoke to both riders. "No more than a half-hour with reporters at the news conference, for either of you. At noon, we'll have the cars here to take you down to the valley, three hours easy. And at four we'll meet to see how everyone's feeling and plan our strategy for tomorrow." He paused, then smiled back into the room. "I know you guys can do it."

Kurt fell back on the bed. For the first time, he started to think about the next six days and what it would take to protect such a slim lead, let alone increase it. He wasn't sure if his six surviving teammates could withstand the pressure of fighting off Comtec, a team with age, experience, and ruthlessness in their arsenal. He wasn't even sure if he would be up to it.

Patterson had not gone back to reading his newspapers. Instead, he sat back in his chair, hands locked behind his head looking out the window. It was a breathtaking view down the side of the mountain, framed on all sides by jagged, snow-capped peaks and, visible way down below, the twisting band of asphalt that had carried them here yesterday, struggling and sweating on their bicycles.

Kurt got up from his bed and pulled the other chair over to the table under the window and poured himself a cup of coffee. He followed Patterson's gaze down the mountain and was struck by the contrast this tranquil scene provided compared with the chaotic, hysterical experience he had on the road below just the day before. Gone were the screaming people, the helicopters, the motorcycles, and the bizarre tunnel of darkness he had ridden in and out of. The pain in his body and the desperate images that had driven him so hard up the mountain were gone, hidden somewhere deep in his mind. The only physical evidence left of that day was the temporary soreness in his legs, the piles of newspapers that Patterson had collected, and the symbolic yellow shirt lying on the floor.

Patterson had also fallen into an unusually pensive mood. "Ya know, mate," he said as he gingerly, almost reverently picked the *maillot jaune* off the floor and held it in his hands, "no matter what 'appens during the rest of your life, no one can ever take away what ya did yesterday. Very, very few men ever get this far in the Tour or, for that matter, ever get this kind of recognition for anything they do in their whole friggin' lives. Ya've reached the top of your profession in a very short time. If anybody 'as the brain to appreciate that, it should be you." He turned away, gazing somewhere way off down the valley.

Dufour looked at Patterson and at the jersey draped respectfully over his loyal friend's hands. For fifteen years this tough, sinewy Australian had ridden his heart out for others, accepting somewhere along the road that his talent and the hours and miles of suffering that he endured would never be enough for him to lead the Tour. Yet he loved being part of it and knowing that his effort and his presence made a difference for someone else. They both knew without ever saying it that Patterson's dream of ever wearing *le maillot jaune* could only be realized vicariously through Kurt. For the young American, this suddenly engendered a deeper sense of obligation, a need beyond his own personal ambition to hold onto this symbol for Patterson and the rest of his teammates, his family, and for the others·who cared about him, no matter what the cost. And there was in him, also, a realization that this was the redemption he had been desperately seeking for himself since his life had been so radically changed five years ago. At this moment, a new feeling crystallized for Kurt Dufour. His destiny, now seemingly within his grasp, was to be the best.

***

The rest day in the ski village of L'Alpe d'Huez was almost over. The small resort town swarmed with the Tour de France entourage of racers, team personnel, race officials, international press corps, and several thousand race followers and sponsors who had been lucky enough to have reserved a room a year in advance. The town had taken on a festive air, with every restaurant booked, and brightly painted team cars speeding around the streets and up from the valley, their drivers intent on gathering hard-to-find supplies for the final week.

The surviving *Tourmen* basked in the glory of it all. For most of the day, they had hung out around their hotels making telephone calls, visiting with families or girlfriends, eating big meals, and getting massages. Virtually every one of them had ridden his bike for at least a couple of hours, pedaling slowly in the flat valley below to keep legs supple, giving local children and the older *cyclo-touristes* a chance to ride along next to them, and perhaps get a smile or maybe even a team cap.

For the most part, the big stars—the ones who held the top positions with a week to go—had to be careful not to be swept into the heady world of reporters intent on spending time with them, smiling, and nodding at every comment the racers made as if the questions being answered about families, their health, or their bicycles were of extraordinary importance. By contrast, the lesser lights paraded up and down the streets or openly hung out in front of their hotels, hoping to be asked to give a quote or be photographed.

No one was more elusive to the press, and perhaps more sought after, than Jacques Poulain. Gone were the boastful press conferences and the hourly waves from his hotel window that had become, in years past, a rest-day tradition to the swarming sea of reporters. This year, Poulain had gone into seclusion right after the finish, but not before he had thrown a few angry punches at a French reporter and shoved nearly everyone else he could out of the way. The Frenchman was no longer the undisputed king of cycling, and the reality of his sudden vulnerability caused him to act in strange ways.

***

"Bon soir, monsieur Dufour. Entrez-vous, s'il vous plaît."

Kurt Dufour did not expect to be greeted at the door by a servant in a tuxedo. But then he hadn't expected to be a guest at a mountain chalet that looked more like a small castle, either. As he stepped into the large open foyer, he took a deep breath, trying to ease the apprehension he felt about meeting Jérôme Garnier face to face.

"May I remove your jacket, *monsieur*?"

"No thank-you. I'd like to keep it on if you don't mind." Kurt smiled politely and pictured his thin GTI team jacket being hung amid a closet full of substantial Comtec apparel and thick sheepskin coats.

"As you wish. Please be seated in the library. Monsieur Garnier will be with you in a few minutes." After showing Kurt to the room, the servant bowed politely and disappeared.

The library could have been a room from a medieval royal hunting lodge. Although not overly large, its ceiling was high and peaked, supported by massive trusses of rough-hewn logs set into the stone walls every few meters. The centerpiece of the wall to the right of the door was a huge granite fireplace, above which appeared a coat of arms and two crossed broadswords. A small fire was burning brightly, giving off just enough heat to take the chill out of the cool alpine evening. The wall to the left was mostly leaded-glass windows, set into sills of polished pine and stone, and overlooking the front of the house. The view from these windows was a breathtaking panorama of jagged mountains that made the town of L'Alpe d'Huez far below seem tiny and insignificant.

It was approaching dusk and a few lights twinkled here and there across the barren gentler slopes that formed the sides of the valley and the base of the sharp snow-capped peaks. The young cyclist stood transfixed in front of the windows, captivated by the magnificence of the setting and the endless view of mountains, the sweeping valley, and the twilight orange of the sky.

"I challenge you to find a better view than this anywhere in the world."

Jérôme Garnier had quietly entered the room and was standing just a few feet to the side of Dufour. He was several inches shorter than Kurt but solidly built, and the thick ski cardigan he wore over a silk turtleneck contributed to the sense that he was a powerful man. He extended his right hand to Kurt, who noticed that, in the thick fingers of his left, he held both a cognac glass and a thick, freshly lit cigar.

"I am sorry you could not join me for dinner, but I am pleased you took the time to at least visit my charming chalet. And, before I forget, congratulations on taking *le maillot* yesterday. It was a truly impressive performance."

Garnier smiled as his massive hand closed briefly and firmly around Kurt's. His eyes bore steadily into his guest's and Kurt had the instinctive feeling that the smile was practiced and rarely used.

108

"I'm sure you understand that it was important for me to eat with the team tonight. But I thank you for the invitation, and I'm glad I could at least get up here for a brief visit." Kurt wanted to be polite and very cautious. He had not told anyone about the invitation, delivered to him early in the day by Comtec's *directeur sportif*, Guy Leguerre. He had called Leguerre as soon as he knew he would be free for an hour after dinner and, on the pretense of meeting Jennifer Scott when she arrived back at her hotel, had managed to score a team car for the evening. Garnier's chalet was only a five-minute drive up from town.

Garnier motioned for Kurt to sit on the sofa in front of the windows. "In that case I would like Guy to join us, and I can get right to business."

As if on cue, Leguerre entered the room, looking a bit nervous and much more the subordinate than Kurt had ever seen him. Strangely, Leguerre's presence made Kurt feel more comfortable. Two people who practiced sport instead of business, even though they were on opposing sides, should be able to establish some kind of rapport. Maybe that was the point, Kurt thought.

"Guy tells me that you are one of the best cyclists he has ever seen. And I can see that you are tough and determined." The practiced smile again, this time through a blue curl of cigar smoke.

"I'm flattered," Kurt said.

"Good. But I'm not here to flatter you. I want to make a business proposition that could make us both very happy...and you very rich."

"Actually, I'm pretty happy right now and I haven't really cared about being rich...but I'm listening." Kurt was curious about the motive and the deal.

Garnier, sitting higher in front of Kurt and framed by the window, leaned back in his throne-like chair. Kurt thought he looked like a medieval king, about to render a sweeping pronouncement that would determine the fate of a young knight under his control. In fact, Garnier first felt it necessary to explain the power he had over his team and how he controlled areas of the sport of which Kurt was only vaguely aware. He talked of how he influenced the officials and the Tour organizers, ensuring that the annual route they chose favored the skills of Poulain, and how he was able to buy good riders from other teams so they would pose less of a threat to Comtec. And he made sure that Kurt knew that he, himself, had been a racer many years ago and that his career had ended in controversy when he was accused of supplying drugs to riders eager to improve their performances. Kurt was well aware of the first big drug scandal that had ripped through the sport in the mid-sixties, culminating in the tragic death of Tom Simpson, a top British rider, and of Otto's and his own father's brush with dopers in the Tour of Britain that ended his dad's career. And just two years ago the Tour was nearly ruined when several of the European teams were implicated in a widespread doping scandal. It wouldn't surprise him if Garnier had somehow been involved both times.

"They never proved a damn thing, but they still tried to ban me from the sport," he said. "But I came back with money...money I earned from being smart at business and knowing how to win the game. And now I like to spend my money in ways that make no sense to others...."

He then turned his attention to Kurt.

"You are young. You have not even worn the jersey for one day. You will be nothing unless you win the Tour once, twice, maybe five or six times. You are young enough and talented enough to do that...so few are." Garnier sat back and took a long pull on his cigar, never taking his eyes off Kurt's.

"I intend to win this Tour, and as many more as I can." Kurt returned the look and made the statement with as much bravado as he could muster.

Garnier took another long pull on his cigar and leaned forward until his face was less than a foot from Kurt's. His serious, deadly stare fixed squarely on Kurt for an uncomfortably long time. Kurt stared back, mentally noting the bushy eyebrows over dark, deep-set eyes, the thick lips, and deeply furrowed, pock-marked skin—an altogether sinister countenance. Then, suddenly and without warning, Garnier rocked back in his chair and erupted into a rasping, uncontrolled laugh that shook his body back and forth, subsiding only when the billowing cigar smoke set him to coughing.

After a moment, he stood up and, with a handkerchief offered by Leguerre, wiped his eyes and regained his composure. When he looked at Kurt again, the laughter was gone.

"Listen to me," he said. "You have much to learn. You will never win this Tour or any others without…shall we say…the right breaks. You need a *directeur sportif* like Guy here. A man who knows the ropes and can build the right team around you. One who can work with the other team directors. And you need a sponsor with very deep pockets, one who can afford the best doctors, the best soigneurs."

Kurt knew this to be true, but his loyalty ran deep. He had spent five years with Otto Werner and the GTI squad. They believed in him, and they had worked hard to help him get to this point.

"I'm happy with my team," he said.

"Of course you are. They are good boys." Garnier's smile was patronizing, as well as fake. "You can keep the best of them if you like."

"What's that supposed to mean?" Kurt knew the deal was coming now. Out of the corner of his eye, he saw Leguerre fidget.

"I want you to ride for me…for Comtec, starting next season. I will give you an initial, guaranteed three-year contract at three million U.S. dollars per year. Tell us which riders you want from your team to come and we'll get them. The team and the schedule will be built around you and the Tour. If you win it next year, I'll add two more years to the end of your contract." He paused, took a sip from his cognac glass, and looked squarely at Kurt. "I think you realize that such a deal has never been offered to a cyclist before."

Kurt tried to hide his astonishment. He thought the quarter-million dollars Otto paid him this year was a large sum, and he knew that Poulain, with five Tour victories, was making around two and a half million. There had to be something else behind this.

"What about Poulain? He's your man, and there's no way we'll ride on the same team."

Garnier, his face contorting into an unpleasant, arrogant smile, looked at an unsmiling Leguerre and then back to Kurt. "After this Tour is over, Poulain will be the first man in history to win six consecutive Tours, and he will retire. Of that there is no question."

Leguerre nodded slightly.

Kurt's first impulse was to leap to his feet and smash his fist into Garnier's arrogant face. In his mind, Poulain's sixth victory was far from assured, and the implication that Kurt would surely lose the jersey caused a hot rage to surge through him.

Garnier was watching closely. He spoke only when he saw that Kurt was able to keep his emotions under control.

"I know this is a lot for you to think about, particularly on the eve of the first day you will ride as the leader of the Tour. Perhaps you could take Guy back down to town for me. He will be able, I'm sure, to answer any questions you have."

Garnier stood up, signaling that the meeting was over. He motioned Kurt to the window. "Please, take another look."

He gave Kurt and Leguerre a few moments to view the sunset and the seemingly endless mountainscape. The sky had become more crimson than orange, and the disappeared sun backlit the granite spires, turning them into a row of jagged silhouettes, silently and powerfully guarding the soft slopes and spreading valley below.

"Before you go," Jérôme Garnier said, "you should know that the entire town was against me building on this land. The view, you can see, is priceless. But I got it, swiftly and decisively, by offering more money than was ever paid for a piece of property up here. And I built this *petit château* with stone from a Tibetan monastery hauled up piece by piece. And now, when they look at what I have created, they thank me for my vision, and they point to my house and say that it is the most unique structure in *les Hautes-Alpes*...and that it is a credit to L'Alpe d'Huez.... It is the way I do everything."

He paused, again leveling his deadly stare at Kurt through the practiced smile. "You will be smart to take my offer."

* * *

Dufour drove slowly, but his mind was racing. His initial flash of anger had subsided, and confusing thoughts now ran through his mind. He was no fool. The deal Garnier offered would set him up for life and give him the assurance that obstacles in the way of becoming a great

112

Tour champion would be greatly reduced. The past five years of hard effort, of learning how to race smart and win, of proving to himself that he really did have the quality of greatness, was paying off. And now, the wealthiest and most powerful man in the sport recognized his talent and was willing to pay for it. Garnier, as unpleasant a character as he seemed, was quite obviously a very successful and shrewd businessman. After all, he had stood behind Poulain all these years while, at the same time, Comtec had grown into a multibillion-dollar global company. And, as far as Kurt knew, there was no more talk, openly at least, of a drug connection. At least, if he took such a deal, he knew he would not turn into the arrogant fool Poulain had become.

"It is much to think about, eh?" Kurt had almost forgotten that Leguerre was in the car. Now he turned to him, realizing that this was the man he most needed to talk to.

"Guy, I need to talk to you for a few minutes."

"I am with you for that reason," Leguerre said. "Pull the car into the next side street. I know where we can go to talk in private."

In a moment they had parked the car and entered through the back door of the *Hôtel le Refuge*. Leguerre knew the owner and, without question, he and Kurt were ushered into a small, comfortably furnished sitting room. The only window looked back toward the mountains, now so dark that their jagged outlines were barely discernible against the deepening darkness of the alpine sky. There was no one around.

Guy lit a candle on the small table in front of the window and brought over a bottle of Beaujolais and two glasses that he pulled from a cupboard in the corner. "I come here every year during *Le Tour*," he explained. "There is always a need to talk privately with someone, and all I need to pay the owner is a new team jersey. In English, I think you would call him a *groupie* for cycling."

Leguerre smiled and motioned for Kurt to sit across the table. He poured them each a glass of wine and waited for Kurt to speak.

"You were different up there," Kurt said, hoping to put Leguerre off guard. "I see that Garnier is very much in charge of things and he's used to getting what he wants."

Leguerre took a slow sip of wine, his eyes lowered from Kurt's. When he finally looked up, Kurt could tell that the man was not about to telegraph his thoughts, not just yet anyway. But Leguerre seemed slightly uncomfortable and Kurt sensed that he might open up a little, perhaps if the wine took hold. He had seen him down a couple of glasses at Garnier's earlier.

"He is a very powerful man, this is true. He buys and sells companies as if they were trinkets." Leguerre chose his words carefully. "And...I know this from being with him for many years...he does what he says. I have learned how to get along with him."

Kurt's impulse was to pour out his thoughts to Leguerre, to say how his gut told him that Garnier was an evil man but that his mind was attracted by the deal, perhaps the only real chance he would have to achieve the greatness that he had decided was his destiny. But Leguerre was not Otto Werner, and Kurt, too, chose his words carefully.

"If you don't particularly like the man, why have you stayed with him for so long?" As soon as the question was out, Kurt realized how naïve it sounded.

Leguerre's lips twitched a faint smile. "We are here to talk about you and your future, not mine. But since you asked, I will tell you." He paused to drain his glass. Kurt reached across and poured more. "You see, Garnier pays me very well and he allowed me to make Poulain into a great champion. I am happy to be recognized as a great *directeur sportif* and to be able to make a good life for my family. C'est tout. *That's all.*"

He looked squarely at Kurt. "And now you. Do you want to be un vrai champion? *a true champion?* Are you willing to pay the price?"

"I'm willing to work hard and make sacrifices, if that's what you mean."

Again the faint smile. "That is...appropriate. But sometimes the kind of sacrifices you have to make may not be to your liking...."

Kurt decided to put it right on the table: "Like throwing my first Tour win in the hope that that control freak up there will guarantee me a future.... It would be easy, wouldn't it?" Fourteen seconds wasn't much, and Kurt knew that losing it to Poulain was almost expected, particularly in the final time trial on the next-to-last day. He suppressed his anger at the thought.

Leguerre chose to ignore Kurt's comment. Instead, he started to paint a picture of what could be. "Next year, right after Christmas holiday, we take three weeks in a warm climate, possible le Côte d'Azur, Southern California, wherever you like. We make the training and we plan, plan the season around you to win *Le Tour*. You and me, we have chosen the riders, *les équipiers,* and I have contracted the best soigneurs, *mécaniciens*...we can have Berclaz, Patterson, Chimello, Langlois if you want...all the uniforms and *les vélos*, they are state-of-the-art...."

Leguerre went on. He became increasingly enamored with his own description of how the team and the seasons would be built around the young champion...how the cycling world would praise the campaign to produce another great Tour champion, how America, France, and all the world would fall in love with the likable young hero.

He finished his speech by gently setting his wine glass, emptied for the third time, on the table. He was leaning forward and his eyes, slightly bloodshot now, looked into Kurt's for a reaction.

For a moment, Kurt did not speak. He had never pictured Leguerre like this. To Kurt, he had always seemed the tough and decisive team director, Poulain's most trusted ally, and a man who took a bottom-line approach to his profession—results, not dreams counted.

"You hate what Poulain has become, don't you?" Kurt needed to know.

Leguerre's head drooped. He stared down at the table for what seemed like a long time and, when he looked up, his expression was serious, unmasked.

"I helped make Poulain a great champion...but I...I did not teach him to be a man of character. No, I do not like what this man has become. If Poulain wins this year, he will give up the bike, and for me he will be gone. I will stop also unless...unless I can do it over with another champion, someone I can help to handle better the fame...a good person. *Comprenez-vous?*"

"Sure, I understand. Throw my first Tour now so I can become a man of character later."

"Sometimes we must compromise." Leguerre shrugged his shoulders. His eyes seemed almost pleading. "Poulain is still very strong. He had one bad day, and he will give everything he has for the time trial. You will disappoint no one if you lose to him. And the future...for you, is very, very good."

"What if I win?"

Leguerre stiffened. "Poulain will not retire. You will have no deal with Comtec. And I will have to make sure Poulain wins next year. It will be hard for everyone."

Crazy thoughts ran through Kurt's mind. He could refuse the deal, try his hardest, and still lose. Or, he could take the deal and have Poulain gone next season, forever. He would stand next to him on the podium this year, his first attempt at the Tour. Second place is better than most rookies ever dreamed of. He had put up a great fight already, shown people that he had what it takes. No one would be disappointed. And his future would be very secure, likely with many years as a Tour champion. But what if this was all a game, a trick to get him to lose now...and then...screw the American.

"How do I know this is for real?" He had to ask.

"You have to trust me. I can put nothing on paper." Leguerre was back to himself, all business. "I will show you what we can do. Tomorrow, the last day in the Alps, you will win again. The stage finishes in Morzine. The last twelve kilometers is all downhill *après le Col de Joux Plane*.... Comtec and Chimello's team, Favolti, will make the tempo all day—it is natural, eh?—they will want to see if your men will crack."

"You mean Chimello's in on this too?" Kurt interrupted, dumbfounded.

"Next year, he will ride for you...." Leguerre caught himself. "...if, of course, you want him to."

"It doesn't sound like I would have much choice."

Leguerre smiled faintly and made sure Kurt was listening carefully before he continued to lay out the plan. He told Kurt when to attack, assured him that the others would let him win tomorrow. But they would make it look real. No one would know.

"This will show you that we can control the peloton, that we can do the same for you next year. If, of course, you decide to cooperate."

"You mean lose the time trial on Saturday."

"Of course..." Leguerre fidgeted slightly, "...by enough to put Poulain back in *le maillot*." He looked away.

Dufour stood up, the color drained from his face. He paced as his mind rolled through conflicting emotions, thoughts of the temptations he'd faced...the dead girl, his transformed life. And now he was within reach of the very top of this game, this sport that had channeled him into a new, focused life. He savored yesterday's victory and wanted more with a burning, driving desire. The power of being a great champion called to him, and yet, at the same time, made him afraid. Maybe this was a freak year; there were many one-time champions who had faded quickly from this sport. On the other hand, maybe he could grab it all...take Garnier's money, get rid of Poulain after this year—only a week, really—and bring his own people with him to help secure a long reign at the top. Patterson, Berclaz, maybe even Otto. It could work....

"Okay," he said. "I'll play along tomorrow."

"And Saturday?" Leguerre looked up at Kurt. His eyes pleaded.

Kurt took a deep breath. He decided to take the chance, his gut telling him to get some sort of guarantee, a way to test them, just in case. He thought quickly and then leveled a menacing look at Leguerre.

"Tell Garnier that for me do this, I need more than a stage win tomorrow. Tell him to deposit one million Swiss francs—a down payment—in a new Swiss bank account in my name. I want you to tell me the name of the bank, the account number, and an access code by Friday."

Leguerre was visibly surprised. This was clearly a new twist. But he nodded and slowly got to his feet. His face was only a few inches from Kurt's. "I know it is a dirty business. But you have earned the right to make the rules. You make the correct decision...to plan wisely for your future. You will become as great a cyclist as there has ever been...."

Kurt Dufour turned abruptly and left the room. *Oh, shit*, he thought. *What have I done?*

****

Chapter Fourteen

Morzine

The red, white, and blue GTI team car, roof bristling with shiny matching-colored bicycles and carrying the new *maillot jaune*, could barely get through the massive crowds to the starting line the next morning. The village of Le Bourg-d'Oisans at the foot of the climb to L'Alpe d'Huez had tripled in size, straining to accommodate the influx of bike racing fans who wanted to be part of this history-making Tour de France. Despite the early-morning hour, shop doors were open, and festive music blared, filling the town center with a holiday atmosphere for the thousands who strained and pushed at roadside fences, hoping to get a look at the wheel idols as they disembarked from their team vehicles and off-loaded their bicycles to take to the start.

Finally, the GTI car, piloted carefully by a smiling and waving Otto Werner, maneuvered into the number-one position, parking at the head of the ragged line of twenty team vehicles close behind the racers, each one designated as the primary road service car for a surviving team in the race. Press and assorted official vehicles stretched for several more blocks in front and behind. People milled about, getting ready.

The leader of the Tour could be excused for arriving late, it being understood that part of the burden of wearing the *le maillot* was constant distraction by autograph seekers and journalists. Only within the zone reserved and secured for the racers and officials could Kurt Dufour safely step from the car into the bright sunshine. When he did, the crowd cheered and whistled, and a dozen or so small children strained over the fence. They frantically waved tiny American flags, hoping to get the young star's attention. His casual, two-fingered salute and faint smile in their direction caused squeals of delight, particularly among the young girls, each of whom was sure his acknowledgment was just for her.

Dufour looked the part. Two weeks of hard riding had deepened the bronze tone of his arms, legs, and face. He had become the ultimate athletic machine, lean and sinewy, with the characteristic bulging thighs of a pedaling specialist tapered shapely into thin ankles, all shaved smooth and still glistening from oil rubbed in during the morning's massage. His light-brown hair was cropped short and showed neatly from beneath the white cotton cycling cap he wore perched toward the front of his handsome face. Its small brim was tilted down just overlapping the top of his sunglasses, in-vogue, titanium-framed ones whose small oval lenses covered each eye. The *maillot jaune* fit snugly over his slender, deep-chested torso, and its bright yellow color radiated a special glow that was a beacon to every person in town that day.

With Werner at his elbow and bicycle at his side, he made his way through the group of milling personnel that was the Tour de France entourage, not saying much and nodding distractedly to the dozens of people who wanted to shake his hand and wish him well.

Only when Jennifer Scott appeared, TV crew in tow, did he stop. Otto left him for a moment.

She touched his arm and looked up to his face. "Everyone is so proud of you," she whispered, her eyes welling with tears.

"What about you?" He had missed seeing her last night. She had arrived late and he had gone to bed right after leaving Leguerre.

"Me…most of all."

He suddenly wanted everyone, everything to disappear but her. He wanted to hold her close, to feel the warmth of her body, breathe the fresh scent of her hair. He wanted to share the wild thoughts that had occupied his mind during the long, restless night. He knew she would understand. And he wanted her to tell him all about the finish at L'Alpe d'Huez and her mad dash to Paris, how they put the show together, and how she had managed to get back to the race. She looked fresh, happy, and beautiful. For all these reasons…and more, he wanted her.

The curtain fell with the arrival of Jacques Poulain. The Frenchman shouldered Scott aside, wrapped an arm around Kurt and grinned into his face. Suddenly, there were cameras and microphones everywhere and shouted questions from all sides.

"Voici le grand vainqueur *Here's the big winner!*" Poulain, still grinning broadly, pulled Kurt tight to his side and, with his free right hand, pointed to the American's face, holding the pose. Dufour stiffened, uncomfortable with such clowning, Poulain's unusually close presence…the man himself. Camera shutters whirred. Never had the two been photographed together off their bicycles, and it was well known that avoidance of the other had, to this point, been a top priority for each.

It was obvious, however, that the Frenchman was no longer smarting from his loss on L'Alpe d'Huez, and Dufour's proximity had suddenly become non-threatening.

"Hey, Kurt! Can you keep the jersey all the way to Paris?" It was Jeff Martin's familiar voice booming above the others.

Dufour suddenly felt stifled. He looked for Otto or Patterson, anyone who would help him get free. But Poulain squeezed him harder and without hesitation shouted an answer toward Martin.

"He may wear it to Saturday. Mais…après le contre la montre, *But... after the time trial….*" He released Kurt, exaggerated the shrug of his shoulders, stuck out his lower lip, and held up six fingers for all to see, again holding the pose. The reporters laughed and the photographers clicked away. Dufour, nauseated, somehow found Otto's arm and allowed himself to be guided through the jostling media to the starting line.

***

Katherine Anderson, standing in the center of Morzine's rain-slicked *ligne d'arrivée*, stood facing the television camera while, in the background, members of the Tour de France stage crew prepared the area for the arrival of the *caravane publicitaire*, the funny-shaped cars and trucks that would entertain and prime the growing audience for the official stage finish in just under two hours' time.

"Welcome to Morzine, France, where, soon the winner of the Tour de France will wheel into town…."

"Hold it, hold it…cut! Jesus, Katherine, you forgot the *seventeenth stage*. Say the winner of the *seventeenth stage* will soon wheel into town." Jennifer Scott, standing facing Anderson and next to Wayne, the cameraman, shook her head. It had been a hair-raising four-hour drive over the mountains to reach Morzine well ahead of the racers and they were all a little frazzled. Still, this was the fourth botched take of what should have been a simple run-through, and Scott was insisting on a flawless opening. Her instincts told her that the show would need a very strong lead in order to set the stage for a dramatic final hour of coverage. They had less than forty-five minutes until they would start getting pictures from the road, and the early day's footage still had to be edited so Martin could intelligently voice over a four-minute recap to open the show. Scott, having easily taken to the role of director, had to keep things moving.

Anderson lowered her hand mike. She glanced at Jeff Martin, standing just off-camera, and shrugged her shoulders.

"Okay, let's start over. Jeff, step in on cue and let's go straight through. We're running out of time here so *please* get it right." Scott paused to make sure Wayne was rolling tape. "Okay, whenever you're ready."

The pro in Anderson finally took over. She smiled easily, raised her microphone, and looked straight into the camera: "Welcome to Morzine, high in the French Alps, where the racers in the seventeenth stage of the Tour de France will soon wheel into town, including the overall race leader, American Kurt Dufour.... Hi, I'm Katherine Anderson, and here to tell us about today's action is our expert commentator and former pro cyclist, Jeff Martin."

Martin shouldered close to Anderson, smiled at her, and then turned to face to the camera. He spoke easily, managing to convey excitement with his voice. He had adapted well to the role of expert commentator.

"Well, Katherine, it's the last climbing stage of the Tour and the question in everyone's mind is, Can Kurt Dufour hold his slim fourteen-second lead, or will Jacques Poulain and his Comtec boys try to take it back?

"It's a long stage—two hundred fifty kilometers, with four really tough passes to climb—and no one knows just how Dufour, Poulain, and their *équipiers* feel after that brutal finish at L'Alpe d'Huez two days ago....

"Only one thing is for sure..." he turned back to Anderson, pausing for dramatic effect "...a mistake today *could* cost either one of these riders the Tour."

Scott, behind the camera, nodded vigorously, pointed to Anderson and drew her hand across her throat, the signal to wrap it up.

Anderson, flawlessly into the camera: "We'll be back with all the dramatic action from the final mountain stage of the Tour de France...stay tuned."

"Beautiful, that's a wrap." Jennifer Scott jumped up and clapped once. "Be in the booth in twenty minutes, we'll be ready to go." On to the next.

Scott had blossomed with this, her first big assignment. She had a talent for directing, a good eye for story angles, and she cared intensely about getting things done right and on schedule. The network had developed confidence in her and, with Dufour taking the race lead, had decided to clear an hour during prime time for special coverage of the last day of racing in the Alps. It was a big gamble, but viewer response to the dramatic scenes from L'Alpe d'Huez on Sunday had convinced the brass that this was an important story to follow. It wasn't often that an American had a shot at winning the world's most important bike race. And just to ensure that the show played well, the network had sprung for the services of Phil Sterling, the British commentator whose legendary insight into the sport would bolster Martin and Anderson in the booth.

Because the stage finish was expected to be at around 5 p.m. French time, the show would be shot as if it were being covered live even though it wouldn't air in the Eastern U.S. until some eight hours after it actually happened. To the viewer, it would look live and feel live, except for the periodic on-screen display of the words *"Recorded Earlier."*

"You know, you've gotten pretty good at this," Katherine Anderson said as she walked with Jeff Martin toward the network trailer. It was drizzling steadily, and she leaned into him and put her arm in his.

Even though the two had enjoyed a few passionate flings in the past two weeks, it wasn't like Katherine Anderson to pass out compliments.

"Thanks," Martin replied, raising his eyebrows. "I guess I know the subject and can get excited about it." Then, with a sideways glance, he added, "Maybe you should get into it a little more...."

Anderson, having heard this kind of comment before, replied, "You know, you color guys are all alike, you love your sports so much. Frankly, I don't see the point...a bunch of grown men with big egos racing around on bicycles...." She stopped, reaching in her jacket pocket for her cigarettes. "Who gives a shit who gets to the top of the mountain first?"

She lit up and looked at Martin, challenging him for a reply.

He stopped, facing her directly. "Who gives a shit about anything," he said, exasperated. "Why care about being a good reporter...why go after an anchor position...why bother getting up in the morning?"

Just then, Jennifer Scott trotted by, intent on her mission to have the broadcast booth ready on time. She smiled as she passed, flashing them a thumbs-up.

Anderson shook her head and blew out a long cloud of smoke. "At least, *she's* excited about this. Maybe I've been at this too long...I guess I need a little more sleaze. All this 'go for the gusto' stuff is a little too noble for me." She looked intently at Martin and said, "Don't these guys ever *cheat*?"

Martin avoided the question. He turned quickly and set off toward the media area at the finish line. He didn't want Anderson to probe *that* angle any further. God knew the sport had its scandals, and Martin knew it didn't need one to surface now, especially around Kurt Dufour. But his experience as a pro told him that something was up. Poulain's carrying-on, his boastful collaring of Kurt this morning before the start, was not the act of someone who felt challenged, particularly after he had been so soundly beaten, humiliated even, on L'Alpe d'Huez. And Dufour himself, distracted and preoccupied, was clearly not focused the way Martin would've expected him to be after taking over the jersey. No, something was going on and Martin could guess, pretty accurately, what it was.

He flashed his credential to the security guard now posted at the entrance to the media area and hustled up the platform steps in search of Jennifer. He found her near the end of the second tier where their broadcast location had been assigned. Dozens of technicians were climbing about, making sure that the banks of television monitors and microphones were connected at each of the fifty-or-so commentator booths. It was the usual organized chaos that occurred each day in the finish-line media area as expert stagehands wired the area to receive the live TV feed from the race.

Martin slipped under the rail and was into the small space that would be the network broadcast area for the next several hours. A table with TV monitor, two headsets, and three folding chairs made up the "booth," separated from the ones on either side by a canvas divider, and sparse only because no one would be on camera here. Jennifer Scott looked up from straightening the chairs as he came into the small space.

"We're set," she said. "Sterling will be here any minute. Where's Anderson?"

"On her way." Martin leaned against the rail, waiting for her to finish and hesitating about what to say. "Uh…Jenny, did you speak to Dufour at the start this morning?"

"Briefly, why?" She put down the last chair and looked at Martin.

"Did he seem different to you…tense, maybe?"

"Of course he was tense. I'd kind of expect that. You know, yellow jersey for the first time, minuscule lead, five-time winner breathing down your neck. Jesus, Jeff, I'd be worried if he *wasn't* tense." She shook her head and looked over the rail, obviously for Anderson. The booths all around were filling with the other commentators.

Good, he thought. She was aware of nothing.

Scott disappeared and returned momentarily with Anderson, who took the chair on the end. Sterling arrived. He was a distinguished middle-aged gentleman with thinning hair and an angular face. He smiled and made small talk with the group while a technician ran cable and connected his headset, placing it on the table beside Martin's.

Sterling's presence energized the American broadcast team and particularly Martin, who, for years, had admired the Englishman's professional and insightful delivery. He was the undisputed English-speaking authority on professional cycling, having covered the Tour and most of the other top races for nearly two decades. During all that time, he had moved in the innermost circles of the sport, exposed to the scandals, the tragedies, the dirt. But Sterling made light of such things. He was an expert at creating the positive spin, in defining the sport as he saw it—a tough, no-nonsense business that created many heroes and provided the public with unforgettable moments of drama and excitement. Martin, in his first year of television, was thrilled to be working with him. Certainly, the Dufour question would be easier to deal with.

The flickering lines on the TV screen turned into a picture—a long line of cyclists curving through a small French town filled with families waving at the speeding racers from their porches and, now that rain was falling, from underneath brightly colored umbrellas.

"Get your headsets on," Scott commanded. "We'll run the intro, then the recap, cut to break, and then back to Phil and Jeff with the live action. We only have time to run it twice, the second one counts...."

Anderson nudged Martin, prompting him to look at her as he reached for his headset. "Tell it like it is, big boy," she said.

***

It was nearly seven hours into the stage, well into the *Haute-Savoie* region of the French Alps, and they'd raced through kilometer after kilometer of roadside fans, screaming his name, before Kurt Dufour started to think straight.

Typically enough, the Comtec and Favolti teams had been setting a hard tempo, creating the natural selection that inevitably occurred in the mountains. The GTI riders, always in the position to defend their *maillot jaune*, did their best to keep near the front, making sure that Dufour did not falter over the first three major passes of the day: the Col du Glandon, Col de la Madeleine, and Col de la Colombière.

There was little need to worry so far. Dufour showed no sign of weakness, comfortably remaining shoulder-to-shoulder with Poulain and Chimello, and always turning the pedals with the ease and power expected from one who wears the *maillot jaune*. Lesser riders had been peeled off the back with each col, and a dozen or so had crashed on the descents, made slick and treacherous by the steady drizzle they had encountered upon first entering the high mountains.

Dufour, after a restless night's sleep and the disconcerting contact with the Frenchman at the start, had shut his mind down. He rode like an automaton and forced himself to think only about the mechanics of his job—stay in the front third of the *peloton*, eat carefully, watch the wheels, stay near Poulain. It had worked for seven hours, but now, as

126

the group of twelve-or-so leaders began to power up the Côte de Châtillon, a lesser climb that indicated there was less than an hour of racing left, Dufour began to focus on the thoughts that had kept him awake most of the night. Mostly, it was Leguerre's parting words:

"You have earned the right to make the rules"

He knew the game plan. His mind was clear. He *could* make the rules. And his body was operating at an even higher plateau. It was as if the *maillot jaune* pumped energy into his legs, his heart, his lungs.

The pre-determined attack point, the "one kilometer to go" sign before the summit of the Col de Joux Plane, finally emerged through the mist. Dufour let himself drift back to the middle of the group, where he found Berclaz, climbing steadily, watching his leader for any instructions or sign of weakness. *Poor Claude,* thought Kurt, *he has no idea.*

Dufour slid next to Berclaz and leaned his head close so no one would hear. He placed a hand on his teammate's wet shoulder and whispered into his ear, "I'm going to attack. You know what to do."

Berclaz, normally stone-faced, was caught off guard. He looked down, not wanting to telegraph his surprise. He came back up, stone-faced again, but between clenched teeth muttered forcefully in Kurt's ear: "You're fuckin' crazy, they'll have you for lunch on the descent!"

But Berclaz, ever the loyal lieutenant, instinctively reacted by increasing his tempo until he reached the front rank of Alcarta and Langlois. He must be in position to disrupt any chase, foolhardy as his leader's attack might be.

The group was still pounding steadily, fast and hard, but not so uncomfortable that any of the top contenders would falter. Gone from this day had been attacks and counterattacks on each of the earlier cols. It was strange. Hard but not hard, a day of attrition to peel off the weak. It was unlikely that the overall standings would change even if there had been attacks, although it would have been an ideal stage for someone several minutes down and not a threat to the leaders to gain some time or grab a stage win. Maybe it was the rain, maybe it was a sense that the Tour had been hard enough already. In any case, no one in the front group seemed to object to the controlled pace.

Dufour hung back, waiting for his moment.

***

The picture Jeff Martin and Phil Sterling saw on their TV monitor was clear. It came from moto 1, the television camera motorcycle positioned with the leaders as they pounded up the last climb of the day. The road was wet, all the top contenders were there. Anything could happen.

Martin was on the edge of his seat. Sterling leaned close to Martin, his experienced eyes watching every move on the screen. Their headsets were on and the mikes were hot. They would call the race live, offer their insights and opinions on the action the viewers would see in their living rooms. Katherine Anderson, miked with headsets on too, sat a little to the side, ready to jump in when a voice in her earphones told her to go to break. Beyond that, she didn't have to know what was going on.

"Phil, it looks as if Berclaz has been told to go to the front. That's him moving in between Alcarta and, it looks like Langlois, at the head of the group." Martin was a little stiff, not quite warmed up yet.

"Indeed, Jeff. A moment ago we saw Dufour whisper something to Berclaz. They have to watch Poulain and his men very carefully now. They only have a kilometer more to the summit of Joux Plane, followed by a quick bump to the Col du Ranfolly. Then it's a fast and wet run-in to the finish, about twelve kilometers, mostly downhill. Pretty treacherous I should imagine, Jeff." Sterling's authoritative British accent oozed drama.

Just then, the picture went haywire. For an instant, the road swirled around and the screen was filled with tree branches, the backside of a motorcycle helmet, indistinguishable bikes and riders. The picture recovered. There, full frame, was the *maillot jaune*. The motorcycle accelerated forward and the camera pullback revealed Kurt Dufour in full cry, blurred images of his competitors struggling behind.

Sterling, hunched over the TV as if he was in the race himself, immediately picked up the action. "A moment's confusion and Dufour, the yellow jersey, the leader of the Tour de France, has launched a powerful attack and his rivals...seem completely caught off guard!

128

"Jeff, this is unheard of. Dufour, the rookie, has taken the initiative against Poulain, Chimello, Koopman, Alcarta, in the face of a slick mountain descent and only fifteen kilometers to the finish...."

Martin struggled to keep up: "It seems like a crazy move, Phil. Dufour's a cautious descender, particularly in the rain. There's no way he can stay away from these guys...."

The camera stayed on Dufour as he strongly topped the final summit and shifted into a higher gear to start the long, twisting descent. He glanced over his shoulder.

"He's ten seconds clear at the summit," Sterling remarked. "I think you're right, Jeff. He'll have to show us a new talent if he can stay away all the way to Morzine. You can bet Poulain and his men will do everything they can to keep him from gaining any more time."

This was Sterling's cue for the producer to switch the picture feed from moto 1 to moto 2 so the commentators could see what was happening behind. The camera didn't switch, leaving no sense of the distance back to the chasers or how hard they were riding relative to Dufour.

Several agonizing moments went by. Sterling started getting impatient. With his left hand, he made a circular motion for Martin to keep talking. With his right, he hit the "talk-back" switch in front of him so he could shut off the on-air channel and speak, instead, to Arnie Campbell, the show producer, back in the control trailer.

"Where the hell is moto 2?" he demanded into his mouthpiece. Martin continued to vamp, analyzing the descending technique of Dufour, the only rider on the screen.

"It's out of commission, my moto 2 screen just went blank," came the tense response from Campbell. "We don't know what happened, Phil. Stand by."

Sterling looked up from the monitor to see what was happening at the other broadcast positions nearby. He could tell from the confusion that no one else was getting pictures from moto 2. It seemed like every production assistant on the platform was scrambling for a radio.

The image of Kurt Dufour, hunched over his bicycle in the driving rain, faded magically into the network logo.

"You're watching network coverage of the Tour de France" came the soothing voice of Katherine Anderson. "We'll be right back with Kurt Dufour and the exciting finish of today's stage."

Sterling and Martin tore off their headsets, practically in unison.

"What the fuck happened?" Martin exclaimed, looking for someone to provide an answer.

Sterling was already out of the booth and two locations down where Dutch television had their position. Hari Verkerk, Sterling's counterpart from Holland, had his ear glued to a radio tuned into the race caravan. He looked up at Phil and rolled his eyes. "*Godverdomme*, no one chases," he said.

Sterling quickly made it back and slid into his chair next to Martin. "Pity. No one wants to chance it, they're letting him go," he said as the headsets slipped back on. "So our boy's having another great day, let's make America proud."

Less than fifteen minutes later, Kurt Dufour, his *maillot jaune* nearly obscured by mud and grime from the long, wet road, pedaled in solo triumph into the jammed finishing straightaway in the alpine village of Morzine. He raised his arms heavenward. He clasped his hands together. He punched at the sky. He blew kisses to the adoring crowd.

Phil Sterling and Jeff Martin, along with hundreds of other commentators and broadcast journalists, none of whom ever got pictures from moto 2, had a solid ten minutes to tell the sporting world that a new champion had arrived. A fearless young man who attacked when others would have defended, an "in your face" kind of guy, who suddenly breathed new life into a sport that had been dominated for years by an arrogant Frenchman. He won in the Alps two days in a row, first to capture, then to solidify his hold on the coveted yellow symbol. All in his first year. The sport was exciting again.

Jacques Poulain rolled across the finish line in second place. He was not as tired as he was when he had struggled up to L'Alpe d'Huez two days ago, nor did he look so defeated, despite the boos and catcalls that accompanied him through town. He glanced up at the timing clock as he crossed the finish line, just slightly ahead of the dozen or so men who had remained with him in the lead group all day.

The rolling numbers stopped at twenty-three seconds, three more than Dufour had been promised. Poulain smiled to himself.

***

A favorite pastime for those who follow the Tour, the insiders on the race, is to buy drinks for each other and hang around the bars at night, speculating—especially the journalists and the TV crews. As soon as the last interviews are conducted, the final story filed, and the *Salle de Presse* closed for the night, the dimly lit bars and the hotel lobbies start to fill up with small clusters of this sometimes boisterous, sometimes subdued group.

The Americans were headquartered at modest alpine digs near the center of town, the *Hôtel le Crête*. The place had a nice lounge, plenty of big comfortable chairs, and a long wooden bar. The soft yellow lighting would be inviting to the weary journalists, particularly on this chilly overcast evening, the last one the Tour would spend in the mountains of France's *Haute-Savoie* region.

It had been a very long day for Jeff Martin, Katherine Anderson, Jennifer Scott, and the others. The edit truck and the RV were packed and on their way to St. Claude, tomorrow's stage finish somewhere north of Geneva. Their show had gone on the satellite several hours earlier. Word from the network execs back in the States was good. There had been heavy promo and they were expecting good ratings, especially since word of Dufour's increased lead would be aired on the evening news, previewing the Tour special by half an hour. America was waking up to its new hero.

Arnie Campbell, producer and ranking network crew member, had suggested they toast their success tonight in the bar. Phil Sterling would come, and maybe even Otto Werner and some of the GTI team personnel, if they felt relaxed enough. The riders, of course, would all be in bed.

Katherine Anderson had invited Sterling to meet early at the bar. They moved to a table in the corner after he had ordered a triple *Trappist* and she a glass of red wine.

"You were phenomenal today, as I understand is usual," Anderson said, as she offered her glass in a toast.

Sterling smiled. "I reckon it was a bit dicey there for a while, wasn't it. It makes it hard when you don't have moto 2 you know."

"Fortunately, you guys had enough to say about Dufour", Anderson said. "Good thing you remembered that package we shot last spring—everybody else forgot we had had it. Guess that's why you get the big bucks." She referred to the pre-recorded piece on Dufour's background that was shot earlier in the year. Sterling had reminded Campbell to have it ready in case they needed to vamp for a while. He had made the transition to it perfectly, buying them precious time to find out what was happening with the chasers on the radio. It had saved all of them three minutes of potentially embarrassing banter.

"Important to roll with the punches, isn't it." Sterling was like that. He didn't jump to take the credit like most other commentators would, most of whom had huge egos.

Anderson took a sip of wine and returned her glass to the table. She cleared her throat and looked straight at him, trying to sound nonchalant. "So what do you think happened to moto 2?"

"Gaston, the driver, said the bloody microwave went down, right when Dufour attacked. It's happened before, you know. Especially on a wet day like this." Sterling seemed quite satisfied with this explanation.

"I heard Claude Berclaz speaking to Otto Werner right after the race. They didn't know I was there", Anderson said, leaning a little closer. "He was pretty upset, said he saw Poulain speak to the camera guy. He said Poulain's effort was half-assed when Dufour attacked. He said he thought it was a dangerous and stupid move for Dufour to break away like that, without it being part of a team plan. He said Poulain and the others kept their brakes on so he could stay away." She paused, waiting for Phil's reaction.

"Come on, did he really say all of that?" Sterling seemed only mildly surprised.

"Yes, I heard it all. Right after the race. He wasn't making it up, Phil. Jeff was right there. He heard it too. *He* said it looked pretty fishy."

"Well, I should think something's going on then, isn't there?" A little more sarcasm than surprise this time.

Anderson, realizing she may be sounding naïve, reached for her cigarettes and sat back, continuing the nonchalant approach. "Come on, Phil. I know there's a little hanky-panky that goes on in every sport." If she'd been sitting next to him, she would've given him a friendly elbow to the ribs.

"Oh, I don't doubt that a bit," he replied, smiling. "And I'm sure you've seen a lot of it now, haven't you?"

She lit her cigarette and leaned back, studying him closely for a long moment. "Why do I sense that you wouldn't tell me anything anyway?"

He smiled a very friendly smile. "Why, I shouldn't think there's anything to tell. It's a great sport, Katherine." He looked past her and waved in the direction of the bar. "My mate from the BBC just popped round. See you later." He winked at her as he got up and was gone.

Anderson angrily crushed her cigarette in the glass ashtray on the table. She exhaled a long cloud of blue smoke, forcefully in the direction of where Sterling had been. "Shit," she muttered. "*Shit!*"

"What's the matter?" It was Jennifer Scott. She slid into the seat where Sterling had been. "Weren't you happy with the broadcast?" She was smiling, flushed with the outcome of the day, and sure that Anderson's bad mood was not related.

"Oh, it was just lovely."

"So what's wrong, then?" Scott leaned toward her, still smiling broadly.

Anderson slammed her hand on the table and put her face a few inches from Scott's. "Call a production meeting, *right now*." She was dead serious.

Jennifer stopped smiling and leaned back. "But why? Everybody's done for the day, and we already went over tomorrow's plan. Katherine…what's wrong?"

"Because there's another story here, Miss cub reporter." She was determined to take control. "And I don't want us to miss it because we're focused on a fairy tale."

"Fairy tale?" Scott was dumbfounded.

"Something nasty's going on in this race, honey. I can smell it." She leaned back and lit another cigarette. "And my gut tells me our hero is right in the middle of it."

"What on earth are you talking about?"

"Just call the goddam meeting." The smoke from her nostrils spread out in front of her and then drifted around her incredulous assistant. She looked straight at Jennifer and slowly drummed her fingers on the table.

***

Arnie Campbell wasn't happy about opening his cramped suite to the broadcast team at such a late hour. It had been a long day, and a successful one at that. He was pleased that they had scored well with this obscure sport, that they were right there when the young American burst on the scene. This was rare for an American network—they were usually too late by at least a season whenever an American showed promise in the Tour de France. He wanted to be at the bar celebrating. But Katherine Anderson, the queen of sleaze, had smelled something and it was his duty to at least hear her out.

"So what's on your mind?" Campbell, the veteran TV producer, was used to tight schedules and brief meetings. He liked to get right to the point.

The rest of them were there, crowded together in a small sitting area made even smaller by several metal cases of camera equipment piled up against one wall. The gear had forced the two small couches and battered armchair to be pushed nearly on top of each other, squeezing Jeff Martin and Jennifer Scott on one with Campbell facing them on the other. Katherine sat in the chair at the end, fingering an unlit cigarette. She looked at each of them and then stopped on Campbell. She knew what she was about to say had to come out the right way if she wanted to get anywhere.

134

"I have reason to believe," she paused dramatically, "that there is some serious cheating going on in this bike race."

"Oh, for chrissake, Katherine." Campbell was exasperated already. "Is that all you think about? You've barely been paying attention to this race and now you miraculously uncover what no one else has even so much as hinted at." He shook his head.

"I have reliable sources. I know it happens a lot in this sport." She looked at Martin.

"Who are your sources? How do you know this? Why are you looking at Jeff? Get to the fucking point, Katherine." Campbell looked ready to throw her out.

"Ask *him*...." She nodded at Martin and put the still unlit cigarette to her lips.

Martin squirmed, causing Scott, seated tightly next to him, to push back for a better look at his face. Campbell, suddenly softening, smiled at Jeff. He liked the ex-bike racer and depended upon his expertise to know what to cover in this often-confusing sport. "C'mon, Jeff, what's this bullshit she's talking about?"

"Beats the hell outta me." Martin seemed nervous enough for Campbell to feel he should probe further. His instincts, his duty as a veteran sports producer was to know the whole story behind an event before he decided what their two camera crews should cover.

"Jeff," Campbell's voice was soothing now, "is there something you saw that we should know about?" Scott's eyes had widened and she watched Martin intensely for his answer.

"Tell him about moto 2, Jeff." Anderson's voice was forceful.

Martin tried not to show the panic he felt. He was torn between his own growing instincts to get the inside story and the need to protect the sport that had made him. He truly didn't know the details of what he guessed was happening between Dufour and Poulain, and he didn't want to speculate in front of these people.

"So, Jeff, what happened to moto 2?"

"I really don't know." Martin held his composure, although not convincingly. "After the stage, Berclaz bitched to Werner that somebody...he thought Poulain...signaled for moto 2 to shut down. Berclaz said Poulain and the others who should've chased, just let Kurt go."

"That's preposterous."

"I agree. I think Berclaz was a little crazed. Sometimes your mind does strange things after seven hours out there." Martin's confidence was coming back, slightly.

"But we *both* heard it. I think someone's trying to control the outcome of this race." Anderson wasn't about to give up.

Jennifer Scott spoke up for the first time. "What are you all saying? You think someone's trying to fix the *Tour de France*? Kurt won the stage. If they were trying to fix things they would've run him off the road or something. And why would Poulain want moto 2 to shut down? This is ridiculous. It makes no sense."

"Unless wonder boy's in on it." Anderson's words were cold, cutting.

There was silence around the room. Scott looked fiercely at her but held her tongue. Campbell was clearly confused. He couldn't make sense of it either. Martin felt he had said enough.

"Katherine, we can't make a story out of speculation. Besides, our man is winning. That's enough of a story. We're getting everything we came for."

"Right, Arnie. But what if somebody else discovers a big scandal. We'd look pretty foolish."

Campbell thought for a moment. Even though his two crews were doing behind-the-scenes coverage, he wasn't prepared to dig into a scandal that probably didn't exist. And he feared Anderson. Once she got the scent, she could turn into a loose cannon and embarrass them all. Not long ago, the network had talked to him about canceling her contract and just for this kind of shotgun reporting. He had supported her ouster, as had several of the other line producers. She was brash and hard to work with, and she made them all nervous. But somebody upstairs saved her, largely because the one big story she nailed led to

136

the discovery of rampant drugging of show horses. The network broke the story and it won them a news Emmy. But in that case they had enough people to gather the facts and others to corroborate the story. Please, not on my watch, Campbell thought.

"We're doing a low-budget sports show here, folks. We don't have the money or the authorization for an investigative piece...not to mention the right reporters." He looked directly at Anderson and scowled.

"Go fuck yourself, Arnie."

He didn't react; he was used to this from her. Instead, the producer searched the other faces in the room. His job was to make the decisions on what to cover and how to cover it. He could tell Martin was aware of something out of the ordinary, and he knew Anderson would harass him relentlessly until he authorized some kind of effort to check it out.

"Okay. Katherine, I'll give you Wayne. You direct him for the next three days and try to dig something out. But for chrissake, if you start pissing people off...."

Jennifer jumped up. She couldn't bear the thought of Katherine Anderson dogging Kurt now, with only a few crucial days to go. "No, wait! Martin should take Wayne. It would be better if he did it. They trust him and...it might be easier for him to find something...without, as you said, pissing anyone off."

Anderson laughed, a deep, rasping sound from somewhere down in her chest. "Come on, honey. He's a color guy, not a dirt sniffer. Plus, he's not going to rat on his friends." She caught herself and looked at Martin, realizing that maybe she'd gone too far.

He gave her a look of disgust. "You're right on that one, *honey*. I'm here to report what I see on the screen. You can go look under the fuckin' rug."

"Hold it, children, hold it. This is getting out of hand." Campbell had a better idea. "Jenny", he looked in her direction, his mind running. "*You* take the crew. You've been doing a great job getting the shots we need. They trust...."

"Oh that's really good, Arnie." Anderson interrupted bitterly, realizing that the first assignment she could really get into was being pulled right out from under her. "She wouldn't see it if it ran her over. That's her white knight riding out there."

"Sorry, that's the way it's going to be." Campbell was relieved. With luck, the whole thing would disappear. His mind was working. Maybe he could neutralize Anderson by giving her a few days in Paris.

They spent the next few minutes going over the revised schedule. They wouldn't have another show until Saturday. Arnie would take Katherine back to the editing studio in Paris where they would start building segments for the new show, an hour-long recap of the week with a live report from the crucial time trial stage on Saturday, still five days off. He would leave Martin and one crew to stay on top of race coverage, and Jennifer with Wayne's crew to probe the inside stuff and get more background material.

Katherine was the first to leave the suite, her anger somewhat mitigated by the opportunity to spend a few days in Paris instead of following the bikes. Martin followed, leaving Jenny alone with Campbell.

He walked her to the door and, before letting her out, touched her arm so she would face him directly. He was near fifty, balding on top, and somewhat stoop-shouldered—likely from so many years spent in editing rooms staring at TV monitors. At this moment, he seemed older than she had ever thought of him.

"Jenny", he said. "I have a feeling that there may be something to this. But half a story is no story, and we'll have a big problem if we don't have hard facts and sources who'll talk on camera. You have a journalist's eye for a good story. If you see or hear anything, call me and, together, we'll figure out the best way to handle it."

Scott nodded, patted him on the arm, and let herself out. As she walked down the hall and into the elevator, her legs felt weak and her stomach nauseous. She couldn't believe what she had heard in there. Suddenly, the heady feeling the day had brought was gone, replaced by the sickening realization that she would have to confront a subject she had no stomach for.

Her first impulse was to get out of the stifling hotel and into the cool mountain air. Her second impulse was to find Kurt Dufour. But it was late and she knew it was past when she could find him up. In a way, she was glad. She couldn't imagine what to say to him or how she would talk to him about her new assignment.

She passed through the lobby and into the night. There was a bench just outside the front door of the hotel and, with no one around, she thankfully sat alone and breathed deeply of the fresh alpine air. At least the initial shock of the meeting had worn off and she was beginning to think rationally about what had been said in there. The hardest part to swallow was that this bike race clearly wasn't all she thought it was. She had been told that many, if not most, pro sports were plagued by people who tried to control things, that under-the-table money and drugs were often part of the game. She sensed that the first time she met Poulain. But Kurt Dufour? He had to be above that. Still, his past nagged at her. That girl who died, the trial that put his desires on public display, and the strange way both he and Poulain had acted today. It added up to doubt about who the man really was. Suddenly, she wished she hadn't been sent here at all, that she'd never met Kurt Dufour, and, worse, fallen in love with him.

***

Jeff Martin knew what he had to do. It had been very uncomfortable in that room and, even though it was well past eleven, he hoped that Phil Sterling was still at the bar. He was, huddled at the far corner talking intently with Hari Verkerk, several empty beer glasses in front of them. Phil sat up and smiled when he saw Martin approach.

"Have a brew, mate, it looks like you could use one." The tenseness on Martin's face was unusual and easy to read. Verkerk, half in the bag, turned his drooping head and gave Jeff a smile. There was a broad gap between his two top teeth. He muttered something unintelligible and went back to his drink.

Martin went around to Phil's side, hoping not to involve Verkerk in the conversation.

"Phil, I've got to talk to you for a minute."

"Need help getting into her knickers? Thought you had that down by now." Sterling smiled. They all knew Martin was doing Anderson and had taken bets on when it would get too hot for him.

"She's a real piece of work, Phil."

"I'll bet she's a screamer."

"Yeah, I think that's part of the problem."

Sterling chuckled. He had been amused by her attempt to uncover something earlier. And he hadn't missed the fact that she had demanded a meeting with her people after their conversation. One of the things Sterling enjoyed about these Americans was how seriously they took everything, how determined they were to get to the bottom of things. The truth, no matter what.

"So who's assigned to the investigation? Not her, I hope."

"No, thank God. I don't think Arnie really wants to know anything. He put Jennifer on it."

"Poor girl. She won't have the stomach for that. And what about Anderson?"

"Arnie's taking her to Paris tomorrow morning."

"At least she'll be out of everyone's hair now, won't she?"

"Yeah, thank God."

"Take it easy, Jeff old boy." Sterling gave him a friendly shoulder pat. "Nothing to worry about, mate. You know this bloody business. We just have to report what we see, nothing more, nothing less."

"Phil, what do you think's really going on?" Martin leaned closer and looked around to make sure no one was near. Verkerk had staggered out and the bar was now empty. He pushed the full beer glass meant for him off to one side so he could lean closer to Sterling.

"I reckon you know as well as anyone." Sterling's face suddenly got serious. "That bloody bastard Garnier's going to cop another one."

"I can't believe Dufour would stoop to that level."

"I hope not, too, Jeff. But Garnier knows how to find everyone's price. Leguerre seemed rather chipper today, and you saw what happened on the road."

Martin shook his head and finally reached for the beer.

****

Chapter Fifteen

The Party

The toughest parts of *Le Tour*, the high cols of the Pyrenees and the Alps, were behind them. From Morzine, the race dropped out of the clouds, pedaling for two days in a roundabout way toward Dijon and from there on to Paris. They stopped for one night in Bourg-en-Bresse—partly because it was Poulain's hometown and, more importantly, because Comtec Internationale was headquartered there and the global corporation had paid two-thirds of the city's bid to host a local overnight stop. It put an arrogant and confident Jérôme Garnier in the limelight for a day. He seemed to particularly relish the moment he got to help place the *maillot jaune* on Kurt Dufour during the post-stage awards ceremony, this time in *his* town, on the platform *he* had paid for. Strangely, Garnier seemed to fawn over the American, even though his own man, Poulain, was losing to him. Dufour was cordial but somewhat aloof, and Otto Werner and the rest of the GTI squad fumed. The rumors flew.

Throughout the day, and to the legions who asked, Garnier registered no concern over the thirty-seven-second lead the American had over his man. Both he, and Poulain himself, had adopted the same response: "Attendez jusqu'à samedi et le contre la montre....*Wait until the time trial on Saturday.*"

So the crowds grew thicker and the cheering grew louder as these final days of *Le Tour* rolled under the wheels of the one hundred thirty-four surviving *Tourmen*. They traversed the sun-drenched hills of *Bourgogne*, wound past the *grande cru* vineyards, and took the quiet and varied training roads that had produced Jacques Poulain and many of the great French champions before him. Here the cheers were loudest for Poulain, *L'Homme Choisi,* the modern-day Duke of Burgundy, who, for five consecutive years, had dominated the most impassioned event in all of France. Like him or not (and most didn't), he was a native son. The fact that it had taken a young American to make Poulain an underdog for the first time since anyone could remember threw French fans into near-crazed excitement and drew a distinct line between those who supported la gloire de la France, *the glory of France* and those who felt it was about time to unseat the arrogant champion.

All the speculation centered on Saturday's time trial in Dijon. The three stages in between the Alps and the time trial—from Morzine to St. Claude, St. Claude to Bourg, and Bourg to Dijon—were tightly controlled by the leading teams so the standings at the top would not change. As in so many past Tours, such a close margin—only thirty-seven seconds between the top two contenders after the most critical stages were over—meant that the final overall winner would undoubtedly be the one who was best against the clock. It was called *l'épreuve de verité*—the race of truth—an all-out test of speed with no teammates to block and no pack in which to hide. It would come down to the power, talent, and desire each man had, on his own, to make his bicycle fly. Dufour held the slim advantage, Poulain was the superior time trialist. The results would cement the top two positions in the overall standings. Sunday's one hundred ninety-two-kilometer final leg from Creteil to Paris would be largely ceremonial.

On Friday afternoon, they swept into Dijon, a massed pack sprint taken by GTI's Hans Vokel. Much to the pleasure of Otto Werner and his upstart American team, this final jab rubbed salt into the wounds of Comtec and established a psychological advantage for the next day.

***

"I just don't understand this goddam race, Jeff." Katherine Anderson was talking into the phone as video images rolled through the bank of TV monitors in front of her. The table at which she sat was strewn with newspapers. "Every one of these rags has pages and pages on the Tour, and I can't read a goddam word."

"Even if you could, you wouldn't find the story you're looking for." Martin smiled into his hotel room phone, glad that Anderson was still in Paris.

"So what's our cub reporter up to? I can't imagine she's uncovered anything she'd tell us about." Anderson had practically given up hope on the scandal she wanted.

"Dufour's uptight, doesn't want to say too much to the cameras. That's about it."

"Yeah, thanks for the bland interviews. But I liked the pretty pictures, the sunflowers, and the vineyards—at least we'll have a nice travel log for the folks back home." She referred to the video footage the Paris studio had been receiving twice a day from the crews on the race.

"Save the sarcasm, Katherine. We've got a great rivalry here, and Dufour just might pull it off." Martin closed his eyes and crossed his fingers, hoping she would back off.

"Cut the crap, Jeff. We both know the kid's on the take. If I were you I'd take a hidden recorder and get him to spill his guts. You could do it if you had the balls."

"You're a real piece of work." Martin's anger was rising. "You don't know that for sure. No one does. So back off."

"Oh, Jeff, Jeff, Jeff." Anderson made a scolding noise into the phone. She paused for a moment and then, softer, "So why don't you buzz up to Paris tonight and convince me I'm wrong."

"Good-bye, Katherine." Martin hung up the phone and fell back on his hotel bed. He was tired from the long day into Dijon. He was glad she had gone to Paris and, at least for the moment, had left him in peace. In a few days it would all be over.

***

Comtec Internationale, as had become a five-year tradition, threw its annual lavish party the night before the final race weekend. No expense was spared to make this the most opulent evening on *Le Tour*. In fact, with five consecutive victories behind them, Comtec had come to be expected to take the lead in the race to entertain as well. Each year, the company's parties had become grander, more indulgent, and, in some people's minds, more *gauche* than the one before. Besides its extravagance, this affair had built a unique tradition that only Comtec had been able to consistently guarantee—a personal appearance by the current *maillot jaune* with only a few days left in the race. The special guest, of course, had always been Jacques Poulain.

For the first time, Comtec was faced with an embarrassing break in this tradition and, for that reason, Garnier's party was the hottest ticket to be had. Would Kurt Dufour be there, or not?

The Tour organizers, top officials from the French cycling federation, the big- money sponsors, and a select few team directors and media people—a total guest list of two hundred fifty—were summoned to Château de Vougeot, twenty kilometers south of Dijon, for the affair. As a palatial former Cistercian abbey in the small town of Gilly, Vougeot was the perfect venue. Its vaulted-ceiling banquet room, dining alcoves, manicured gardens, thirty-nine fully appointed sleeping rooms, and nine suites were at the disposal of Garnier and his guests. For this night, he owned the place and he intended to use it to his fullest advantage.

***

"I'll come on one condition, Guy. No interviews, and I'll stay for one hour. Not a minute more." Dufour spoke on the phone from his secure room at the *Hôtel Pullman La Cloche*, one of Dijon's better hotels and only a few minutes from the start of tomorrow's time trial.

"That is no problem, *mon ami*." Leguerre closed his eyes and breathed a sigh of relief. Dufour's consent to come would avoid another nasty confrontation with Garnier. Things were still going smoothly, one step at a time.

"I'm bringing my people, too, Guy."

"*Combien?*"

"Werner, Patterson, maybe Jennifer Scott and Jeff Martin. Five of us altogether." He knew this might not sit too well with Leguerre, and he wasn't at all sure they would all come. But he needed to have Americans and at least one teammate around. Better to prepare him than not.

There was a short pause at Leguerre's end. "Okay, okay. I will fax you the map to this place. Make sure you bring the car to the back gate. We will have people to bring you in with no problems."

"And I don't want to have any embarrassing moments with Poulain. No big presentations. *Comprenez-vous?*"

"*Bien sûr*. I understand." Again Leguerre closed his eyes. It would be all right since Poulain was already excused and such a small contingent of Dufour's team wouldn't disrupt. "Please, arrive by seven."

Dufour nodded to himself and hung up the phone.

"You reckon you should really go to this shindig?" John Patterson was lying on his back, eyes closed.

"You're coming too." Dufour leaned back in his chair and looked across the room at his teammate.

"Fucked if I am."

"C'mon, John. I can't go there by myself." He desperately wanted Patterson to come.

"Otto says we stay put. Besides, you're the leader of the fuckin' Tour, mate. I reckon ya don't have to go anywhere ya don't want to, especially tonight." Patterson still lay on his back, eyes closed. He knew he was getting into dangerous territory.

"I think I should go...look at this." Dufour took a piece of paper from the nightstand and dropped it on Patterson's chest.

The Australian opened his eyes, fumbled for the page, and rolled onto his side to read it. It was a fax that had just been delivered to the room:

> *Dear M. Dufour. On behalf of the Fédération Française de Cyclisme, I offer you congratulations on gaining the yellow jersey and wish you the best good fortune for the finish of Le Tour. I would be most honored to meet you at Château de Vougeot this evening. Perhaps we could speak for a moment about your experience in the most important event in our sport. With all sincerity, Claude Gervais, Secrétaire Générale.*

"Ya get the jersey, they all want to stick their noses up your ass. As soon as ya lose it, they shit all over ya." With disgust, Patterson threw the fax on the floor. "Bloody bastards just want to be on the fast wheel."

"So what's wrong with that? Maybe that's the smartest way to get to the front."

Patterson, now sitting on the edge of his bed, stiffened and snapped his face toward Kurt. "Yeah, particularly if ya pay the right bloke."

146

"What's that supposed to mean?" Dufour's anger rose.

Patterson stared at him for a painfully long moment. His face was taut and his jaw muscles rippled, as if he was fighting himself to speak. He stood up and took a step so the two would be eye to eye. "Listen to me, mate," he said in an even, serious tone. "I'll go to the friggin' party with ya. Just like I've given ya the sweat off me balls for five bloody fuckin' years. And I'll watch your ass, just like I always do...." He paused.

"But..." Dufour gently interjected and looked down, hoping to soften what he guessed was coming.

"But...ya better chew that French fucker up tomorrow."

"What makes you think I can? Nobody expects it."

Patterson grabbed his friend by the arm, forcing Dufour to look into his eyes. "*I* expect it, mate. *I* expect it."

They were interrupted by a sharp knock on the door, Otto Werner's, followed immediately, as usual, by the man himself.

"Gotta go over the schedule, men." Otto seemed a little tense.

Patterson, sharply, turned from Kurt to Otto, just in the doorway. "No time, boss man. Duff 'ere's goin to the shindig."

"Bullshit!" Otto flared, looking at Dufour. "If you think you're going to that goddam party, forget it." He was unusually agitated, and he moved between Patterson and Dufour so he could be face to face with Kurt. Patterson flopped on his bed to watch.

"Otto...it's a tradition for the race leader to go. I thought we'd all...."

"Oh, bullshit!" Otto interrupted. "What tradition? It's Garnier's tradition, started to honor his own man and stroke his own ego. Now he's only trying to save face. You've got the most important ride of your life tomorrow—and you want to hang out with those pricks? You need to rest, stay away from them." Otto shook his head and turned toward Patterson.

"Couldn't've explained it better meself." Patterson, hands behind his head, smiled up at Otto.

Kurt's anger rose. "Well I'm going. For an hour. I don't want to stay holed up in this shitty little room with nothing to do but think about tomorrow." He softened and moved to his suitcase, searching for the right clothes. "Besides, I'm rested. I feel fine. And I need to get out."

"Oh, for chrissake." Resignation had crept into Otto's voice.

Kurt turned to face him. "Honestly, there's nothing to worry about. John said he'd come with me. I promise, one hour max."

Patterson shrugged his shoulders, to no one in particular.

Otto shifted gears, knowing too well that it was not wise to create more tension with his star performer. He was much like the other good ones, a high-strung racehorse; sometimes a few carrots paid off. Better to make a concession than risk a bigger blow-up.

"Okay, Kurt. One hour. And I'm sending Oberman with the two of you so there's no screwin' around."

"You should be there too."

"Sorry, I've got too much to do. I want to go over the bikes with Ramos, and Berclaz needs some attention—he's fried. And listen, Kurt, I want to talk to you as soon as you get back. Nine o'clock. We have a couple of issues to discuss…about tomorrow."

"See you then, boss."

Otto moved toward the door, pausing by Kurt to look directly into his eyes. He wasn't sure what was there. Still, he winked and squeezed Kurt on the shoulder.

"Bike room. Nine o'clock." The door closed gently behind him.

Otto Werner was tired. He walked slowly down the hall toward his room and, quite easily, decided it was time to make the phone call. He only hoped he could get through so close to the party.

***

"Of course he comes, sir. He knows it is his duty." Guy Leguerre stood, somewhat nervously, in front of Jérôme Garnier who occupied a vast wing chair next to the window. They were in the Château de Vougeot's heavily decorated bridal suite, which Garnier had made his headquarters for the evening. The wing chair was positioned at enough of an angle so Garnier, when seated, could both preside over the room and gaze out on the gardens and graveled drive below. He wore a white dinner jacket with black bow tie and cummerbund and, with his left hand, massaged a near empty cognac glass. A freshly clipped Cuban cigar rested on the little tea table to his right along with a small intercom box.

"Then why do you appear so nervous?" Garnier's level gaze bore into Leguerre, making the usually cool *directeur sportif* fidget even more.

"Perhaps it is nothing, sir. But, you understand, this one is difficult to read…."

Garnier, irritated, cut him off. "You had the money wired, didn't you?"

"*Mais, oui.*"

"And he knows this?"

Leguerre nodded.

"So then, Guy, what is the problem?" Garnier casually picked up the cigar and brought it to his nose. His eyes never wavered from Leguerre.

"Well…he's coming with a few other Americans. And I really haven't had the chance to speak with him since Morzine. He has been very cool."

"Do you think he dares to play with me?" Garnier took the fat cigar in his mouth and repeatedly rolled it over his tongue. A three-inch flame shot from his lighter, and heavy cheeks sucked in and out until clouds of smoke billowed upward.

Leguerre closed his eyes for a moment, as if to carefully think through his answer. "No. I think he will honor the deal. We kept our word on the road to Morzine and he knows it. He has nothing to lose and everything to gain."

"Well then, Guy, you must make the boy and his friends feel welcome. Use those wonderful coaching skills of yours so he knows he made the right decision. And make sure everyone knows Poulain rests, like the true champion he is, for his big day tomorrow." He dismissed Leguerre with a wave of his cognac glass.

There was no more discussion. After Leguerre had left and quietly closed the heavy wooden door behind him, Garnier sat for several minutes, taking long draws on the cigar and watching the first cars arrive on the driveway below. Finally, when he was sure Leguerre was well away, he pressed a button on the intercom box.

"Ja, Herr Garnier?" A thin male voice responded immediately.

"Has Leguerre gone downstairs?"

"Ja, mein herr."

"Then come in ten minutes, Heinrich, and tell our new friend to give us a moment alone first."

***

Dr. Oberman had a team car with Dufour and Patterson as his passengers and clear instructions from Otto to make sure they were back by nine. And Otto had told him to remind any medical officials at the party how important it would be to test carefully tomorrow.

Before leaving, Kurt left a message for Jennifer saying he hoped she would be there. They hadn't spoken since the start at Morzine, even though there had been several interviews with Martin and the crew since then. Kurt knew the TV people were jamming to be ready for tomorrow and only held slim hope that she would even get his message, much less able to get to Vougeot tonight. He worried, too, that she had seemed aloof these last couple of days and maybe she didn't want to see him.

Leguerre's directions were perfect. He met them at the back entrance, avoiding the throng of media that waited for Dufour at the front, but weren't invited in. Only a select few journalists had made it onto

Garnier's guest list, and then with the understanding that they were not to turn the evening into a press conference. Besides, with Poulain in bed, the promise of fireworks was all but extinguished.

Leguerre graciously welcomed Dufour, Patterson, and Oberman. He ushered them through the kitchen past smiling and nodding wait staff, into the large banquet hall, and, with little fanfare, introduced them around to small groups sipping drinks and making small talk.

In years past, the race leader had been presented with much more of a ceremony, an elaborate grand entrance by Poulain, who, last year everyone remembered, was dressed handsomely in a black tuxedo with bright yellow tie and cummerbund. The outfit and the music to introduce him had been Poulain's own idea, to show that he had style and could command attention off the bike as well. The wife of France's prime minister, who was very sophisticated and had been there, even said the yellow cummerbund was a nice touch and *très chic*.

But this year, of course, had to be different. Although it was still Comtec's party, and the tradition of introducing the race leader had to be maintained, the hosts didn't dare show any kind of control over Dufour. As a partial consequence, the GTI men were an island of denim in a sea of silk and linen, waiting only for the moment when Garnier himself would come down to make this year's far briefer presentation.

***

Upstairs, the harder Jérôme Garnier thought, the more smoke he generated.

By the time Heinrich Kemptka entered, Château de Vougeot's bridal suite was enveloped in thick purple haze. The huge Cuban cigar had rarely left Garnier's mouth, and now it appeared to be nothing more than a steaming moist nub that, when Kemptka took his position in front of the throne, Garnier removed from his mouth and crushed into his now empty cognac glass.

"Tell me *Herr Doktor*, is the plan in order?" Garnier placed the smoking glass on the table, leaned back in the wing chair, and gazed at his new guest over hands that, had Garnier been at all religious, would have been described as coming together in prayer.

151

"*Jawohl.*" Kemptka, a small wiry man, smiled wickedly.

"And how is Poulain?"

"Tonight he sleeps like the baby. Tomorrow he flies like the cheetah."

"What about the dosage?"

Kemptka turned his back on Garnier, pretending to look out the window. "Only a slight increase, *mein herr*. He vill haf the legs."

"And Leguerre?"

"He knows nothing, as usual." Again, the wicked smile as Kemptka turned his large head, close-cropped and bespectacled, to face his boss. His arms were crossed tightly to his chest and he shifted from one foot to the other as if trying to control himself. It was his nature.

"Then bring in our guest. Quickly. I must be downstairs in a few minutes." Garnier shifted to look out the window, noting to himself that the gravel drive and surrounding lawn was filled with cars.

Heinrich Kemptka rubbed his small hands together and scurried from the room. This was his moment. He knew what he had done for this assignment would please his very powerful and important boss, the man who empowered him to do what no others could be trusted with, not even Leguerre. His projects were special and very important. He made sure all of Comtec's pharmaceuticals had a secondary market. He tested them and he covered tracks, always a step ahead. He was able to keep his cover during the last scandal, despite the investigations, the panic, and the finger-pointing. He had engineered the elaborate frame-up that had sent two doctors and three soigneurs to jail. Nothing could be proven beyond them. Kemptka smiled at the memory of how he'd laid the trap, how they had been convinced to remain silent. And he found people, smart people, to do the things that had to be done, to move the money and to eliminate the obstacles.

Kemptka knew his boss would be especially pleased with this one.

***

Only a half-hour had past and Dufour was already regretting that he had come. Everyone wanted to talk to him, to shake his hand, and to make some kind of comment about how honored they were to meet him or how they had known all along that he would be a great champion. At least, that was the drift. His French was passable, at best, so he smiled and nodded a lot, forgave the bad English he heard and frequently gave his own apology: "Excusez-moi, mais je parle un peu de française, seulement." Excuse me, but I speak only a little French.

He was relieved when a distinguished-looking gentleman purposefully approached. He knew, from the navy-blue blazer with the embroidered breast emblem that this was Claude Gervais, secretary-general of the French Cycling Federation and the man who, via the earlier fax, had hoped to connect at the party. Gervais smiled and stood politely to the side while Kurt gave his bad French line to an attractive middle-aged woman. When she smiled and moved off, Kurt turned to Gervais and extended his hand.

"You must be monsieur Gervais."

"I am. And perhaps a poor substitute for the prime minister's wife." Gervais nodded in the direction of the woman Kurt had just met.

"The prime minister's wife? No wonder we didn't understand each other." Kurt smiled and noted the twinkle in Gervais's eyes. He felt he would be comfortable with this man.

"I assume you got my fax."

"I did."

"May we go somewhere to talk quietly for a moment?" Gervais was polite and professional. He stood straight, slightly taller than Kurt, but in good shape for a man about his father's age. His dark hair was wavy, streaked with gray, and thinned on top, and his face, tan and angular, indicated a level of sophistication beyond his life as a cycling official.

Kurt nodded and Gervais motioned toward some French doors at the back of the hall. In a moment they were through them and on to a slate verandah that overlooked the manicured back gardens of Château de Vougeot. No one seemed to notice their departure, and only one amorous couple was outside, way down at the far end. It was apparent that they were too busy with each other to notice the company.

For a moment they stood at the stone railing, gazing over the gardens. Daylight was nearly gone and the only real illumination on the verandah spilled in wide swaths from the several sets of French doors at the back of the banquet hall, some of which were open to let in the cool evening air. The gardens were pleasantly lit by well-placed lanterns, leaving everything else in shadow. Music and conversation from the banquet hall was pleasantly muted out here.

Gervais stepped into the light from the nearest door. He turned so Kurt could see his face and also so he could see, over Kurt's shoulder, if anyone might come out from the hall.

"It is a nice evening," he said as he lowered his glass from his lips. "It seems so far removed from the Tour."

Kurt nodded, waiting for Gervais to continue.

"In a few moments, you will be introduced to the people in there by Jérôme Garnier."

Kurt spoke. "I hope it will be brief. You know, I didn't come for that."

Gervais smiled. "I have been told you are much like your father. I can see this."

Kurt was taken aback. He looked closely at Gervais and searched his mind for the connection. He didn't recall his father speak of this man.

"You know my father?"

"I raced with him over twenty years ago. I was next to him when he went off the road in England." Gervais paused for this to sink in.

"Wait a minute...." Kurt touched his head as if trying to recall. His eyes widened and he hesitatingly pointed a finger at Gervais. "You're...you're the Frenchman he was trying to beat...you were caught with drugs...."

"Actually, it was a vial of urine."

Kurt backed away slightly, suddenly not sure of this man's past or why they had been brought together.

Gervais was quick to explain. "I made a mistake back then. I paid for it, and so did many other Frenchmen. We went through a bad period...we learned some things. I eventually came back to the sport...."

"You raced again?"

Gervais looked down and shook his head. "No.... No, I couldn't do that." After a pause, he looked up and smiled faintly, as if he had told this story many times, as if Kurt should've known. "We were disgraced. It was a long time for me to get over it. I did not want to carry such baggage, so I started to work in the sport, to help make it clean, I suppose." He smiled and twirled his hand in the air. "So now I am the big official."

Kurt thought for a moment. "You must know Otto."

"Of course. I have come to know him during the past years. We believe the same things. In fact, I spoke with him just before I came here this evening."

Kurt leaned on the railing and gazed over the lit gardens. He shook his head, smiling to himself. How bizarre this life had become. Kurt finally turned to Gervais.

"So why did you want to talk with me this evening?"

"Besides wanting to meet you to offer my congratulations, I must tell you something about this cycling game." Gervais lowered his eyes, suddenly looking as if he carried a heavy burden. "You see, Kurt, we are at a difficult...how would you say it...crossroads right here at this Tour."

"What do you mean...crossroads?" Kurt suddenly felt nervous, as if Gervais knew something more than he should.

"I will tell you straight." He looked directly into Kurt's eyes, mentally rehearsing what he was about to say. He cleared his throat and began.

"There is an evil man connected…deeply…with our sport. He was one of the worst ones when he raced with us. Only, he didn't learn the same lessons we did. Instead, he decided to get even. I think you can guess who he is."

"Garnier." He really didn't have to guess.

Gervais nodded, looking steadily at Kurt. "His fingers have spread like a cancer, so much so that we are on the verge of another scandal that could kill professional cycling for sure this time. He has manipulated and controlled people for so long, and we could not catch him two years ago during the big crisis…." Gervais stopped himself, struggling to keep his voice calm. "It has gotten to the point where we have no choice but to try and expose him."

"Expose him for what?" Kurt felt a sudden panic rise within him. Gervais couldn't know about his meeting with Garnier.

Gervais continued, not noticing Kurt's discomfort. "He has always had a fascination with drugs, how they can affect people, change them…sometimes help them, sometimes ruin them. When they do good for people, he looks at that as business, a chance to make money…."

Kurt's panic gave way to curiosity. "But all that money he makes, surely he doesn't have to supply drugs to riders…?"

"Of course not. He does not push drugs. He tests them, he finds new ones, just so he can stay ahead of what is on the banned list. For his team, it increases their chances of winning, for his business…let us say he has a unique test group…."

Kurt blanched. He knew all about the doping scandal of two years ago and knew that the guilty ones had been caught and expelled from the sport. He was confused and not wanting to believe what he was thinking. He looked at Gervais. "Poulain…?"

Gervais responded as if this had come up before. "Maybe not early in his career. But now…it is more than speculation…."

Kurt leaned on the rail for support. "Holy shit…." His mind flooded with questions—*what was he using?…for how long?…how many were involved this time?* He chose to avoid looking at Gervais and asked only one question.

"What does this have to do with me?"

Gervais stepped in front of Kurt, making sure his face was fully lit. His jaw was set and his eyes burned deeply into Kurt's. He spoke forcefully. "You are the leader of the Tour, and tomorrow is the day when you will win or you will lose. We will make a surprise test, after the stage on all the riders…."

Kurt thought for a moment. "Why every rider? It's always been the winners and a few randoms. If the testing procedure changes, you have to tell everyone in advance." He was well aware of how indiscriminate, surprise testing the last time had resulted in riders being dragged from their beds and pulled out of showers. There had been assumption of guilt that wildly fed the media, and it had resulted in so much protest from riders and teams that the Tour had almost stopped. As a result, a new set of ground rules had been adopted. Even though more-thorough testing had become routine, some sort of new surprise test was asking for trouble.

Gervais nodded. "Of course we know this. There are the normal blood test to reveal each rider's hematocrit level and then…" He paused for dramatic effect. "We have found a way to further breakdown the blood to finally detect the presence of EPO in the urine. These new findings will be leaked to the press and, at the same time, certain riders will come forward to reveal that they have been given the drug all along and have been using masking agents to hide its presence." Gervais watched closely for Kurt's reaction.

Kurt didn't answer. He knew all about the Epogen, or EPO, phenomenon—although Otto and Dr. Oberman had insisted that he and the rest of the team stay away from it. It is a synthetic form of a naturally occurring protein that stimulates the body to produce oxygen-rich red blood cells, a wonder drug for very sick patients with severe anemia. *And* a wonder drug for endurance athletes who, by increasing normal red-blood-cell count, get an unnaturally high amount of oxygen in their blood, enough to increase endurance by as much as thirty percent, a phenomenal competitive advantage. Plus, the drug is a synthetic form of a naturally occurring substance in the body and thus, at least until now, impossible to detect. Only if a cyclist's red-cell count, or hematocrit level, is found to be abnormally high—

above fifty percent—is there suspicion that the drug has been used and the rider "for health reasons" is suspended from racing until his hematocrit level falls back under fifty. The health dangers are real. A high red-cell count means abnormally thickened blood and increased risk of heart attack and stroke in young, otherwise healthy athletes. Suspicious deaths of very fit cyclists had been reported. Kurt believed it was nothing to mess with.

Gervais continued: "You know we have been trying to develop how to detect this EPO for some time. Just a few weeks ago, we found a way to determine if hematocrit levels were high because EPO had been introduced from urine samples...and now we have several cyclists, I cannot give their identity, who will come forward to say how this substance is still coming into the sport."

Kurt's mind started to spin. He suspected that he knew some riders who would be involved. But who would speak out? He tried to imagine the likeliest ones, who might blow the whistle. Certainly not Poulain...but others on the Comtec squad? Although many riders wanted to see the end of doping once and for all, most preferred *omertà*, to keep quiet. He tried to think rationally.

"Wait a minute," he said. "You can't suddenly say you have a new test. There'll be so much protest...it'll stop the race."

Gervais smiled. "We may require a physical examination or an unannounced urine test at any time during the last week of a stage race to protect the health of the riders—you know it is the new rule just passed this year. And now we can, for the first time, detect the presence of EPO in urine." He shrugged. "Of course the press will know we are sampling the whole peloton. It is almost expected that somehow the results are leaked."

"Still, if Garnier is behind this, and he got through the last scandal, there's no guarantee that he'll be caught. He must be able to cover up anything...buy his way out." Kurt was thinking beyond the drug issue.

Gervais watched him closely. "This is true...we've been hoping for other ways to catch him."

The two had been talking so intently that they hadn't seen John Patterson approach across the verandah. His tap to Kurt's shoulder startled them both.

158

"Sorry to break this up, mates, but the host man wants to make 'is announcement." Patterson's head motioned toward the banquet hall, his eyes fixed on Kurt's.

Dufour felt a sudden sense of panic. He had to go in there as the honored guest, the leader of the Tour…and he had to pretend that his mind was clear, that his focus was exclusively on the next two days of racing, not swirling with the pressure of living with lies and with the knowledge that much of the sport was in a cloud of deceit and, if exposed, he would once again be under the lights…like he was before this all started. His judgment, his ethics would again be questioned, his life turned upside down.

He felt a strong hand tighten around his arm, interrupting his thoughts. It was Patterson, tightly pressed to his side and squeezing the arm hard. Their heads were close and his teammate, after waiting a moment until Gervais moved out of earshot, whispered forcefully into Kurt's ear.

"I 'eard it all mate…and, besides, I know the whole fuckin' story anyway. You think, now…and ya listen to me. Snap the fuck out of it and do what ya were made to do. You walk out there with your 'ead 'igh and ya remember that bloody fuckin' jersey is yours." He shook Kurt and pulled him closer. "Look at me, cocksucker."

Kurt tried, unsuccessfully, to wrench his arm free. But he turned to face Patterson. They were nose to nose, and Patterson's teeth were clenched and his eyes, like twin lasers, bore into Kurt's.

"I know where your 'ead is mate. And I'll tell ya what to do…ya fuck Garnier. And ya destroy Poulain. Ya ride your bloody balls off. That's it. And no matter what 'appens, ya never look back."

Patterson, the unwavering. Dufour stopped. This time, when he twisted away, Patterson let go of his arm. Kurt glanced quickly toward the building then leaned toward his teammate. His eyes were clear and a calmness had settled over him. He spoke softly, "Listen, John, I've had to think a lot lately…about my future, maybe yours too."

Before he could say more, a smiling Guy Leguerre burst through the doors. He spread his arms toward Dufour, completely ignoring

Patterson. "Ah, there you are. Please, come quickly. Your public waits."

Leguerre stepped between the two friends and took Kurt by the arm, steering him from the darkness into the bright lights of the banquet hall. As they entered, cheering and loud applause arose from the assembly, and, from the band, a rapid drum roll and fanfare music filled the room. Leguerre guided the young star through the smiling and nodding crowd straight to the curving staircase, where, halfway up and flanked by tuxedoed dignitaries and potted plants, stood Jérôme Garnier, arms outstretched to receive cycling's newest hero.

Oberman and Patterson watched from the sidelines as Kurt Dufour, looking much smaller than when on his bike, especially in comparison to the thick men around him, politely smiled and received the framed yellow jersey Garnier presented to him.

As the lone representatives from Team GTI watched the presentation, they were joined by another with a vested interest in the celebrity being honored. Jennifer Scott had just arrived and was glad to have found Dufour's teammates off to the side. She touched Patterson's arm to silently announce her presence.

Patterson immediately straightened from the wall on which he had been leaning. Both he and Oberman smiled, obviously glad to see her.

"I wondered if ya would show up," Patterson whispered in her ear, noting the fresh smell of her soft hair and the fragrance of French perfume. She was quite lovely. He also noticed the absence of her camera crew. "Night off, eh?"

She smiled and nodded toward the presentation in front of them. "He invited me. I thought I'd come as a human being, just to wish him luck." She searched Patterson's face for a clue as to the mood of the evening.

"Reckon 'e'll need it, dearie. They all want a piece of 'im." Patterson showed no emotion, but he watched closely as Garnier shook Kurt's hand.

Suddenly, he turned to Jennifer and grabbed her arm. He pulled her around and through the door where they couldn't be seen by anyone in the hall. With a hand on each of her shoulders, he looked into her face and spoke softly but firmly. "Talk to 'im, lady. I reckon 'e'll listen to you. Tell 'im to win the bloody time trial, tell 'im to bury that bastard…'e can do it, 'e can do it on 'is own."

He released her and sighed, shaking his head. Scott's eyes had widened, and she stood staring up at him. She shrank back.

"Is…is it true…are they really…controlling him?" She could barely get the words out.

"Dunno. Don't wanna know…'e's been actin' strange." Patterson looked at his watch. "We'll go get the car. We'll pick 'im up at the back entrance, where we came in, in ten minutes." Patterson, noting that the presentation was over, signaled to Oberman and headed off to get the car.

Dufour, as soon as he could politely break free, clutched the framed jersey and pushed through the well-wishers toward where he had left Oberman and Patterson. Although he smiled and nodded, his eyes darted around the room, looking for the familiar faces of his teammates. In their place, he spotted Jennifer and quickened his pace toward where she was standing.

As he got to her, he motioned for her to follow him out the door and onto the verandah, away from the crowded room. As soon as they got outside, he stopped and turned to her.

"Jenny, we have to talk." He spoke rapidly, then caught himself. "I'm glad you came." He smiled and rested the frame on the ground so he could touch her arm.

She felt her pulse quicken and fought her desire to throw her arms around him.

Instead, she stayed where she was, even backing off some. "You *better* talk to me," she said, "or I have this all wrong. By the way, you have less than ten minutes; your ride will be at the back by then. And you've got a serious job to do tomorrow." She watched him closely.

"Jenny, I…I know everyone is wondering. I don't have time to explain it all now. But I can tell you this, I won't make the same mistake again. I've got a once-in-a-lifetime chance, and I don't intend to blow it." His eyes were steady and strong and he looked hard at her to drive home the message.

Her knees felt weak but she felt compelled to ask the question.

"You...you mean you'll ride to win tomorrow?"

"Absolutely." His eyes never left hers.

She swore she wouldn't weaken. She swore she was going to keep this man at a distance until all doubt was gone, until she was sure who he was, who she expected him to be. But she lost. She fell into his arms and buried her head in his shoulder, fighting to hold back the welling tears. How could she have ever doubted him?

"Oh, Kurt...Kurt. I want you so much."

He drew her closer and whispered into her hair. "Just stand by me, Jenny. Please. It'll be over soon."

She responded by clutching him tighter, pushing her body hard against his. For a long time, they held each other, silently pressed together in an embrace that, for each of them, had been too long in coming.

***

Not far from the spot where they hugged, a man, hidden in the shadows of the banquet hall, watched them intently. He could hear parts of the conversation and, because he, too, was an American, understood what was being said.

He remained in the shadows, watching them embrace and then move off, arms around each other, toward the back of the castle. When they had gone, he smiled to himself and leaned back to light a cigarette. His hands shook some, but that didn't matter now. It had been more than five years since he'd seen Kurt Dufour, and his smile was one of satisfaction...satisfaction that the young man was finally in his sights. And that slut that he was with...she didn't have near the class that his Leslie had.

For five years, he swore he would avenge her death, his beautiful little girl, his lover. He was made to leave the firm in disgrace...to find refuge with others like him in strange places. Bangkok, Morocco, and, finally, Paris. Then the headlines. The same Kurt Dufour who had taken her from him. The bastard. It wasn't hard to get to him. It's always easy when one knows where to look, to find those who despise the heroes. Kemptka, a man like him....

Donald Conway, in his newly issued black leathers, emerged from the shadows and slowly walked to the parking lot. There were still many vehicles there—the party went merrily on for those who could stay up late.

It didn't take him long to find the motorcycles, big, high-powered Kawasakis parked in neat formation and plastered with official *Tour de France* stickers. He double-checked the key chain he had been given, noting that number 32 was marked *"Sécurité Spécial."* The bike was at the very end of the row, just like they had said. He slid his hand over the fuel tank, along the black leather seat and, before finding the ignition, he kissed the key and whispered to himself, *"Thank you, Herr Heinrich. Thank you, monsieur Garnier."*

Conway chuckled as he threw his leg over the machine and carefully inserted the key. In a moment, the motorcycle roared to life and he gently feathered the throttle until he was satisfied with the pitch of the deep-throated rumble.

He straddled the bike for a moment while he adjusted his new helmet and methodically donned his new leather gloves. He leaned forward and then, with a violent twist of his right hand, leapt the bike forward into the night.

***

"Sorry I'm late." Kurt Dufour walked purposefully past Otto Werner at the hotel entrance and headed straight through the lobby toward the bike room, trailed by Oberman and Patterson.

Otto, relieved to see his star performer safely back, said nothing. Instead, he fell into step and glanced questioningly over his shoulder at Patterson.

The Aussie clapped Otto on the back and gave him the thumbs-up sign. He winked and then pulled Otto close so he could whisper in his ear. "Clean and green, boss man."

Otto looked closely at Patterson and then steered him aside. Dufour and Oberman continued toward the bike room. Otto's eyes were wide, incredulous.

"What happened?"

Patterson smiled and pushed Otto to keep going. "I reckon I made 'im see the light, or maybe 'e figured it out on 'is own. No matter, Otto, 'e wants the jersey. Real bad."

Otto breathed a sigh of relief and rolled his eyes. He stroked his chin as he walked, thinking deeply. Suddenly, he turned again to Patterson. "He talked to Gervais?"

Patterson nodded, "Spilt the 'ole plan."

"How's he feel?"

"Pissed, tough…ready to kick some serious ass…'e's the Duff on Alpe d'Huez." Patterson smiled broadly and again gave a thumbs-up.

Otto didn't return the smile. Instead, he looked forward, again lost in thought. His worry transferred from wondering about his boy's integrity to his safety, suddenly a much bigger issue.

They were at the door to the bike room, and Kurt and Oberman had stopped to wait for them.

"So, open it," Otto said.

"It's locked." Kurt rattled the door handle.

"So knock."

Before he had a chance, the door swung open, revealing a small room filled with people and bikes—the entire GTI complement and a few others, some fifteen people in all. They shouted in unison: "Sur…pri…ize!" and several pairs of hands pulled him inside.

Dufour shook his head and smiled. "Oh, for chrissake" was all he could manage. His eyes quickly scanned the room. All his teammates were there in front, the loyal *équipiers* who had fought hard for nearly three weeks to help him get, and keep, the yellow jersey. There were only five of them left, each a toughened survivor of brutal days in the mountains, torturous cobblestone roads, bad weather, and crashes. One by one, they clapped him on the shoulder or shook his hand, smiling and offering words of encouragement.

The rest of them were also there to wish him well: Otto, Tomi K, Dr. Oberman, Ramos, and Jeff Martin, Van Brugen the soigneur, the various drivers and helpers. Even Kurt's father had flown in for the final weekend, standing slightly apart, and grinning proudly.

There was considerable throat-clearing and awkward shuffling as these grown men sought to express their feelings. It was the eve of possibly the greatest achievement they, as a team, would ever experience, and one that could quite possibly change their lives forever. To be part of this maverick squad, to have accomplished the ultimate in their sport, meant future recognition and riches that, a few seasons ago, seemed all but impossible. The long march was almost over.

When Patterson took to the center of the room, everyone fell silent. From a linen-covered table at his side, he passed out champagne glasses, filled with Perrier for the other riders and the real stuff for everyone else, including himself.

When each had been served he raised his glass and began.

"I reckon most of us thought we'd never get 'ere." He looked slowly around the room, making eye contact with Spain, Vokel, Hoban, and finally Berclaz. "And, as the senior member of this 'ere team and by the oath I first swore five years ago at Ramos' bloody cantina...."

"Si, *La Cantina*!" Ramos's shout from the side of the room caused a stir of laughter.

"...I 'ereby say to Poulain, Comtec, and all the rest of them bloody bastards...our boy 'ere...." He looked fondly at Dufour.... "Our boy 'ere is gonna do us proud, 'e's gonna chew 'em up and 'e's gonna keep that fuckin' yellow shirt!"

The room erupted. Some whistled, some clapped, and all shouted words of support and encouragement, like "Go for it" and "Bury the bastard!"

Despite their weariness, despite the stress and strain of some three weeks of energy-sapping and unrelenting pressure, the team was both relieved and rejuvenated. Their morale once again soared to its peak and, to a man, they openly and silently pledged that they would give everything they could to protect their leader for the remaining two days. Whether they had talked about it or not, they all knew that Dufour was now with them, that he wouldn't sell himself, or them, to the other side.

The gathering dispersed and the departing faces turned serious as they began to mentally prepare for the individual test the next day.

Otto held Kurt behind and brought him to Ramos, who was straightening up his work area in the back of the room. They confirmed 9 a.m. as the reporting time for Kurt to do a final road test of his new custom time trial bike. The race would not start until the afternoon, and Kurt, as the *maillot jaune* and last one off, had until four to get ready.

"It's time to hit the rack." Otto tapped Kurt on the shoulder and they walked out together. When they emerged in the lobby, they were met by Peter Dufour.

"That was quite a send-off." The father smiled warmly and put a hand on each of their shoulders.

Otto nodded but smiled only faintly. "You two need to talk for a minute, I'm headed up." He disappeared in the direction of the elevator. In a moment, the father and son were seated at comfortable club chairs in a quiet corner of the lobby.

Peter Dufour spoke first. "I got wind of some foul play from Otto." He paused for a moment. "I guess you sorted it out."

Kurt sank back into the thick, richly upholstered chair and closed his eyes. He exhaled deeply and shook his head.

"You wouldn't believe it, Dad."

"I think I would. What was the offer?"

"Everything. Nothing. Nine million dollars and my pick of the litter. No opposition for years, just like Poulain. All I had to do was pedal soft tomorrow. It was tempting."

"You had trouble saying no?"

He was reluctant to confess to his father, admit another lapse in judgment. But he had to get it out.

"Actually...I had a lot of trouble saying no. Maybe it was the moment right after Alpe d'Huez." He looked searchingly at his father. "You can understand, you must have been driven to be the best at some point in your career...and then an offer comes along, not just money, that's so tempting, that will make it so much more likely to happen...."

The father registered no emotion. "Then you said yes?"

"Dad, I said yes. But I meant no. I...I guess I thought they were lying. So I played the game into Morzine and it happened just like they said. They controlled it, they let me win. And they put a million Swiss francs in a Swiss bank account for me, I checked this afternoon. Now I owe them." He looked down and shook his head. "I think I'm in deep shit."

Peter leaned forward and looked closely at his son. "Jesus, Kurt, you agreed, you accepted money?" He stopped himself and shook his head in disbelief. His jaw was set and, for a moment, Kurt thought he was either very angry or very disappointed. Probably both. There was a pause while the father tried to sort out what to say next.

Kurt felt a surge of anger spread through him. He controlled it and looked away, despite wanting to lash out at something. When he finally turned to his father, his face had a tortured look and his jaw was set. He spoke evenly, forcefully.

"Listen, Dad. I didn't think it through, okay? Kinda like when I screwed that girl. Maybe I'm not as rational as you, I don't always think of every consequence, you know? I fucked up. I've thought a lot about it, and I know I did the wrong thing. But now I'm prepared to fight my way out...and I want to win, even if it might only be once." He stopped, letting the anger subside, and then sunk back into the chair, exhaling deeply.

Peter shook his head slowly, thinking to himself. He wondered why his son still couldn't see far enough ahead to avoid acting on impulse, particularly when it could lead to nothing but trouble. And not just a minor transgression. He had been able to accept the situation surrounding the girl's death five years ago. That was an adolescent mistake, driven by hormones. But this was different. He was old enough now to know better, to not be tempted by a man clearly devoid of ethics, a man with enough power and ego to crush a young athlete.

He looked at his son and wondered. Maybe what took him to the top of this sport was what made him different. So very few had the right mix of mental toughness and superlative physiology. The great champions before him were not necessarily rational, and certainly not normal. In fact they were usually stubborn, impulsive characters who acted first and thought later. Eddy Merckx, the Cannibal. Bernard Hinault, the Badger, a French superstar with legendary stubbornness. And even Poulain, whose talent and mind combination made him as strange a package as Peter had ever seen.

Kurt was watching him now, waiting.

A slight smile twitched across Peter's face, the one Kurt recognized to mean his father had come to some kind of realization.

"Kurt…." Peter put his hand on his son's shoulder. "I think I know why you're so goddam good at this game. And your greatest strength is also your greatest weakness."

"Right." This time it was Kurt who shook his head. He rolled his eyes.

Peter Dufour looked at his son and then across the lobby toward the front entrance. He thought about himself, the times when he had been tempted to do the wrong thing, or, more often, when he had held back because he didn't have enough information to make the right decision. Those decisions had generally been good—in cycling, in business, in his personal life—but he knew he had missed some big opportunities because he hadn't acted on instinct. And here was his son, just the opposite. And now *he* was in trouble. The irony didn't escape him.

Peter turned back to him. "Kurt, I never came near the level you've achieved. I never had the balls to do what you've done, regardless of what the decision was or the consequences. And, you know, that's what it takes. That's what it takes to win a race like this, to survive the pressure, to fight when most people would give in. Only the very best have it...caution is not a word that describes winners of the Tour."

He paused for a moment, looking for the right words, struggling to articulate what had happened long ago. "I think, sometimes, that I thought too much when I raced...my instincts were more to analyze the situation, weigh it too rationally. Maybe I backed off, maybe that's why I went off the road and nearly killed myself."

He looked up at Kurt. "You don't back off."

"You back off, I don't. You almost died; I'm probably about to. What's the difference?" Kurt sniffed at the irony, although he understood that his drive both made him good and got him into trouble.

Peter slowly shook his head, thinking. Finally, he spoke again: "How you got to this point doesn't matter now, Kurt. You made a gut choice last week. Thank God you have the sense to know now it was wrong and you're willing to fight to change it. It's now become a question of character...if you're tough enough and committed enough to carry out the fight."

Suddenly, Otto's repeated warnings rose up in his mind, about the cloud surrounding Garnier's past and his current tarnished reputation...about Gervais and his mission to rid the sport of the latest, highly dangerous drugs at whatever cost. The father tried to think clearly, to think of solutions, and, most of all, to try and remove the fact that the central player in this sordid affair was still his son.

There was a long pause. "So what are you going to do?"

Kurt had already decided. He leaned forward and, with more conviction than Peter ever thought he'd seen in his son's eyes, looked straight at him.

"I'm going to set the record straight...." Kurt said in an even, controlled tone. "For me, for Poulain, and for that bastard, Garnier. And I don't give a damn what it costs to do it."

Peter Dufour registered no emotion. He nodded slowly, letting Kurt's words sink in. His mind reeled at the possible consequences.

Kurt, sensing his father's concern, continued. "I don't have a whole lot of choices. Just a plan...."

The two leaned close together and talked quietly for another ten minutes.

****

Chapter Sixteen

Options

Otto Werner shot bolt upright in bed. Despite the air-conditioned chill in the room, he was soaked in sweat. It had been a very restless night, and he shook his head to try and pull himself together. The grayness of an overcast dawn lightened the hotel room just enough to make out the clock on the nightstand. Seven o'clock.

He sat on the bed, barely moving in the half-light, alone, and gripped with a pervasive dread. There was no escaping the reality brought by this dawn, the reality that his entire program, his entire life, and everything he had worked for, could be brought down by what might happen today.

His first clear thoughts were of Kurt Dufour, a young man whose star quality eclipsed that of any human being he had ever known. It was still strange to Otto how such talent emerged and grew in a person. The kid was so different. In the last five years, he had seen the transformation from a raw, headstrong youth struggling to find himself to a determined and focused athlete as good as any in the world. He seemed afraid of nothing and he seemed to get stronger with the intense pressure that piled on him. He had the nerve to play games with the most ruthless of people and yet, somehow, seemed totally oblivious to the potential consequences. Part of it was youth. A bigger part of it, Otto mused, was genetics. The brains and the engine undoubtedly from Peter, and the instincts from Sharon, once pretty wild, he'd heard.

He sat round-shouldered and quiet in the middle of the bed for quite some time. The energy that constantly drove him was absent. He was over fifty now and, for the first time, was beginning to feel tired, the years of constant travel and the cumulative stress of relentlessly directing his stable of high-strung players wore on him. And now this.

He had grown close to Kurt Dufour and, despite their professional relationship, had allowed the young man to become the son that he had never had. And the father too—more like a brother now than even when they had been inseparable, years ago. Otto's primary instinct, his accepted role, was to protect this family.

But for once in his life he wondered if this was too much for him. It wasn't merely to race well and win…that would be difficult enough, particularly if the rumors surrounding Poulain were true…. It was more the fact that he would have to fight a force that Otto feared might be beyond his capability….

The phone rang, rescuing him from these thoughts.

"Otto, its Peter."

"How's Kurt?" Otto's natural reaction was to inquire of the star performer. It pushed the fear aside and replaced it with real priorities.

"Most likely, still sleeping. I suspect we won't see him for another hour or so."

"I hope you two didn't stay up late." Otto slowly got up from the bed while he talked.

"Just long enough to get worried. He told me all about Garnier's bag of tricks—the man's scary."

"I told you three weeks ago, he stops at nothing." Otto stood in front of the window, phone cradled between his bare neck and shoulder so he could pull open the curtains. His ample belly hung over the tight blue briefs he had slept in. There was a light rain falling outside.

"What's Garnier likely to do, Otto?" Peter's voice was low, full of concern.

Otto turned from the window and slumped into a large chair at the foot of the bed. He shook his head and rubbed his chin thoughtfully. He was beginning to focus again.

"Probably nothing…today. If Kurt still has the jersey tonight, there's no telling. For sure, we have to press for much more security from now on, particularly going to Paris tomorrow."

"You're worried about actual physical violence?"

Otto leaned back, searching for the right answer. "Seems pretty unlikely…." He paused for a moment as the thought ran through his mind. "But then again, Peter, he's done some pretty bizarre things."

Otto thought of the new drug revelations that were about to surface. And he wondered how allegations of payoffs could be substantiated and, if leveled, how Garnier was likely to react. He didn't like what he was thinking.

"Shouldn't we meet with the officials...do something to take precautions?" Peter was beginning to sound desperate.

"I've been talking with our old friend, Gervais. As the big muckety muck now, he's assured me that the organizers are adding extra security...more gendarmes, more moto marshals...."

Peter's tone turned forceful. "Otto, we better make sure that happens...because sometime later today the shit could really hit the fan."

Otto sat up, suspecting that Peter was about to share something important. "What do you mean by that?"

"Kurt's written a letter. I think you should see it right away."

**

Katherine Anderson stumbled into the broadcast booth and threw a piece of paper on the desk in front of Phil Sterling.

"What the hell is *this*?"

Sterling calmly raised the paper, glanced at it for a moment and then dropped it in front of Jeff Martin seated next to him. They were busy readying themselves and the booth for the live time trial coverage set to begin in a few hours. It was the typical daily set-up: hastily erected and covered scaffolding above the start/finish line with technicians scrambling to make all the final connections. Due to the day's importance, Sterling and Martin had arrived early to go over their equipment, statistics and start sheets. They didn't want distractions, least of all from Anderson.

"By the look of it, I'd say it's this morning's official communiqué from the organization." Sterling only glanced at the paper and went back to adjusting his headset.

"I know it's the goddam communiqué, *Phil.*" She was obviously very agitated, a state which made Sterling even calmer. "I want to know why they're calling for testing of every rider immediately after the race today. Why are they doing that?"

It was Martin who chose to answer. "New rule, Katherine. Says that once during the last week of a stage race, officials can call any kind of surprise test or exam. You know, a health precaution. They won't like it, but they'll have to do it." It was clear that both Martin and Sterling had been aware of the test and were not concerned with its implication, at least in front of her.

Anderson, in frustration, slammed one of the empty chairs into the table, wedging it sideways. "You bastards are no help at all...." She wheeled around and stormed out of the booth, muttering, "I'll find out *myself* what's behind this."

She pushed past Jennifer Scott who was just arriving. Scott looked over her shoulder, pausing to watch the heated departure. When she entered the broadcast area, she instinctively straightened the chair and moved to behind Sterling and Martin, placing a hand on each of their shoulders.

"What's eating her?"

"Still looking for her story, I reckon." Sterling smiled without stopping work.

"I guess her holiday in Paris didn't take the edge off," Martin said. "She must think we haven't been working hard enough." He patted Scott's hand on his shoulder, as if to assure her that this wasn't true.

Sterling finished his work and put his headset and mike on the table. He leaned back, turned to Jennifer and winked. "She missed Jeff, of course. Nobody to abuse."

Scott, in mock outrage, slapped Sterling's arm and gave him a disapproving look. She rolled her eyes as Martin reached his arm toward Sterling, making sure his hand and extended middle finger were squarely in the Englishman's face.

"You two are awful," Scott said. But she smiled, recognizing that Sterling and Martin had become like brothers to her in the few weeks they had been together. They had helped her get her job done, tolerated her mistakes, and, most of all, didn't ride her about getting the dirt her boss wanted on Dufour. She didn't exactly know how to express it, but she was grateful.

For a moment, she let her thoughts drift, as she had been doing a lot since last night. Kurt's longed-for embrace still wrapped around her, and a deep feeling of being one with him, and that they had actually spoken about their feelings for each other, spread a warmth through her that she had never quite experienced before. It was a delicious feeling and one that she wanted to conjure up at every possible moment.

Her daydream was interrupted by a polite tap on the shoulder. "*Êtes-vous Mademoiselle Jennifer Scott?*"

She wheeled to face a pleasant looking young man dressed in some sort of uniform—not a gendarme.

"*Oui, c'est moi.*" Jennifer smiled and, with a questioning look, reached for the envelope he extended to her. She looked at it and saw that it was addressed to her, care of the network: "*Tour de France Broadcast Team États-Unis au Ligne du Départ.*"

"Please, please, you must place your signing here." The messenger pushed a clipboard toward her and pointed to the place for her to sign.

"What is this?" She asked the question while she scribbled her name as directed. Sterling and Martin, curious, had turned to watch.

The messenger looked at his watch and shrugged. He smiled and entered the time next to her signature. He was clearly excited over his assignment to deliver a letter to someone inside the Tour de France. Still, he seemed anxious to go.

"Who sent this to me?" She watched him shrug and smile again, although this time he spoke.

"*Merci.* I must go fast to find the others before the race starts." He held out a list of several names. Besides her own, the only other name she recognized was Otto Werner's. Martin and Sterling were standing over her shoulder now, also looking at the list.

Sterling pointed. "Look, there's Claude Gervais, he's head of the French Federation. And this one's the Minister of Sport for all of France. There's one I don't recognize." They exchanged confused looks. The messenger shrugged again, attached the paper to his clipboard, and abruptly left.

Jennifer's hands shook as she ripped open the envelope. The two men pressed over her shoulder. She pulled out two sheets of heavy cream-colored stationery from the *Hôtel Pullman La Cloche*, one a brief handwritten note and the other a neatly typed page of text.

She read the note first:

Jenny: Here's the whole story. If it ever gets to the media, you're the only reporter with the facts. Please keep this to yourself and only share it with Sterling and Martin. You'll know if and when it'll be needed.

Thanks, Kurt

It didn't bother her that Martin and Sterling were already looking over her shoulder. In fact, she wanted them to help her understand the longer letter she had now turned to.

It was dated that morning and the greeting listed all of the names on the list the messenger had just shown them.

Dear (names):

I am writing to inform you that on July 15, I was invited to meet Mr. Jerome Garnier at his chateau above L'Alpe d'Huez. To my knowledge, the only other person present at that meeting was Mr. Guy Leguerre, directeur sportif of the Comtec professional cycling team.

During the course of the meeting, Mr. Garnier told me how he influences the sport and how he runs his Comtec team. And he made me the following offer to race for him, starting next season....

The three were so absorbed in reading the letter that they failed to notice Katherine Anderson coming up the steps toward them. She stopped a few feet away, waiting for a clue as to what captured their rapt attention.

Each of them scanned the letter a second and third time, speechless. Scott felt her legs weaken and a sickness well up from the pit of her stomach as she re-read and grasped certain parts of the letter: *"Leguerre agreed to wire the money...I am expected to purposely lose Saturday's time trial."* She could barely get the words out as she slumped against Martin: "Oh, God, no. Please, no...."

It took both of them to try and steady her. In the confusion and shuffling of the moment, Scott's hand fell to her side and unconsciously released the letter.

Anderson was there in a flash. She scooped it up before Sterling could intervene and jammed herself into the corner of the booth, simultaneously kicking a chair in front of her to keep Sterling and, by now, Martin from grabbing it back. Scott collapsed into the one chair in the opposite corner.

"What's this?" Anderson held the letter close to her chest, trying to peek at it as the men struggled against the chair.

"For God's sake, Katherine." Sterling finally pulled the chair aside and stood directly in front of her. "For God's sake, woman, bugger off. It was addressed to Jennifer."

"Then why were you all reading it? It's about the *real* story, isn't it?" She looked at the letter and, before Sterling could cajole her to give it up, had gleaned enough to know this was what she was looking for.

It was useless for them to fight her. She had seen the letter now and, as she read it more carefully, her eyes widened in disbelief. "Holy shit, this is more than a story...." She looked at the others for some sort of explanation and didn't resist when Martin at last yanked the paper from her hands.

It was Sterling who spoke first. "So, I reckon it won't be long before the whole bloody world knows, now." He looked threateningly at Katherine.

She nodded, a slight smile playing on her lips. She looked at Jennifer, still dazed in the opposite chair. Anderson straightened up, smoothed her clothes from the scuffle and then, with newfound authority, looked hard at Sterling and then at Martin.

Her voice was surprisingly soft. But it was firm. "I'll go call Arnie, tell him how we should handle this. You guys finish setting up the booth." She looked at her watch and then at Jennifer, who at last was beginning to recover her senses. "Jenny, snap out of it. We have to start rehearsal in forty minutes."

Before she left the booth, she turned to look at all of them, a smile of triumph on her face. "Remember, we just report the facts."

For a moment, they sat in stunned silence, Jennifer unmoved in one chair, Martin in another, and Sterling leaning against the broadcast table. It was Martin who finally spoke.

"Now what the fuck happens? If this opens up now, there'll be a lot of explaining to do, forget about wonder boy and *this* sport." He looked up at Sterling, hoping for the usual wisdom.

Sterling returned the look. "It's a bloody tough one, isn't it?" One arm crossed his chest, the other stroked his chin in contemplation. After a long, reflective moment, he spoke.

"There's only a handful of people who've seen the letter. And apparently they all had to sign for it *before* the time trial. Obviously, Dufour wanted it in responsible hands, people he could tell who would know how to handle it…wouldn't use the information unless…or until…they needed more for a case against Garnier…."

"He accepted the fuckin' money, he was handed Morzine…." Martin wrestled with this, trying to sort out the implications.

"Yes, but Kurt didn't put on the brakes now, did he? He went for the win. I reckon *they* made the decision not to chase. Leguerre tried to bribe him with the money. Bloody fools if you ask me…."

Jennifer sat up at this. "And the letter says where the money is, they'll know he had no intention of taking it." She brightened somewhat.

"He's gonna blow the whistle on the bastards." Martin was a step ahead. "And he made sure the letter was delivered before anyone could possibly know if he'd end up with the jersey…."

"Copies were sent only to insiders," Sterling added, "or people who could be trusted to keep silent until the right bloody time, keep the lid on until after a proper investigation...when the race is over."

They were all thinking the same thing, but it was Martin who put it into words, almost in a whisper, "*She* knows what's in the fuckin' letter."

***

It was just after 8 a.m. and Kurt Dufour awoke from a restless sleep. He lay on his stomach, for a moment coaxing his mind to make the transition from the surreal world of dreams to a new day of hard reality. It took him a moment to remember he was in a hotel in Dijon, France, that he had a slim lead in the Tour de France, and that today would be the most important day in his life. He wasn't sure if he was up to it.

Despite all the turmoil of the last twenty-four hours, he still had to face the real test, the effort that, to him, would more clearly define who he was than any other moment in his young life. After today, he would know, the world would know, if his destiny was to be the very best or just another good player in a game where only a few were selected for greatness. Part of him wanted to slip into anonymity, a bigger part wanted to reach the top step of the podium.

At least, he'd made his decision, the letters were signed and gone. Otto would have his by now, Jenny, and the others, soon. They would figure out how to protect him. He could turn his focus completely to the job now at hand: keeping the jersey. Yet he feared it might not be possible. He wondered about the surprise tiny sample of blood each rider would have to give immediately after the race. How could EPO suddenly be detected from a urine sample when it never could before? Who and how many would be caught? Not his problem.

"Bit of a drizzle out there, mate. Weather report says it could last all bloody day." Patterson was more nervous for Kurt than himself. He drew back the curtains of their unusually spacious hotel room and scanned the centuries-old fountains of Place Darcy. On the street below, a large truck emblazoned with the Tour de France logo rolled through the gray morning drizzle, heading, no doubt, to bring supplies to the starting line which, Patterson knew, was only a few blocks around the corner. At this hour on a Saturday in July, not much more was happening in Dijon.

He scratched his sinewy white chest with birdlike fingers. His thin arms were tanned a deep bronze to mid-bicep and aspirin-white above, matching his torso. He, like the rest of them who had only two more days to go, was pared to ultimate racing weight—in Patterson's case, just above one-fifty on a body designed to comfortably pack one-seventy-five, and this despite the voracious consumption of up to nine thousand calories a day.

Dufour eased out of bed, waiting while Patterson padded over the soft carpet to the bathroom. By habit, he lowered himself to the floor for his ritual of morning stretches. As he methodically went through the half-dozen positions that were designed to wake up his system and tell him how he might perform today, he realized he felt stiffer than normal. His muscles ached and his thighs felt tight. He told himself that the morning test ride and subsequent massage would have him fully ready by show time. But still he worried. He had to be better than he'd ever been, not in the least bit off, particularly if he was to match Poulain. Poulain....

Patterson, out of the bathroom, interrupted his thoughts. "How ya feelin', mate."

He ignored the question, instead asking what was foremost in his mind. "John, how do you think Poulain'll go today?" He lay on the floor on his back, right leg held tight to his chest.

"Reckon 'e'll fuckin' fly with them high-octane chemicals they're shootin' 'im with." Patterson was matter-of-fact, as if everyone knew this.

Kurt stopped his stretching and sat up, looking across the room at Patterson. Suddenly, he remembered Patterson's comment last night, when he ran into him and Gervais at the party. "What did you mean last night when you said you knew the *whole fuckin' story*?"

Patterson finished pulling a T-shirt over his head and put on a pair of sweats before sitting down to answer. Dufour raised himself to the bed, waiting expectantly.

"Duff, ya know I've been around this bloody game a long time...I've seen it all by now...amphetamines, steroids, EPO, saline IVs, masking agents, all the shit you can imagine...can't say I 'aven't sampled a bit of it meself." He spoke as if he had taken more than he wanted to admit.

"John, you never told me you were into this...." He paused, incredulous. They had talked drugs before, many times. But Patterson always seemed to shrug it off, as if they weren't for him. Besides, taking anything on the banned list had always been against team policy. Otto and Oberman made that clear.

"You're not one of the ones who's...."

"Gonna blow the whistle? Naw, not me mate. I'll tell 'em what I know, if they ask. But I ain't one of them that's comin' forward. No way. I got no problem keepin' me level under fifty."

"What the hell does that mean?" Kurt couldn't contain his curiosity. He was taken aback that, in five years, Patterson had steadfastly advised Kurt to stay away from what they all knew others were taking, especially EPO. Suddenly, Kurt felt extremely naïve.

Patterson looked at him for a long moment, thinking carefully about his next words. Kurt sensed he was mentally wrestling with something significant; his face was tense and the jaw muscles rippled.

"Tell me something, mate...'ave you really decided to try and bury Poulain today?"

"Absolutely." Kurt felt a nervousness grab at his gut, his legs weaken. "I...I just hope I can."

"You're really prepared to double-cross Garnier, no matter whatever the fuck ya agreed to?" Patterson watched Kurt closely.

"I made the decision, John. I'm not changing it."

Patterson leaned back and placed his hands behind his head, thinking carefully.

"Well, then, Duff, you're gonna need some 'elp 'cause the only way you're gonna beat that frog is if you're on equal ground with the bloody bastard." As he spoke, Patterson got up and went over to his travel bag and, reaching down and around to the bottom, pulled out a tightly rolled hand towel. He placed it on top of the bureau and then carefully unrolled it, revealing several small vials that had been hidden inside.

Dufour got up and went over to where he could see what Patterson was doing. He looked at the vials and turned to him, speechless.

"I think ya might lose your virginity today." Patterson said this without pleasure.

"You're telling me now, after five years together, that you expect me to take some of this shit to win?"

"Ya never 'ad the jersey before, mate. Ya take just enough to keep it, I reckon about seventeen seconds' worth...."

Dufour, angered, slammed his fist on the bureau, making the vials jump. "I don't need it. If you do, that's *your* problem, not mine. I feel good, the best I've felt since the Alps. I can beat him, John."

"I reckon ya can, mate. Most days, for sure." Patterson looked at him, casually, as if he wasn't convinced. "How ya really, feelin', Duff?"

The question hit home. It was impossible to hide anything from Patterson. Dufour dropped his head for a moment, then looked back up and around at the ceiling, searching for the right words. Finally, he replied, softly. "Nervous...I guess. Scared. Worried." Getting the words out made him realize what he'd been trying to hold back. For a moment, he felt like he couldn't move from the weight of it.

Patterson placed a hand on his shoulder. "It's about time, Duff. Ya've been bloody fuckin' amazin'...to all of us. Ya've been runnin' at two hundred percent...ridin' like no one before you. Ya don't crack, ya don' feel no pain...ya bloody piss on them that tries to buy you. 'ow long can ya keep this up, mate?"

Kurt slumped into a chair, his mind numb. For the first time, he was really on the edge. He knew it. The pressure was closing in and he finally had to admit it...he was deeply and utterly afraid. Afraid that he couldn't do it. Afraid that he couldn't live up to his own expectations, that he'd disappoint all those who now expected him to be the best. Afraid that Garnier would seek revenge.

Patterson spoke softly. "We all go through this, mate. It's bloody inhuman what we do. Look at me." He pulled up his shirt to expose his bony chest. "Ya call this 'ealthy? Look at you. Ya've turned into a bloody scarecrow. We all look like we're livin' in Ash...Az...."

"Auschwitz."

"Right. Bloody fuckin' prisoners of war, I say. And that's just on the outside." He pointed to his head. "What about in 'ere? Now, sometimes, I reckon we all need some 'elp. You, for sure, a 'eap less than the rest of us."

Kurt sat silent, listening to Patterson's logic. Finally, he spoke. "You think I need it? You think I could pass this new test? You think I should risk my whole goddam future?" He was both angry and incredulous.

Patterson nodded his head, accepting the questions as if they were a normal part of the initiation. He got back to the business at hand. He rolled out two small white pills from one vial and held them up. "These two, forty-five minutes before the start." He shook another pill out from a different vial. "This one, as soon as ya finish. Masks the first two. Trust me, it's brand new. It works. You'll feel as good as Poulain and anything abnormal will be gone from your system by the time ya do the piss test. No worries."

"You're fuckin' crazy, Patterson." Dufour shook his head, a million thoughts running through his mind. He felt the anger continue to rise. "You really think I need to take this shit? What is it, anyway? It can't be EPO...."

"You're right." Patterson pointed to a third, larger vial. "*That's* EPO."

"What are you, a goddam pharmacist? I had no idea you had all this shit, particularly after the crackdown." Dufour was shocked, disbelieving.

"Listen, Duff." Patterson turned and walked toward the window, keeping his back to Kurt. "Ya didn't need to know this, you're one of the few who's got the talent without it. Now me, and some of the others, we're startin' to wear a little bit.... If you ask me, Poulain 'specially. I'm careful...I know how much of the shit gets me up to a

183

level just below fifty. And if it looks like it may go 'igher, I just take some of me special thinners." He jabbed with his thumb over his shoulder toward the medications on the bureau. His back was still to Kurt and he continued to gaze out the window. He didn't seem worried about being tested.

Kurt looked at the three pills on the towel meant for him. "If it's not EPO, what is it?"

"No matter. It'll make ya feel confident, maybe a little aggressive, that's all. Just enough to equal Poulain. It's not EPO, ya have to run that in your system all the time. EPO don't work as a charge."

Dufour remained incredulous, looking from the bureau to his teammate's back. "Where do you get this shit? Does Otto know about it? What about the others...Oberman?"

Patterson turned around to face him, in a way relieved that there was no reason to hide it any more. "Nobody likes this, nobody wants to use it, least of all Otto...'e looks the other way, 'specially with an old dog like meself...'e wants ya to keep away from it, long as possible. Oberman don't allow anything illegal...."

Dufour got to his feet, still incredulous, pressuring. "How do you monitor this, how do you know you're not fuckin' up your system...where do you get the shit?"

"Whoa, Duff...easy, boy." Patterson, in mock panic, held outstretched hands toward Kurt as if to hold him back. He waited until Kurt sat back on the bed before he dropped his arms. "I got nothin' to hide from ya mate, so take it easy."

The Australian, without emotion, continued. "There's a little German guy, a doctor supposedly, with Comtec, what supplies the soigneurs— in our case, Van Brugen."

"You get it from *Van Brugen*?" Kurt thought of the jovial, heavyset Belgian who, every day, massaged his body back from fatigue. He had never offered anything beyond vitamins to Kurt, probably was told not to.

Patterson nodded. "Through the German guy. Nobody ratted on him last time so 'e's still in the game...'e's a pipeline to Comtec's labs, ya know, where they make the stuff. This friggin' bloke works for Garnier." He smiled and shook his head, looking as if he were about to laugh. "And 'e supplies all the same shit to everyone else what's supposed to be just for Poulain. The ol' double dip. And Garnier, the dumb fuck, thinks only 'is own guys get the shit. Damn, don't that beat all?" He stopped smiling when he turned to Kurt, who wasn't.

"John, who's *everyone else?*"

"Not to worry, not *everyone*, mate." Patterson spoke matter-of-factly, as if it were no big deal. "Just them's that's on Comtec or strugglin' to keep up, like me, mostly *équipiers*. But then there's some that 'ave a shot at Poulain...Koopman, Chimello. They're 'ittin it pretty 'ard, I reckon, and word is they'll be the big names what blow the whistle for Gervais at the end of this bloody race. I reckon they'll finger the Kraut...lead 'em to Garnier."

Patterson sought his roommate's eyes with his own and spoke, for the first time, with emotion in his voice. "Listen, mate, you're the only one who's good 'nuf to beat Poulain, with or without the juice. You gotta bury 'im today. It'll put the stake through Garnier's heart, and they'll all rally 'round. It's gone too far, this shit. If you lose, the sport's fucked again...'e stays in control."

He looked over at the vials and pills on the bureau. "Just this one time, for insurance, mate. Ya won't get caught."

Kurt stood up, his eyes leveled at Patterson. He understood the twisted logic, and he raged against it. Finally, he spoke—forcefully.

"Not this time, John...not ever. I go clean. For me, the temptation's over. You can take your drug store and shove it up your ass."

Patterson didn't try to defend himself. He shrugged his shoulders as if the moral issue escaped him.

"Facts is facts, mate. They takes it, you gotta take it. If ya wanna beat 'im, ya gotta do the dirty deed, mate. Ya said yaself, ya're about to crack."

Dufour jumped up and grabbed the front of Patterson's shirt. "You just said I can do it with or without the shit. *You* were the one who begged me not to sell out to Garnier. How's this any different? Where does it stop, John?"

Patterson gently pushed him away and turned to the window again. He spoke quietly, with his back to Kurt. "Dunno, mate. I reckon when Garnier's behind bars and that little German fuck is hung by 'is balls."

"No John. It's when we all decide not to participate in this...this farce." He thought about the new test, shook his head and thought to himself, *And who knows who'll get caught today.*

"You're a bloody fuckin' dreamer, mate. Long as blokes wanna go fast, they'll invent new 'elpers...and new tests and new 'elpers." He turned from the window, a look of resignation on his face. He looked at Kurt and shrugged his shoulders.

"Keep your pills, John, and use them if you must. I've got to get ready for the race. And not with this..."

He swept his hand across the bureau, sending the vials and their contents clattering to the floor.

***

"This is your rocket sled for this afternoon." Otto spread his arms toward the machine in the stand and then patted Ramos on the shoulder. "Bassini himself brought it in from Milan late last night...he only finished it three days ago." Otto was determined to focus his thoughts on something other than the letter he had just read. There was a job to do first.

They all stood—Otto, Ramos, and Dufour—in front of the bike stand set up in the center of the equipment room. Otto and Kurt willingly focused their attention on this new arrival, relieved to have something more practical to think about than the pressure cooker they were moving toward later in the day.

Kurt gazed at the machine and let out a low whistle. His now trained eye immediately realized that the position of the saddle and the specially created "aero" handlebars would pitch him forward and flatter over the bike, a scientifically measured tuck that had been wind-tunnel tested and refined several months before to achieve the ultimate in aerodynamics, particularly crucial in the time trial. And he noticed the broader, flattened single tube of the main frame swept, almost wing-like, from the front to the solid back wheel of the bike.

"This is legal?"

Otto grinned. "Of course. Fabio brought the prototype to UCI headquarters in Switzerland last January, just in case. They approved it."

"What about Poulain's bike?"

"New, radical. Also legal."

Dufour and many of the other riders, builders, and mechanics had been closely following the official reaction to recent design innovations, some so radical that the bicycle had to be more carefully defined in the rule book. Most controversy had to do with marginal accessories and design elements created to reduce wind drag and artificially boost propulsion, particularly when such things created a riding position so outstretched that the bike became hard to control. Because interpretation of the new rules was largely subjective, some machines had been banned, literally, on the starting line. Protests were rampant, mostly directed at those officials who opposed change. It paid to pre-register.

Ramos took the bike from the stand. He grinned and handed it to Kurt. "Ligero, muy ligero, *very light.*"

Kurt gingerly took the bike by the saddle and handlebars, raising and lowering it slightly to test the weight. He whistled again.

"Only seexteen pounds. But very strong." Ramos was obviously pleased with the design. He quickly went over the bike with Kurt, pointing out that all the components were titanium or forged aluminum, and the wing-like frame was made from the latest carbon fiber.

No excuses here, Kurt thought. He was dressed in black leg warmers and light rain jacket for the morning warm-up, an easy team spin around the thirty-eight-kilometer time trial course to test bikes, loosen legs, and gain some familiarity with the course every rider would face a few hours later.

One by one, the rest of the GTI team shuffled in, each connecting with his own time trial bike. The machines were all carefully polished and lined up along the far wall, each specially designed, though none quite the same as Kurt's. Otto's players were all dressed the same, well covered for the light rain falling outside and carrying their bike shoes. Normally, they would warm up for a time trial on their own schedules, but Otto had insisted that this final one be *en masse*, to build on the solidarity expressed last night. Privately, he did it for security, and he made sure every spare vehicle and motorcycle would accompany them. From here on in, they could take no chances.

Kurt waited for the others to finish getting ready in the shelter of the hallway outside the bike room. He sat on the floor with his bike leaning on the wall next to him, mentally rehearsing the tightly programmed day leading up to his own 4 p.m. start time, the very last rider off, and two minutes behind Poulain.

After this morning's ride, a quick shower. Then Van Brugen's full massage with extra work on the legs. A big meal around noon then an hour's nap, that is if he could sleep. At 2:45, he'd dress for the race and, at 3:15, leave on his road bike for the staging area, only a few blocks away. Then on the trainer for a vigorous warm-up right up until start time. All the time, he'd be surrounded by Otto, Tomi K, Oberman, Ramos, and maybe Berclaz who, lying seventh overall, would start about fifteen minutes before him and might roll with him to the start.

They would all help him get him through the crowds and keep the reporters at bay. There would be an area roped off under an awning just behind the start ramp, GTI's private sanctuary in a sea of chaos. There, his time trial bike would be waiting and stationary trainer for a good twenty-minute warm-up. He could get a last-minute drink there, and maybe one of Tomi K's energy concoctions. He would be too nervous to talk to anyone, wouldn't want any more distractions.

He visualized the time trial itself, the power that would have to flow from him into the bike. The race was only for thirty-eight kilometers, about twenty-three miles, and it would only take him about fifty minutes. But the effort would be intense. It would require total concentration and the need to be at his absolute limit, the knife-edge between peak power and total collapse. He could fly, he knew he could fly. But so could the others, especially Poulain, the master at this game; and now, Kurt was sure, helped by chemistry. Kurt had never beaten the Frenchman in a time trial. No one had in five years. For sure Poulain would be juiced but maybe, just maybe, the new test would get him.

It didn't matter. If Kurt could just hold on to at least part of his current thirty-seven-second lead, the Tour would be his. He would win. He would break Garnier's vice grip on the sport, and show he couldn't be bought. He would be the first and only man to stop Poulain, and at the one event the Frenchman needed on his record to be declared the greatest cyclist of all time.

And maybe, just maybe, he could help Otto hold the team together, and bring in some new blood that would keep them at the top of the sport after the Comtec dynasty was toppled.

He sat alone in the hallway, thinking about these things and how his conviction would have to give him the strength he needed.

***

Katherine Anderson hated French carnival music. And she thought grown men racing bicycles was silly. To her, putting the two together for three weeks in a foreign country was the height of absurdity, especially when reasonably intelligent men like Phil Sterling and Jeff Martin lived for it, regarded it with a kind of lofty nobility that escaped her.
Like most sports, it was a silly game to her, a "guy thing" that made usually attractive men sputter for hours over meaningless statistics, road surfaces, and bike parts. She leaned against the RV, closed her eyes, and took a long drag on her nearly finished cigarette, trying to shut out the wretched music and excited French commentary of the start-line announcer.

She smiled as she slowly exhaled. Strip it all away and you find the real story. Human greed. Payoffs. Drugs. It could be show horses or bike racers, it was all the same. Her challenge, the only one that made her like this job anymore, was finding out how it was put together, and then pointing the finger. She liked taking the credit for exposing things others wanted to hide. In the end, she was right and they were wrong; everything else, except maybe a little sex here and there, was boring.

"Katherine!" She opened her eyes to Arnie Campbell, both his hands slammed against the trailer on either side of her head. She could smell his breath, stale with garlic and cheese.

189

She gently pushed his chest, moving the breath out of range. "What's the matter, Arnie?" She smiled up at him, as sweetly as she could.

"Now what?" he asked, exasperated. "We've got thirty minutes to show time and you want to discuss our *approach*?"

"In light of the new evidence, yes."

"What *new evidence*? What in God's name is it now? We don't have time for another one of your half-baked theories."

Anderson straightened to her full height, still several inches shorter than Campbell's, and took a deep, deliberate draw on her cigarette. She exhaled directly into the producer's face, making him back away farther, coughing.

"Jesus Christ, Katherine, you can really be foul." He tried to wave the smoke away as he retreated.

"Me foul? *Me* foul?" Anderson threw her cigarette down and advanced on Campbell. "The bicycle boys are the foul ones, Arnie. Wonder boy's sent a letter around—they're bribing him with millions of dollars. He's supposed to throw the race. They *did* let him win, that day with the broken motorcycle. And drugs…they're all still on drugs. I read the letter, Arnie. *I* read the fuckin' letter!" She pounded her chest with her finger, crowding him again.

"What letter? What money? What drugs? What on earth are you talking about?" Campbell held his hands up, defensively. He was angry. Confused.

"The fucking letter from Kurt Dufour that I wasn't supposed to read. It was given to Jenny and some others, officials, important people. It says the French guys tried to bribe him. Millions. They offered him millions, Arnie. He even gave the Swiss bank account where the money was wired! And he's going to blow the whistle…*we're* going to blow the whistle. Foul, Arnie! Wake up! Wake up!" She flailed her arms madly.

Campbell snapped. He grabbed her by the shoulders, shook her hard, and slammed her back against the trailer. "Now listen to me. I don't know a goddam thing about this letter you're talking about. But I'm going to have to see it first. And you're going to have to shut up until then!" He shook her again, keeping her pinned hard to the trailer. "Jesus fucking Christ, Katherine. We go live in a few minutes. You pull yourself together or I'll yank you. I don't give a shit what they say in New York. And if you say one thing about this on the air...."

She spit in his face. When he dropped his head, she spit on his bald spot. She kicked at his legs, but he still held her against the trailer. "You sonofabitch!" she shrieked, trying with all her might to wriggle free. But he was too strong, and he had the advantage of being able to lean his weight into her.

"Katherine...Katherine." Campbell changed, making his voice as calm and firm as possible. He had to control her, bring her back. "You have to forget this, Katherine." His eyes pleaded. He shook her, gently this time. "Please. I promise to look into it. But after today's show. We can always file a news story later, once we're sure of the details."

Her tense body started to capitulate. She looked at him, trying to read what was in his eyes, if he was being truthful or just patronizing her again. A drop of her spittle fell from the tip of his nose. Finally, she nodded and he released her.

"Please, Katherine, go to the booth now."

She nodded again, without saying anything or showing any emotion, and then headed off in the direction of the French carnival music.

****

Chapter Seventeen

Race of Truth

Kurt Dufour sat rock steady on the trainer, his legs a blur as he pounded tempo to *Gonna Fly Now* that blasted from his Walkman into his sweat-soaked ear phones. He and Berclaz, the last two GTI riders to start the time trial, spun next to each other, sheltered from the light rain by a canvas awning that projected from the GTI equipment truck to the center of the narrow side street. The side street, well away from the immense and boisterous crowd, was secured as the racers' ready area just off Dijon's Boulevard Maréchal Joffre, the heavily festooned start/finish straightaway that was today's main stadium.

Secured by high barricades surrounding bumper-to-bumper team vehicles, the block-long ready area allowed the world's best professional cyclists to perform their last-minute and private pre-race rituals and warm-ups in relative quiet. To ensure this, the few breaks in the fencing were guarded by gendarmes and burly officials who stood attentively, making sure that only properly credentialed team personnel and competitors passed into the area, now even quieter since most of the riders were already out on the course. At the far end were the medical vans, many more than usual, to handle the urine test required of each rider after the race.

Kurt could hear the constantly recycled music blaring over the public address system a block away, punctuated every couple of minutes by the rapid-fire French of the race announcer, and accompanying loud cheering, as each rider launched himself from the starting platform.

As Berclaz dismounted from the adjacent trainer, he gave Kurt a nervous thumbs up and disappeared into the trailer, first wrapped in a towel offered by Tomi K. Kurt slowed his tempo and thought back to the earlier massage done by Van Brugen's thick, strong hands. They had pushed supple and well-oiled muscle from ankle to knee, knee to thigh.

"Loose as goose, soft as mama's big tits." Van Brugen had said as his huge and creased face smiled down at him. There were beads of sweat on his brow and his bushy eyebrows blinked in unison because, Kurt and his teammates had mused, he had never mastered the art of winking one eye independently of the other. He had said nothing about drugs.

Despite the tension of the moment, Kurt smiled. He felt warm from a vigorous twenty minutes on the trainer and his mind, for the first time today, spoke to him of awesome power. He conjured up the mental image of that power surging through his body, from his hips to his thighs to the pedals. He could feel the speed of his wheels on the road, the wind and rain rush by his face. He was clean, he was right, and he had nothing to lose. And he felt like he could fly.

"It's time." Otto gently patted him on the shoulder and motioned for Kurt to dismount from the trainer and towel off the sweat. Ramos stood to the side, waiting with the polished blue bike that looked like an inverted wing. He grinned broadly, trying to hide his own nervousness. Tomi K was there and Dr. Oberman, ready to surround him for the short roll to the starting line.

Otto toweled Kurt's face, ending with his customary pat on the cheek. Silently he helped secure and close the zipper of Kurt's *maillot jaune*, today the top half of a specially designed one-piece skinsuit made of the thinnest Lycramax.

As they made their way from the ready area to the officials behind the start platform, TV camera crews hurried to get in front of them, and flashbulbs from the press photographers popped all around. And above the increasing jostling and shouting, Kurt could hear the announcer building the next introduction....

"Mesdames et messieurs...s'il vous plaît...bienvenue à le plus grand champion de la France...cinq fois vainqueur du Tour de France ...aujourd'hui, seulement trent-sept secondes derrière le maillot jaune, il cherche sa sixième victoire consecutive...voici Jacques Poulain!"

The crowd response was deafening. Wild cheering and air horns, even cowbells not heard since the Alps....

***

"And here he is, Jeff. Certainly the favorite to win today, if not to take back the jersey of overall leader."

193

Phil Sterling and Jeff Martin leaned close together, watching the screen in front of them. They were two stories above the start line in their broadcast booth, one of nearly fifty press cubicles erected from scaffolding on one side of the boulevard. In addition to their TV monitor, they had a good view of the street below, and the covered start ramp from where each rider was sent off at two-minute intervals. Anderson sat on one side of them, Scott on the other. They were broadcasting live, via satellite, to the United States.

"Just listen to the crowd, Phil. Despite Kurt Dufour's popularity, there's no doubt that many, if not all, Frenchmen here want Poulain back in yellow for that final leg into Paris tomorrow."

The screen filled with the image of Jacques Poulain mounted on his bicycle and enclosed in the elevated start platform. An official in a maroon blazer stood behind him, holding him upright until the clock's sweep hand would signal release down the short ramp and out onto the course. The boulevard was lined with thousands of spectators packed against the barricades for as far as one could see or jammed into temporary bleachers, twenty rows high, for several hundred yards closer in.

"Well, he's starting today with a thirty-seven-second deficit behind Dufour. And you'll recall, Jeff, the last time they met in this kind of time trial was in the Tour of Italy two months ago...

"That's right, Phil. And, as you've pointed out, Dufour only lost that one by thirty seconds. And that was over fifty kilometers, not today's shorter thirty-eight."

As they waited the last few seconds for Poulain to start, Sterling took over, doing what only he had the talent to do, convey the drama of the moment for a television audience thousands of miles away....

"Jacques Poulain is ready, taking the last few deep breaths before he's off.... A superb athlete who must win this time trial to capture his sixth consecutive Tour de France, a record that no other professional cyclist can claim in the history of the sport. And this is his specialty, the individual time trial, the race of truth...."

The sweep hand of the huge official time clock ticked straight up and Poulain, throwing himself forward, powered his bicycle into motion, his legs straining and his face grimacing with the sudden effort. In an instant he was down the ramp and onto the wet road, lunging and driving his bike to top speed as quickly as possible. The crowd roared as one, a deafening tribute that carried Poulain like a wave up the road, the loudest send-off by far.

The image of Poulain hurling himself through the enormous crowd to the cheers of his countrymen faded into a spinning-wheel graphic and the silky smooth voice of Katherine Anderson.

"Stay tuned for American Kurt Dufour and more from France's Race of Truth...."

***

The windshield wipers thumped out a tempo that nearly matched the smooth pedaling cadence of Kurt Dufour. From inside the following car, four pairs of eyes focused intensely on that cadence, a smooth powerful flow that propelled Dufour and his bicycle over the wet road as fast as they'd ever seen him ride.

"Hot damn!" Otto Werner pounded his steering wheel. "He's fuckin' flyin'!"

The official seated next to him, obligatory for this event, sat impassively staring ahead. Ramos and Tomi K leaned forward from the back seat. No less than seven motorcycles, two with television microwave towers and camera operators, and another official car, the race director himself, cruised even-paced all around them, careful not to be so close to Dufour as to interfere or offer him wind protection.

On this early part of the course, the roadway was wide and smooth, headed into the teeth of a steady northwest wind. It was here and through the subsequent Burgundian hills where Dufour had to at least hold Poulain even, hoping to create enough of a time cushion to hold off the Frenchman's superior ability to negotiate the tricky wet turns near the end of the course.

The car radio crackled: "*Allô, allô. ici Radio Tour.* At the second check point, kilometer 7.5 at Messigny, Poulain 11:05, Dufour 10:47."

Otto bounced in his seat, slamming his fist on the dashboard. "Holy shit, eighteen seconds already! Haaa!"

195

"Going veddy, veddy fast," said Tomi K in the backseat. "Could vin, maybe minute or more."

"*Caramba!*" shouted Ramos.

Otto's eyes darted furtively from side to side, focusing on the phalanx of motorcycles that protected them and the crowds that, so far, seemed nothing but supportive, cheering wildly as they passed.

They accelerated down a short hill and over the river bridge at Val-Suzon, the point marking the beginning of the toughest hill on the course, two miles to gain six hundred feet of elevation before the final, mostly downhill blast back to Dijon.

Otto geared the car down for the reduced speed on the curving road leading to the summit. They were close behind Dufour now. He climbed strongly with a still-powerful cadence between the massive banks of cheering fans, rocking his shoulders only slightly as he absorbed the more difficult terrain.

Otto grabbed his mobile phone halfway through the first ring.

"Otto, he's doing it! He's gonna win!" Peter Dufour, back at the finish line, shouted into the phone.

"Peter, listen to me!" Otto shouted back. "Make sure you're at the finish line with some help. We'll get him back to the truck as soon as possible!" He flipped the phone shut and tossed it over his shoulder into the back seat.

The radio crackled again: "*Allô, allô, ici Radio Tour.* At the summit of Val-Suzon, kilometer twenty-two, Poulain 33:01, Dufour 32:36."

Otto and his men cheered, pounded each other, and bounced up and down on their seats. The official stared straight ahead, a slight smile on his lips.

"Possible to vin Tour by vun minute!" Tomi K had become the statistician.

Their speed increased dramatically on the downhill. Dufour had shifted into his biggest gear and his legs turned slower and more powerfully. He had a tailwind now as well.

196

The car became quiet. Dufour was hitting close to fifty miles an hour on wet roads. They were straight and wide now, but everyone in the car knew the last four miles would be along narrow, twisting back roads through Hauteville and Ahuy before hitting the wider streets of Dijon—a daunting series of blind turns and tricky ups and downs, undoubtedly jammed with spectators.

"Take it easy, Kurt, take it easy." Otto spoke softly. In the back seat, Ramos crossed himself.

They hurtled toward the sharp left turn at the end of the fast descent. The crowd grew thicker, a mass of multicolored umbrellas that obscured the sight line into the turn.

"Going too fast...." Tomi K saw it first. Dufour, trying to swing as wide as possible to make the turn, wavered then tried to correct his line. His rear wheel skidded on the wet pavement and in an instant he was down, sliding, and slowly rotating as if on ice, his feet still locked into the pedals.

"Shit!" Otto pumped his brakes then slammed them hard. The car slid sideways into the turn and then spun around backwards, coming to a stop inches from the barricade and the screaming spectators. Dufour sat on the wet street a few yards away, awkwardly trying to free himself from the twisted machine. Most of the motorcycles had detoured around except for the camera bike, which stopped to record the chaotic scene.

"He's okay! He's okay! Get him up!" Otto shouted as he struggled to get his door open. The official looked shaken but didn't move.

All three leaped out of the car at once, knowing instinctively what to do. Ramos ripped the spare bike off the side rack and ran it to Kurt. Tomi K disengaged the fallen bike and helped Kurt quickly to his feet. In an instant, they had gotten him onto the spare and helped push him off. Otto pushed the hardest, running as fast as he could until Dufour was clamped into the pedals and gaining speed on his own. The fans cheered wildly, some of them jumping the barricades to help while the gendarmes blew their shrill whistles to try and keep them back....

***

197

"Oh my God. *Oh my God, Phil!*"

The TV monitor showed a chaotic scene. The GTI team car, doors open wide, facing backward in the middle of the turn and men scrambling to pick up Kurt Dufour from the pavement.

"He's down! Kurt Dufour has fallen off on that tight, rain-slick turn. This could be a tragic moment for the young American!" Sterling's voice took on new drama.

"He's lost time, but they got him back pretty quick, Phil! That was Otto Werner, Dufour's team director who pushed him the longest. He doesn't look hurt!" The picture showed Werner's portly body and short legs reach top speed before falling out of the way of the camera bike, now right behind Dufour.

The camera was back in action, closely following Dufour's redoubled effort to gain back the lost momentum. He was riding hard, out of the saddle on the short hills and shaving the corners close, despite the wet pavement and certain pain from the recent spill. The camera stayed right behind his shoulder, recording the outstretched arms and screaming faces that cheered him on, appearing and falling away in an endless frenetic stream.

There were less than four kilometers to go and the question in everyone's mind was how much time had been lost.

The camera picture suddenly switched from the motorcycle with Dufour to a fixed position above the finish line, looking way down the broad finishing boulevard. A digital Swiss Timing clock displaying running time rolled across the bottom of the screen and, within seconds, a lone rider swung into view and started his long drive through the canyon of spectators to the line. Official cars and a brace of motorcycles formed a curb-to-curb wake behind.

"Jacques Poulain has started his final drive to the finish! Seemingly out of it just a few minutes ago, Dufour's unfortunate crash may have put the French champion back in the running!"

"We're waiting for the final time check, Phil. There's no telling yet just how much time Dufour lost in that crash."

"Jacques Poulain has been here before. He has the undisputed claim as the world's greatest time trialist and, now, here he is with just a few meters to go, desperately trying to coax every bit of speed out of his shuddering machine!"

Poulain lunged and rolled over his bike, throwing every ounce of effort into reaching the finish line. He knew, they all knew, that this was his last and only chance. To the crowd's deafening roar, he passed by the "100 meters to go" sign and stood out of the saddle, making one last driving effort to beat more speed out of his already speeding bicycle.

Poulain flashed under the finish-line banner.

"Forty-eight twelve! The fastest time so far by over two minutes! Jeff, this man has done the ride of his life!" Sterling was clearly shocked. But no sooner had the clock stopped than another deafening roar arose from the far end of the boulevard.

"*And here comes Dufour!*"

The camera switched from overhead to right next to the American, inches from his straining body. Helmetless, his head was lowered, and his short brown hair was wet and matted. And his side was covered with a smear of mud and blood, the *maillot jaune* in shreds. His eyes looked up and his face, a fierce determined mask with mouth open wide, seemed as if from another world. His arms, his shoulders, his back, his legs shuddered and strained with the effort.

Sterling raised his voice to a rapid-fire near-shout: "*Kurt Dufour, the brilliant young American, is giving everything he has! He's running on adrenaline now, concentrating only on driving his bike these last few meters, using every ounce of energy he has left. He's been hurt but he's not out of it yet.... He's got the kind of determination, the kind of class that will make him a true champion...the yellow jersey, torn and ripped now...but still on his back....*" Sterling glanced at the overhead clock and did a quick mental calculation. "*To keep it, he must cross the line in forty-eight, forty-nine or better....*"

Dufour gave one last thrust to the finish then slumped over his bike, immediately swallowed into the sea of crazed reporters, photographers, and officials jammed between the high crowd barriers.

"Forty-eight, twenty-two! *Forty-eight, twenty-two!*" Martin shrieked into his mike, "Omigod, omigod…Dufour's kept the jersey by *twen-ty sev-en sec-onds!*"

All around them, American journalists leaped into the air, the crowd roared and cheered wildly. Sterling and Martin slammed each other on the back and Jennifer Scott, completely swept away by the moment, slumped over the table and sobbed into her arms. Even Katherine Anderson, momentarily forgetting her mission, was caught up in the pandemonium.

Only Campbell's voice, shouting in her earphones, brought her back.

"Wrap on the slo-mo! Go to break, go to break!"

The screen filled with the replay, Kurt Dufour in slow motion, mouth agape, straining and rolling over his bike, the jersey torn from his side, his eyes looking upward toward the clock above the finish line.

"Kurt Dufour, the new American hero, crosses the finish line to keep his yellow jersey and now certain victory in the Tour de France…. This is Katherine Anderson from Dijon, France. Stay tuned for continuing coverage."

***

The same slow-motion replay of Kurt Dufour's finest moment instantaneously appeared on television screens around the world.

One of these, a very large one, was the only source of light in the closed-curtained bridal suite at *Château de Vougeot*, less than twenty kilometers from the finish line. In this semi-dark room, Jérôme Garnier and his attendant, Heinrich Kemptka, intently watched the scene. The party of the previous night was long over, even the last women and hangers-on gone to Dijon where they could continue their brush with fame, their connection to Poulain's celebrity, in the thick of the action.

The light from the television screen eerily illuminated the faces of the two men, silently watching the huge worldwide event they had become used to controlling—with intimidation, huge amounts of money, and pharmaceuticals.

Garnier's face contorted when Kurt Dufour's finishing time froze under the slow-motion image of his triumphant and defiant drive to the finish line.

He sat transfixed. His thick eyebrows narrowed and his mouth became tight-lipped, twitching with anger. He tightly gripped the arms of his chair, and his eyes, glued to the screen in outraged disbelief, began to blink and twitch uncontrollably. Suddenly and violently, he brought his fist down, shattering the plastic remote control on the table next to him. The screen went dark.

Kemptka jumped to his feet, then, just as fast, dropped back into his chair. He squirmed and glanced sideways at his boss.

Garnier sat motionless for an uncomfortably long time, staring at the black TV screen. The only light now came from the gray sky outside, further muted and diffused through the closed curtains of the suite. Finally, Garnier spoke, in a low, steady tone.

"You gave Jacques the right amount, *Herr Kemptka*?"

"*Ja, mein herr.*"

"And the money for the American? It was wired into the account as I instructed?"

"*Ja, mein herr.* Yesterday, by Leguerre." Kemptka shrunk deep into his chair, fearing what might come next.

Garnier stood up slowly. He turned and walked the two steps to where Kemptka cowered. He stood over him menacingly.

"Then explain to me, *dummkopf*, why the American won!" As he spoke, he swiftly and brutally brought the back of his hand across Kemptka's face. The smaller man reeled backward from the impact and then tried to scramble from the chair. But Garnier's bulk blocked his retreat and another blow slammed him back. Kemptka raised his hands in defense and started to babble.

"It vas Leguerre, Leguerre! Not me, *mein herr*. Ve should haff checked up on him. He is not like me, *mein herr*, he is veak, he is fool."

Garnier reached down and grabbed Kemptka by the front of his shirt, pulling the much smaller man up to his face.

He shook him hard and spoke through teeth clenched in rage. "I have been defied. No one defies me, Heinrich Kemptka. *No one!*" He thrust the German back into his chair. He looked down at him, his evil countenance speaking with as much authority as the threatening words. "Now I will get rid of that weakling Leguerre and you will execute tomorrow's plan. There can be no more mistakes!"

He planted his thick hands on each arm of the chair and leaned close to Kemptka's face, by now contorted with fear. "Do I make myself clear, *Herr Kemptka?*"

Kemptka nodded vigorously. His voice trembled, "*Ja, mein herr.*"

***

Peter Dufour took most of the impact of his son plowing into the crowd of crazed journalists just across the finish line. But he was ready for it, and so were the four burly officials on loan from Claude Gervais.

They pushed and shoved to blanket themselves around the wounded American. His chest heaved and he gasped for air as flashbulbs popped and fists and elbows flew from the men whose job it was to record the anguished face at its most dramatic moment.

From somewhere, Otto Werner's portly body torpedoed into the melée. He pushed through to Peter Dufour, grabbed his sleeve, and shouted, "Quick, this way!"

Displaced gendarmes blew their whistles, wrestled to regain control, and struggled to help the human cocoon surrounding Kurt Dufour, still on his bicycle, surge toward the relative safety of the ready area.

In a few moments, they had squeezed through the barricades and a wall of gendarmes and officials sealed the opening behind them.

In another moment, they were back at the GTI truck, safely under the awning and surrounded by euphoric teammates. There was hugging and backslapping as Dufour was peeled from his bicycle and eased into the aluminum lawn chair awaiting him. He slumped over, grimacing with pain, as his raw side scraped one of the chair's arms.

In a moment, expert hands were all over him, rubbing his face and neck and gingerly peeling the shredded jersey from his body. They probed and checked and, within a minute or two, had him covered with his sweat suit and wound-dressings where needed.

Throughout all this, Kurt Dufour had been in a daze. He knew he had nearly beaten Poulain in the time trial, despite the fall. And he knew he still held the jersey by enough of a margin to be all but assured of overall victory. But the ride itself, the roads, the confusion of the crash, and his last agonizing moments to the finish were hazy.

He was starting to recover now and he leaned back in the chair, letting the reality of what he'd done, the congratulations of his teammates and closest friends sink in. "Shit", he said, to no one in particular, "I did it, I actually did it."

He felt a hand on his shoulder and looked up to see the familiar lean and angular face of John Patterson. There were tears in the Aussie's eyes as he slowly and softly patted Kurt's back.

"Well, bloody done, mate. Ya buried the fuckin' bastard, no worries."

He knelt down to be close to Kurt's face, placing his arm around his friend's shoulder, then glanced around to make sure no one was listening.

"Thanks, mate," Patterson whispered.

Kurt turned his face to the Australian and gave him a quizzical look. "What is it?" he said, still somewhat dazed and not sure why he was being thanked.

"Rode the best TT of me life," Patterson said with pride.

"That's great, old man." Kurt was still confused. Patterson was never one to talk about his own performance, especially in a time trial where his ability was weakest and his contribution to the team the least important.

Patterson glanced cautiously around again and then opened his hand to reveal a small plastic bag. It contained three pills.

"Tried me a little experiment...rode faster without 'em." He smiled, stood up, and walked toward the GTI truck. He dropped the plastic bag into a nearby trashcan.

***

The rain had stopped and it was almost dark when the Mercedes coupe slowly turned the corner onto the small side street, which, only a few hours earlier, had been the restricted ready area for the riders. A crew of men worked to unlink and stack the steel barricades that had defined the area. They worked by streetlight, conversing occasionally as the barricades clanged together in ever-growing piles, stacked neatly on the curb for pickup by one of the big equipment semis that would soon arrive. The riders were long gone and the crowd dispersed, leaving the only evidence of the earlier carnival—a few dirty towels in the street and small piles of litter scattered here and there.

Last to go was one medical van, the remainder of a large fleet of antiseptic white vehicles that had been set up to handle the unusual number of post-race doping tests carried out on every rider.

Heinrich Kemptka, the driver of the Mercedes coupe, knew the routine as well as anyone. A doctor in each van would observe the rider urinate into a small sample vial and then, still under careful observation, seal the vial, label it with the rider's number, and place it in a rack to be transferred into a locked case for the trip to the lab in Paris. As a last step, the rider signed the seal, thus confirming that the sample was his. This van, the last one left, was the one in which the samples from the last riders to finish the time trial were taken, including Poulain, Dufour, and most of the top twenty on general classification.

Kemptka parked in the shadows a good hundred meters from the van and got out. He watched for a few moments as the technician and his driver cleaned up, converting the van from testing facility to secure transport. Between now and when the samples arrived in Paris, he knew, would be the only time he could get at them.

At the rap on the car roof, Kemptka's passenger got out, dressed in a white frock identical to the one worn by the lab technician in the van.

The two quietly approached the vehicle, staying in the shadows to avoid detection by the teardown crew and the two men preparing their van for departure.

When they were within earshot of the van, Kemptka touched his accomplice on the shoulder and gently pushed him into the light, less than twenty meters from the vehicle. He nodded and shrunk further into the shadows.

A shrill whistle drew the technician from the van, looking first for some kind of recognition and then motioning to his driver to stay put. The smile and the imposter's uniform worked. The teardown crew had moved off in the opposite direction and didn't notice.

"Qu'est-ce que c'est, mon ami?" *What is it, my friend?* The man asked as he approached, unsuspecting.

In a flash, Kemptka lunged from the shadows and was on him from behind. He clapped a handkerchief over his nose and mouth, and the man went limp, quietly sinking to the ground. In an instant, Kemptka produced a syringe and plunged the needle into the man's neck. There had been no chance to struggle or cry out. Kemptka's decoy dragged the body into the shadows.

Swiftly, the two closed on the van and, when the driver stepped out to look for his partner, Kemptka stuck again in the same fashion. The second body was also dragged into the shadows.

Within moments, they were inside the van, with the white frock staying under the cab light so as not to arouse suspicion. Kemptka found and opened the sample case in the back of the van where his work couldn't be observed from outside. With a small flashlight clamped between his teeth to illuminate the sample rack, Kemptka's skilled hands worked quickly, turning the labels of each sample until he found the two he wanted.

The white frock turned to watch and smiled wickedly. "You're good at this, Herr Heinrich."

"You do vut you do, I do vut I do." The heavy German accent and the flashlight between Kemptka's teeth made this barely intelligible. Nevertheless, Donald Conway understood and smiled again, watching with relish as Kemptka expertly applied the last label and then, from a scrap of paper he had placed next to the vial rack, swiftly and accurately duplicated the signature of Jacques Poulain. In an instant, all was replaced as found.

Kemptka glanced at his watch. "Ve haff less than vun minute."

As they hustled the limp bodies into the van and placed them comfortably in the front seats, Conway couldn't help but ask again. "You sure they won't remember?"

Kemptka placed the unconscious technician's right hand on the locked sample case, patted him gently on the check and turned to Conway. An evil grin spread across his face. "You forget, *mein herr*, I am za drug *meister*."

Within minutes, the Mercedes coupe was headed north out of Dijon.

****

Chapter Eighteen

Last Day

The three network commentators stood in the middle of the sun-drenched Champs-Élysées in Paris. Their backdrop was the Arc de Triomphe, and their audience was millions of American TV viewers who were tuned in to see and hear just how a young countryman of theirs was about to seal victory in the world's biggest, if barely understood, annual sports event.

They were dressed for the occasion in network-logoed navy blazers, blue oxford shirts, and red-and-blue striped silk neckwear—ties for Phil Sterling and Jeff Martin, a matching scarf for Katherine Anderson. A slight breeze gently lifted Anderson's blonde hair, and the thin strands on Sterling's head wafted back and forth. Martin's hair, slicked back for the occasion, stayed firmly in place. All three of them looked unusually tense—and not at all happy.

Jennifer Scott, off-camera with headset on, silently held up one hand, folding down one finger at a time for the five-second countdown. Her eyes, watching the monitor on the street in front of her, were swollen and bloodshot, which contributed to her overall look of saddened detachment. As soon as the raised hand became a fist, Katherine Anderson's face filled the screen….

"Welcome to Paris and the final day of the grueling three-week Tour de France. I'm Katherine Anderson, here on the historic Champs-Élysées, to bring you the conclusion of a most amazing sporting event…an event that now, as the wheels spin finally to this spot, suddenly and unexpectedly swirls in controversy…." She turned her head to introduce Phil Sterling at her side. The camera closed in, revealing the British commentator's unusual look of grim resignation.

"Well, it's sad but true, Katherine. The brilliant riding of young American Kurt Dufour all during the Tour…the man who just yesterday dramatically held on to his yellow jersey with a brilliant effort in the key time trial…has been marred by the announcement, only two hours ago, that he is suspected of having taken EPO, a dangerous illegal drug that has crept into the peloton. Those of us who have followed this race for decades just can't believe it but, in an official document obtained by the French press, it was revealed that Dufour's mandatory urine test, required of all cyclists after yesterday's time trial, showed traces of the banned drug EPO that, until this new test, was undetectable...."

This was Sterling's lead-in to a hastily edited package about how the shocking news was gathered. There were shots of officials trying to block cameras from recording scenes at the entrance to a drug-testing lab in the Paris suburbs, and, then, a hand holding up the document that Sterling's voice identified as the official medical report from Dufour's blood test. As the pre-recorded scenes of racers, officials, and yesterday's time trial finish rolled across the screen, Sterling laid out the story:

"Race officials, citing a new medical rule, administered the urine test to every rider immediately after finishing the time trial yesterday and, apparently, an overnight staff of lab technicians was brought in to test the sample of the top twenty riders overall. Despite official efforts to suppress the results, the reports were leaked just after the start this morning, and no less than nine riders were found to have traces of EPO in their system, the most prominent of whom were the Dutchman, Fedor Koopman, Andrea Chimello of Italy, and race leader Kurt Dufour. Apparently Poulain's sample was clean."

The scene returned to the three commentators on the Champs-Élysées, and this time Jeff Martin spoke.

"Phil, this kind of scandal has ripped through the sport before and, in at least one case, the results have been overturned."

"That's right, Jeff. And *if* true, and I want to emphasize the fact that this report is not yet official, we could be in for the same kind of incident that erupted in 1998, when several teams were found to be smuggling and using performance-enhancing drugs. There were accusations and denials flying about and some of the biggest names and teams quit the Tour in protest. It took a year to sort out the problem and clear up the mess. Now it's important to again emphasize, Jeff, that no official charges have been filed against Dufour or anyone else as of the moment."

"Well, Phil, we were able to contact GTI team director Otto Werner in his car behind the riders. He vehemently denied the charge and said that, if indeed the accusation becomes official, he would demand a re-test and B-sample analysis as soon as the race finished today."

The scene changed to live action somewhere on the road to Paris. The riders were strung out, riding hard and oblivious to the scandal unfolding as they pedaled toward the finish....

***

The shocking news ripped through the caravan of team cars following the race. It came from a press car, not from *Radio Tour*, the communications channel reserved solely for announcements from the race officials. And, since virtually every car in the race caravan had radios tuned to several channels at once, the story spread like wild fire.

An anonymous tip from the testing lab had sent reporters scurrying to the scene and it was there that someone had gotten copies of the lab results and the reports showing that nine riders had, indeed, been found to have traces of EPO in their system. Once the French press broke the news, the rest of the reporters had no choice but to cover the story....

Otto Werner slammed shut his mobile phone and dropped it on the seat.

"Bullshit! Bullshit! Bullshit!" He pounded the dashboard and then the steering wheel.

"Report not trrue. Bad guys vurking to destroy good man." Tomi K, from the backseat, shook his head in denial.

"Jesus fucking Christ," said Peter Dufour, seated next to Otto.

Otto drove with one hand, fumbling with the other in his trousers pocket. Finally, he held up a piece of crumpled paper.

"Here Peter. Here's Gervais's cellular number. Get him on the phone right now. We'll get to the bottom of this real quick!"

In a moment, the number was punched in and Otto took the phone.

It crackled then cleared. "Allô, allô...Gervais, *ici*."

"What the *fuck* is going on, Claude?"

"Otto...Otto. I am completely confused by this news...."

"You're not the only one, pal!" Otto shouted into the phone. The car careened around a turn, Werner steering with one hand, desperately trying to stay close to the bumper in front and talk at the same time. "Claude, you have to make an official announcement—this report's bullshit!"

"Bien sûr. *You are correct.*"

In a moment the car radio crackled and the announcement came, first in French and then English.

"Ici Radio Tour. The story of this morning about blood test results is not official. The blood test reports have not been released. Repeat: the blood test results of last night have not been released."

It was too late. The news of Kurt Dufour taking EPO was too hot to hold. Even with the disclaimer from officials radioed from the caravan, the bomb had been dropped. Live-action reports were interrupted by the story, spread uncontrollably by the electronic media.

It hit with one hour to go in the race toward Paris. Roadside spectators, many tuned in to portable radios, turned up the volume, and talked excitedly to those near them. In homes and pubs throughout Europe, the speeding race scenes were interrupted by grim, desk-borne commentators.

And, in the United States, even the channels not covering the Tour broke into their programming....

This just in from Paris...American Kurt Dufour, about to win the Tour de France, has been accused of doping....

The riders knew nothing. They were in the outskirts of Paris now, winding through Issy-les-Moulineaux and pounding toward the magnificent setting of the Champs-Élysées, where they would turn their pedals even faster up and down the broad boulevard for six laps, witnessed by an estimated one million onlookers jammed into the area. It would be the grand finale, the spectacular high-speed parade of bright colors and spinning wheels, chased by honking cars and flashing motorcycles, and all accompanied by the din of whooping police sirens and thumping helicopters overhead.

The adrenaline surge pumped collectively through the riders. Soon, they would race through the tunnel at Quai André Citroën, past the Eiffel Tower, over the Pont de la Concorde, and then, finally, onto the Champs-Élysées....

Kurt Dufour was in the middle of the pack, surrounded by his teammates as he had been all day. They had carefully dogged Poulain and his Comtec men who, as they approached Paris, had started to launch stronger attacks. But it was futile and everyone in the pack knew now that there was no chance to spring Poulain free far enough to gain back Dufour's lead. In fact, all the squads seemed willing to block any attempt by Comtec to regain control of the race. Poulain's reign was over and even the fallen star himself seemed resigned to this fate. He had been subdued both on and off the bike since the morning and now, as his teammates made an effort to show they hadn't given up, his attempts to encourage them were halfhearted at best.

Now, and only now, for the first time in the last four hours, did Kurt Dufour begin to feel that he would make it. That he would actually see Paris as the winner of the Tour de France and that perhaps he could bask in the glory offered to him by the millions who waited to cheer the riders who had survived,—and especially him, the only one to topple the invincible Poulain. His legs turned smoothly and rapidly and, as if joined to the machine he rode, he leaned comfortably in and out of the turns, shifting his weight easily to match the curving undulation of the long line of riders as they wound their way through the last suburb.

He forced himself to concentrate on the wheels around him, to not trade that still-needed focus for thoughts of how he would throw his hands skyward at the finish line or later on the top step of the podium. Jennifer invaded his mind as well. He forced her from it, ignoring her outstretched arms in favor of the handlebars he had to hold for only a little while longer. He forced his mind into a foolish, yet calming mantra: *the victory and the girl...the victory and the girl....*

***

The broadcast team was in the booth above the Champs-Élysées, now calling the live action as the serpentine field entered the outskirts of Paris. For a moment, the scandal was forgotten as Sterling and Martin leaned into their assignment of interpreting what was on the screen. They didn't hear the phone ring. Anderson did.

"Anderson here," she snapped, annoyed at the interruption.

"Kathrine...Kathrine Anderson, *s'il vous plaît.*"

"*C'est moi.* Who the hell is this?" Interrupted during a live broadcast. The nerve.

"Guy Leguerre here."

Anderson shot upright, pressed the phone to one ear and covered the other with her hand. "Leguerre?...Where...?"

"I have not much time to speak."

"Where are you? Aren't you behind the race?" Anderson was searching her brain to figure why, from where, he called.

"I am here. I am there. It does not matter. I have no team. You must hear me."

"I hear you, I hear you. What is it?" Martin and Sterling were too intent on the screen to notice the call. Scott was gone, somewhere.

"Are you alone in this place?" The voice was distant and not altogether clear.

Anderson looked around and huddled over the phone. "Yes, what do you want, Guy?" She softened a little, hoping he would open up. Quickly.

"You tell the good story, eh? You do *la vraie histoire, n'est-ce pas?*"

"I don't speak goddam French, man! What are you trying to tell me?" She sensed he was somehow becoming incoherent and that whatever he wanted to say would be good. But why her, and what was wrong with him? They had barely spoken in three weeks.

212

"After the race, you come to Guy, eh? I know this story, Katrine. You...you, the American television bitch woman, you can tell it for me...." He drifted off.

"Guy! Guy!" Anderson tried to keep him on the line without alerting the others.

There was a long pause from the other end. Anderson shook the phone.

"I...I am still here. You come right after the finish...Hôtel Plaza Athénée for very big story...Suite 120...Okey dokey?" Leguerre chuckled, distracted by this American expression he had remembered from somewhere.

"Guy, Guy! Are you okay?" This time the shouting distracted Martin. He turned to her, angrily.

She said nothing but kept the phone pressed to her ear. Leguerre drifted off again "...it will be hell to pay and no more for me. I was fired anyway, after all the *shit* I did for them. *C'est dommage*, it's too bad for them...they don't tell me these things...." The phone went dead.

She had dropped her headphones around her neck to take the phone call and now Martin was gesturing wildly for her to put them back on. She did it just in time to hear the smooth, British accent of Phil Sterling.

"Stay tuned...we'll be back for the exciting final laps on the Champs-Élysées...."

Then the agitated voice of Arnie Campbell: "Phil! Jeff! Where the fuck is Anderson?"

***

Otto had shut down the press channel. He didn't want to hear more. Not now. And besides, the speed was picking up and he had to be alert. The crowds were huge all along the road. People were screaming and waving their arms. Were they angry at the news, or were they just cheering?

213

On either side of the car, motorcycles drifted up and back, vigilant to control the crowd and leapfrog ahead if there were problems at already sealed intersections. Otto had never seen this many coming into Paris. The organization had put more on, just in case.

He should have seen it. He should have known that one of the security motos was moving too fast, especially with the tunnel coming up. It blasted by, easily at seventy or more, on a mission to hurtle past the team cars and toward the tunnel where the riders had just entered.

They flew over an overpass to a quick right-left jog, and then into the tunnel. Suddenly, everything went crazy. The awful sound of screeching brakes and the unmistakable thumping and crunching of cars piling into each other. Otto braked hard and swerved to the left, sending the car careening sideways into the darkness of the tunnel. They bounced off something and then, miraculously, straightened and were free in the left lane. They skidded to a stop next to a twisted pile of racers and smashed cars. There was the awful din of car horns and men screaming, and more cars, plowing into the tunnel and trying to brake before they too added to the awful crunch.

Otto and Peter were out of the car almost before it came to rest. They ran to the chaotic pile of moaning racers, some trapped under cars, and some already struggling to their feet. They scrambled through the débris and, as their eyes adjusted to the dimness of the tunnel lighting, frantically searched for recognizable jerseys...bodies.

Peter Dufour stopped cold, his eyes looking in horror at the scene on the ground in front of him. He clapped his hands to his face, "Omigod, omigod...."

Otto flew past him and sank to his knees beside the two prostrate forms of John Patterson and Kurt Dufour. Patterson was moaning, his legs trapped under a car bumper. And Dufour, partly covered by Patterson, lay on his back. His eyes were closed and a trickle of blood ran from his ear down his cheek and onto his yellow jersey....

***

Chaos in the broadcast area. All pictures from the motorcycles suddenly went dead. The commentators from around the world scrambled for commercial breaks until things could be sorted out. The scene on every live monitor switched to the long, fixed-camera shot looking from the Arc de Triomphe way down the cleared and waiting Champs-Élysées toward the Place de la Concorde. The lead official motorcycles and cars swung into view, followed by a pack of twenty-or-so racers, and then clumps of riders, alone or in small groups, pounding hard to regain lost distance.

"There's been a crash! There's been a crash! In the tunnel!" Martin was glued to the monitor screen as Anderson, Scott, and Sterling nervously looked around for a clue as to what had just happened.

"From the look of the way the riders are straggling onto the Champs-Élysées, I'd say it was a pretty bad one, Jeff."

Scott, who had been frantically pounding her cell phone, hurriedly scribbled a note and shoved it in front of Martin.

"Phil, we've been unable to reach Otto Werner in the GTI team car behind the riders. I hope that doesn't mean Dufour's been involved in some kind of mishap."

Suddenly, two rows below them, the Dutch commentator, Hari Verkerk, leaped to his feet, holding a set of headphones tightly to one ear. He turned to shout the news to his fellow journalists, "Big crash in za tunnel! Big crash in za tunnel! *Dufour's down...he's hurt!*"

Sterling was on it. "We've just gotten the bad news, Jeff. Kurt Dufour has been involved in an apparently bad pileup in the tunnel, just on the other side of the river. We lost camera contact at that point and can't give any more details at this moment...."

Martin practically leaped out of his chair and yelled, pointing at the screen. "It's Poulain, Phil, *it's Poulain!*"

The entire broadcast team crowded around the monitor in horror as the high-up camera zoomed in on what was the unmistakable flying form of Jacques Poulain, leading the charge of the survivors. His Comtec teammates were strung out in a long, single line behind him, pounding for all they were worth to gain time on the disgraced, and now fallen, American.

Jennifer Scott clapped her hands to her face, numb with the growing realization of what was happening. Even the normally aloof Anderson stood in shock.

215

Only Sterling, the consummate pro, held the show together.

"It's Poulain all right, Jeff. And he's riding like a man possessed. With no sign of Dufour yet, he's assuredly taken back the lead and, I'm afraid, dashed the hopes for America...."

Suddenly the monitor switched to the darkened and chaotic tunnel. A very unsteady camera panned the chaos of smashed cars, littered bikes, and, now, the flashing lights of ambulances as white-suited men rushed to the center of the confusion. Some riders were on their feet, checking their bikes, or scrambling to remount. The camera bounced and jostled closer until it reached the last knot of people, bent and stooped over the injured on the ground. The camera pushed closer until most of those attending the fallen riders were rudely pushed aside.

"It's the yellow jersey. It's Kurt Dufour on the ground, and he doesn't seem to be moving...."

Just then, the unmistakable figure of Otto Werner rose from the ground, his face an angry grimace. He pushed at the camera and then his right fist came slamming down. The screen went black. And then, in a split-second, the picture was back on, now from the camera above the Champs-Élysées. Poulain was still riding madly at the front.

Martin was at a loss for words. Scott sobbed in horror and reached to Anderson, standing next to her, for support. Even Anderson, normally above this kind of emotional display, looked shaken.

Sterling took over again. "Poulain is clearly on the attack now. There's no question that, with Kurt Dufour down and out, the Frenchman will take his sixth Tour de France. And, as if Kurt Dufour's tragic crash with only a few kilometers to go weren't enough, there's still the unbelievable controversy that surrounds his positive drug test of last night." Sterling looked to Martin for comment.

There was none.

Sterling decided to throw the pressure back to Arnie Campbell in the edit room. "We'll be back to try and sort this out after these messages." Sterling watched the monitor fade from Poulain's long victory ride at the front of the field into the network logo. He sat in stunned silence, shaking his head in disbelief.

***

The broadcast was over. After Poulain crossed the finish line to the hysterical cheers and jeers of his countrymen, Campbell decided to cut it short, instructing Anderson to promise to come back with a replay of the closing ceremonies and a report on Dufour's condition, the latest on the doping scandal, and maybe an interview with some of Dufour's teammates. They were granted an hour from the network to sort things out....

Anderson was shouting into the phone, the only sign of energy in the stunned and spent broadcast booth.

"Arnie, Arnie! Get a crew and meet me at the Plaza Athénée, right now!" She was highly agitated.

Sterling and Martin, headsets now removed, turned to watch her, incredulous that she wanted to rush off. Scott appeared dazed. There was confusion all around them as journalists and helpers all scrambled for information about Dufour, the tunnel, anything that would shed light on the last confusing moments of the race.

"*Goddam it, Arnie*, don't ask me any more fuckin' questions! I'm telling you there's a story at that hotel and I'm the only one that knows about it! I did what you said, Arnie...now you do this for me! Get the fuckin' crew and meet me there, in the lobby, *right now!*" Anderson slammed down the phone and, for the first time during the conversation, looked at the others.

"Anybody know where's the Plaza Athénée?"

"What's doing there?" Sterling's interest was now aroused. He stood up to block Anderson from rushing off.

"Arnie says we have to file another report within the hour. Guy Leguerre called me with some kind of tip. He sounded weird, like he knew something." She tried to push her way by him. "I'm going to check it out."

217

Martin leaped to his feet, panicked. "What about Kurt? We have to find out what happened to him!"

The phone rang. Scott, nearest, picked it up. She spoke between pauses, fighting to stay in control of herself, to force the image of him lying still in the tunnel from her mind. He would be all right, he *had* to be all right.

"Okay. Right. They're on their way." She hung up the phone and turned to them. "Arnie wants you three to go to the hotel, it's on Montaigne, just around the corner. You'll do the next report from there. I'll stay here just in case there's any news. Keep your phone on."

Scott struggled to stay focused on the job at hand, to keep from thinking the worst. She turned away and motioned for them to go, to leave her there alone.

Anderson hesitated and gently, firmly, placed a hand on Scott's shoulder. She forced her to turn back toward them. "Jenny...give me the letter."

The letter. She looked blankly at Anderson and then past her to Martin and Sterling, both of whom watched her intently. The words came to her...*"you will know when it may be needed"*.... Sterling, expressionless, nodded slightly.

Anderson held out her hand. "Now's the time Jenny. We need the letter. You'll have to trust me."

Give the letter to Anderson? It was what they all had feared. But now...everything had changed. What difference would it make?

Scott reached into her pants pocket and drew out the two crumpled papers. She gave Anderson a detached, resigned look and then handed her the longer, neatly typed letter from Kurt Dufour. She carefully folded her own note from him and slipped it into the front of her blouse.

Sterling patted her gently on the back and then all three were gone. Scott slumped over the phone and fought to hold back the tears. All she could think of was the image of him lying in that tunnel...so still....

They all arrived at once, past the canopied red windows, through the plushy carpeted and oak-paneled lobby, toward the elevators. Wayne with his big camera, cable-connected soundman, and producer Arnie Campbell had tried to push past a concerned-looking concierge, winking and telling him there was an important person upstairs to be interviewed for American television, related to the Kurt Dufour story, they managed to say in broken French.

At first, the concierge, formally dressed and appearing quite official, was affronted by the way they tried to get by him, obviously a threat to the five-star hotel's discreet, and often hounded, high-profile guests. But the three TV personalities in blue blazers behind them were part of the team and, since they were dressed more appropriately for the Plaza Athénée and looked very official, they gave credibility to the scruffy-looking crew.

Their Tour de France media credentials seemed in order and a check with the front desk verified that someone in Suite 120, occupied as part of the room block reserved by Comtec Internationale, had indeed called down to say that an American television crew was coming to tape an interview. The concierge quickly changed demeanor, bowed politely, and motioned them to the elevator.

***

Jennifer Scott sat alone in the broadcast booth high above the finish line on the Champs-Élysées. She stared, with tears running down her face, at the television monitor in front of her, watching but not believing the picture being fed around the world. Jacques Poulain on the top step of the winner's podium, now in the yellow jersey that had suddenly become his to keep, holding high an enormous bouquet of flowers and surrounded by grim-looking officials and flanked by one dark and portly man who grinned wickedly—Jérôme Garnier. She blinked to clear her eyes, to carefully watch the close-up of these despicable people who were being honored for capitalizing on Kurt Dufour's misfortune. Poulain was jubilant, full of himself, and smiling and winking at the people below him as if he, and he alone, deserved this honor. It made her stomach turn.

She looked up from the monitor to see how the other journalists were reacting. Only the two French booths down below still appeared live and covering the full awards presentation. Everything else was in disruption with staff and commentators scrambling for news from the tunnel, from the drug-testing lab, from anywhere. This would not be a clean wrap. She expected the news and rumors to filter in for hours as all the networks and print journalists vied for breaking stories. They would have to stay with this now all night, maybe for days, as the twisted events slowly came together.

The phone rang, startling her.

"Jenny...Jenny?" It was Campbell calling from the Plaza Athénée.

"We're stuck here, Jenny, 'til someone else arrives. It's pretty grim. We're going to tape a two-minute update and have it run over to the truck. We should just make the next uplink...."

"What about Kurt?" Her voice sounded strange, even to her. "Nobody's called here."

"He's been taken to the hospital." There was a pause as Campbell said something off the phone. He came back. "Listen, Jenny. Are you okay?"

"I'm somewhat coherent." She felt far away.

"Jenny, go to the hospital. We'll do our next update from there as soon as we finish here with Leguerre...."

Something awakened in Scott. "How is he, Arnie?"

There was confusion in the background. Campbell left and then returned.

"Jesus Christ...I think he's dead."

A shot ran through her and her head started to spin, causing her to slump over the table and drop the phone. And then the spreading numbness of shocked disbelief. She started trembling. It couldn't be...it couldn't be.

"Jenny! Jenny!" The phone next to her ear shouted at her.

She slowly slid it toward her mouth. "Arnie...?"

220

"Jesus fucking Christ, Jenny! *Leguerre*...we think *Leguerre's* dead!"

"Leguerre's dead?" She didn't comprehend.

"We *think* he's dead. We're pretty sure Dufour's *alive*. Jenny? Jenny?"

Alive. *Alive?* Her senses slowly returned. She didn't know whether to laugh or cry.

"Jenny, Jenny?"

"I'm here. Barely."

"Jenny, I'm sorry lady." He tried to make his voice sound soothing. "I didn't mean to scare you like that."

"I'm still scared." She straightened up and held the phone tightly with both hands. "How's Kurt?"

"All we know is that he's alive and he's been taken to Saint-Périne hospital by Place de Barcelona. There's cabs in front of the hotel here, right around the corner. They'll know where it is. Come get one and go there now...Jenny?

"I'm here. I heard you."

"Jenny, listen to me. Find a cop and tell him to get some men over to Suite 120, Plaza Athénée. We'll meet you at the hospital in a few minutes." He hung up.

Still trembling, she threw the cell phone in her bag and left, on weak knees, to find a gendarme and then a cab.

***

His practiced kick had landed squarely, and the ensuing panic and colliding bikes and cars told Donald Conway, *Sécurité Spécial Moto 32*, that his aim was true.

As soon as he could, he whipped the bike around, noting that the dimmer lighting of the tunnel would add to the confusion, leaving a good chance that his blow went undetected. Within seconds, he was heading back in the other direction, taking the opposite lane so he could observe the damage and be free to do his job. No one seemed to notice as he cruised slowly by the pile of panicked men, bikes and cars, noting wryly that most seemed intent on getting back in the race with no concern for the fallen hero.

For a kilometer or so after he headed back on the still-closed roadway, he did, as a reinforcement driver, what he had been told to do—warn any stragglers or following vehicles to slow down and watch for danger ahead. Two other security motorcycles were doing the same thing, and with nods of heads and hand motions, the three shared these responsibilities until the broom wagon and the last gendarmes appeared, marking the tail end of the race caravan. At that point, they wheeled again with the unspoken mission of getting back to the crash where more marshaling help would certainly be needed.

Conway lagged back. When he spotted the sign for *Pont d'Issy*, he guided the bike between the temporary barricades, wheeled off the course and accelerated over the bridge, quickly leaving the Tour de France and the havoc he had created behind.

He had his escape route down cold and, within minutes, turned off St. Cloud and slowly cruised into the parking lot of the Parc des Princes soccer stadium, heading toward the north end where he spotted the Mercedes coupe.

All according to plan. Conway smiled at their efficiency. He pulled beside the car and removed his helmet just as his new friend and accomplice, Heinrich Kemptka, got out.

Kemptka greeted him with a sinister, clenched-teeth smile that Conway interpreted as pleasure with the mission that had just been accomplished. He was wearing a pair of sunglasses with small round lenses and when Conway tried to make eye contact, he could only see his own reflection.

"Vell?" Kemptka asked. Despite the dark lenses, it was obvious that the German's gaze was moving, instinctively checking for any possible observers to their rendezvous.

"I knocked the little fucker out of the race. He went down easy." Conway was wild-eyed and flush with triumph, and his wavy white hair was wet with perspiration and stuck to his forehead.

For the first time, Kemptka leveled his gaze directly at Conway. "Sehr gut, you haf done za job vell...."

As he spoke, Heinrich Kemptka raised the long silencer to Conway's forehead and, before Conway could fathom what was happening, squeezed the trigger....

***

Bright lights flooded the hallway outside the door to Suite 120 of one of Paris's finest hotels, the Plaza Athénée. Katherine Anderson, mike in hand, stood in front of the partially opened doorway through which the camera revealed an oak-paneled sitting room, furnished in exquisite Louis XV rosewood.

Arnie Campbell was in charge. It was unusual for him to be unsure of what to do, but he was. This was not your usual news story. There was no one there but them, and a lot of questions about the unmoving body they had discovered. He hesitated.

Anderson didn't. She sensed the reluctance of both Arnie and Phil to start shooting, but she wanted this story and she wanted it bad.

"Jesus Christ, Arnie. We can't wait for the cops. Just stay back from the body." She glanced at Sterling, seeking support. He was looking through the open door, dumbfounded.

"You didn't disturb anything in there did you?" Campbell was starting to come around. "...didn't touch anything?"

"Nope." She shook her head and instinctively pushed the small envelope she had found on the floor next to the body deeper into her jacket pocket, careful to not put it in the same place as Dufour's letter.

Campbell looked searchingly at Sterling, who only shrugged.

Anderson swept them into it. "Let's record this. We've got a story here, boys. We didn't do anything wrong. We got a call, and we're here. It's all ours. Roll tape, Wayne."

223

She quickly moved them into position outside the partially open door. With no resistance, they took the assigned places, Campbell behind the camera just in case he decided to direct.

Anderson, flanked by Sterling, spoke into the camera. "It's been less than an hour since the Tour de France concluded on the Champs-Élysées just a few blocks from here, but already the controversy surrounding the results of that race have taken another bizarre twist."

She held up a piece of paper and continued. "Just hours ago, we were the first to obtain this letter from race leader Kurt Dufour, written *before* yesterday's time trial. In it, he reveals that he was offered a substantial amount of money to throw the race and thus assure victory for the Frenchman, Jacques Poulain."

She lowered the paper and paused dramatically. "And now, as Kurt Dufour lies severely injured in a hospital bed and Jacques Poulain has been awarded the victory, we discover that one of the men named in Dufour's letter, Poulain's team manager, Guy Leguerre, now appears dead...apparently from a drug overdose taken in this hotel suite...." She turned sideways and brought Phil Sterling into the picture. "Phil, what's your reaction to this bizarre turn of events?"

"Well, Katherine, it's a sad day, indeed, for professional cycling. In twenty years of covering the Tour de France and cycling races all over the world, I must say there has never been a story quite like this."

He stopped and shook his head, lowering the mike to his side. Wayne looked up but didn't shut the camera down. Sterling added, "This isn't right. We should wait for the gendarmes." He looked to Arnie for support.

Anderson exploded and pushed Sterling aside. "Goddamit, keep shooting Wayne! If you guys are too fucking scared, I'll do it! We've got to record this!"

Wayne, experienced cameraman that he was, never hesitated. He swung his camera and focused tightly on Anderson. She had instantly transformed herself into calm reporter.

"Kurt Dufour, the brilliant young American, raced courageously throughout the Tour, refusing to give in to Poulain and then, apparently, when offered a nine-million-dollar deal by his biggest rival to throw the race, refused that as well. Of course, we all know by now, he suffered a bad crash only kilometers from victory today and, as we speak, lies critically injured in the hospital.

"But the story doesn't end there and, as if to make this case even more bizarre, we all heard earlier today that Dufour was strangely named one of nine riders who supposedly used the banned substance, EPO."

As she talked, she moved toward the hotel suite door, pushing it open wider so the camera could look within. Sterling and Campbell were transfixed and didn't interfere.

"And now this...." The camera lens probed the room, following the harsh light that stabbed through the outer sitting room and then into another doorway to reveal the bedroom's gold-satin-and-peach walls and the prostrate form of Guy Leguerre, stretched serene and lifeless on the still-made bed.

"The strange and sudden death of the Comtec team director, Guy Leguerre."

The camera turned back to Anderson. She faced the lens squarely, her straight blonde hair and hardened expression presenting the perfect image of a responsible, hard-working journalist. Her Emmy was about to be earned, the second-rate American reporter in Paris who followed her instincts to blow open one of the biggest scandals in sport....

Her voice was calm and dramatic, "Accusations of doping....A serious accident just moments from the finish, the hero in the hospital, and the villain on the podium...And now, a dead team director implicated with them all in a bribery scandal that rocks the foundation of this sport, perhaps of all sports." The camera closed tighter on her face. "The Tour de France may have finished, but serious questions about *how* it finished are just beginning. We'll be back with more...."

Wayne cut the lights and stopped shooting. Arnie Campbell shook his head at Anderson in awed disbelief, pausing them all for a moment. Then, coming to his senses, he grabbed the camera from Wayne's shoulder, quickly removed the videotape and handed it to the crewman standing in the hall. "Get this to the truck and up to the bird instantly! And use the back stairs," he demanded.

They all heard the growing sound of sirens outside.

With tape in hand, the technician ran down the hall in the opposite direction of the elevator. He disappeared through the exit door just as the elevator opened, spilling a half dozen gendarmes into the hallway. In a split second, another elevator opened and out tumbled an unruly mob of reporters and cameramen, each intent on being the first to cover what the Americans were already running to feed in New York.

***

"I finally got through to New York." Arnie Campbell announced this as he sank into the upholstered leather bench seat on one side of the pleasing and private booth occupied by Phil Sterling and Jeff Martin. Campbell sighed, leaned back, and closed his eyes, finally acknowledging the exhaustion brought upon by the highest stress he had experienced as a line producer in many years.

It was past midnight and the three had agreed to meet after it was all over back at the Plaza Athénée in its English Bar, the clubby, mahogany-paneled watering hole that usually hosted any number of after-hour celebrities, musicians and socially elite. Tonight, the last Sunday in July, it was quiet.

"What'd they say?" Martin was as much drunk as he was tired, having come from the hospital an hour before. He slid a full pint of beer in front of Campbell. Sterling, just arrived from a BBC meeting, was already halfway through his.

"They're sending replacements...news guys. Sports is out of here tomorrow as scheduled." Campbell looked at them both, then smiled grimly and raised his glass. "Here's to the bitch. They loved her piece and they want her to stay on the scene here, as principal correspondent."

Sterling shook his head without returning the smile. He clinked his glass to Campbell's. "Reckon that's a good choice. She'll love it now, won't she?" They held their glasses up, waiting for Martin to join the toast.

"C'mon now, mate," Sterling said to Martin, who was staring at nothing in particular, both hands wrapped around his beer. "Raise your

226

glass and move on. The race is over. We'll go round to see the boy before we leave."

"He's still unconscious," Martin said.

Campbell and Sterling put their glasses down without drinking. They exchanged glances and then waited for Martin, who had stayed at the hospital the longest after they had done their final report, to continue.

"Jennifer's a basket case, the old man's beside himself, and Otto's ready to kill somebody." Martin looked earnestly at both of them. "This sucks," he said. He picked up his nearly full glass and drained it in one long gulp.

"You're dead right on that one, mate," Sterling said. He spoke as if his thoughts were somewhere else, shaking his head sadly.

"Phil...." Martin's eyes probed into Sterling's and waited until the Englishman met his gaze. "...this bullshit with Kurt doing EPO...."

Sterling raised his hand, cutting him short. Campbell was paying close attention.

"Dirty bloody business it is, now, isn't it?" Sterling said. "I reckon somebody in Garnier's camp switched the samples, it wouldn't be the first time. The bloody bastards had it all figured out. Caused the crash too—according to one of the drivers, anyway. Bastards figured they'd get him one way or the other...."

They sat in silence for a moment, each in their own thoughts, trying to make sense of it.

"So who's going to nail this guy?" Martin asked.

Sterling looked at Martin then at Campbell. "We're all out of here now, right Arnie? I reckon that leaves the woman now, doesn't it?" He raised his glass to his lips, looking at the beer, and not suggesting anything different.

"I'm afraid you're right," Campbell said.

Sterling looked at them both and smiled. "Reckon she'll get to the bottom of it all right. It's her mission, isn't it?" He paused for dramatic effect, pulling them both in. "Besides, she copped a note from the floor next to Leguerre's body. I reckon that'll be the key, along with Dufour's tell-all letter about that scum Garnier; she now has that one too...."

Campbell's eyes widened as this sunk in. The disbelieving look on Martin's face indicated he'd known nothing of a second note found next to Leguerre's body. After a moment, Campbell spoke for them both. "I knew she went too far. She's got to turn all this in, Phil. For sure, it's crucial evidence. You should've taken it from her."

Sterling shook his head slowly, as if he'd already thought this through.

"I reckon none of us saw Leguerre's note, eh? Let her run with it, Arnie. She's the only one who holds all the cards now. If anyone can piece together the whole story, it'll be her."

****

Chapter Nineteen

Return

He felt better today. The October sun was warm, and the green Adirondack chair in which he sat was turned just right so the warmth touched his face and actually made him feel hot. Later, he'd be able to take his jacket off.

He gazed out over the small tranquil lake and remembered the summer days long ago when he and his sister and cousins played on the little sandy beach. They used to love to paddle a couple of the old aluminum canoes to the other side, where they could play on the rope swing. If you pushed hard from the high bank, it was possible to sail way out and drop into the cold, clear water, far enough from the shore that you wouldn't hit bottom.

He smiled at the memory, those days when the Dufour family came up here, to their little lake in Vermont, to get away from the bustle of Greenwich. Before high school, before Dartmouth, before bike racing.

He looked around at the orange, green, and crimson foliage that covered the hillside to his right and the maple and aspens on the far bank that spread around to the Dufour home site, the one on the south bank that was meant for him when he grew up and decided to have his own family. They were right to send him here to recover. The memories were strong. The roots ran deep.

His headaches were gone now and the painful wounds long since healed. They said he had taken a bad blow to the head that resulted in post-traumatic amnesia. Supposedly, that's why he could remember all of this, why he could remember his team and his teammates, the dead girl, the trial, but not a disconcerting period after his brilliant ride in the Tour of Italy. He always wanted a shot at the Tour de France, but when they told him he was winning it when this happened....

He just couldn't remember. They said it should gradually come back, or maybe in big chunks, triggered by something or someone after his brain had completed the slow process of knitting itself back together. He had been given articles to read, watched video replays, talked to family and friends...but still the things he watched and the stories they recounted remained a strange disconnect. He recognized himself but he didn't remember the events. It had become too hard to deal with. His doctor, his parents, all agreed that the best way to recover was to get away from it all, to go somewhere where the memories were from a simpler time long ago, where there wouldn't be constant calls from people who knew him, or said they knew him, so he wouldn't get distressed over not being able to recognize them or share their memories of things, some of which he had a hard time believing could happen at all...drugs, payoffs, deaths...he almost thought they were playing a cruel joke on him.

He thought of the young dark-haired woman, the TV person who, in the small Paris hospital room, looked deep into his eyes, trying to pull something from him he didn't share. She had hung around for a long time, coming in to talk, to bring him something to drink, to repeat stories he was supposed to know. He felt something for her but whatever it was, it wasn't in his soul the way it was in hers. And it depressed him when he saw how she tried not to hurt when he couldn't respond the way she expected. She tried not to cry when he left Paris for Vermont. But he knew she had, and it upset him.

He leaned back and closed his eyes to again start the slow, meticulous process of trying to merge what he had heard with what he knew. Within five minutes, he had fallen into a deep sleep. He didn't hear the car stop at the top of the hill, nor did he wake up until the car's occupants had unloaded the bikes and brought them down to the little beach.

"'Ey, mate, time to wake up. It's a bloody good afternoon for an easy roll."

Dufour opened his eyes and recognized Patterson and Berclaz, dressed in their GTI cycling clothes, and with three bikes lying in the grass nearby.

Patterson blocked the sun with his face, smiling down at his teammate. "It's me first time back on the bike mate, and I figure we oughta go together. Berclaz, 'ere, says 'e'll tag along, just ta make sure we don't get lost."

Kurt smiled, a strong urge passing through him, an urge that he hadn't felt since before this all happened. He wanted things to turn back to normal, whatever that meant.

"How did you find me?" He had seen them both over the last several months, Patterson at first in the hospital in Paris, and Berclaz as a visitor in between late-season races. They had both come back to the States in September and they had all spoken on the phone. For Kurt, the conversations had been mostly embarrassing because they invariably turned to incidents they had supposedly shared but he couldn't remember.

"Your old man gave us directions. He figured by now you might want to get back on the bike. Who better to start back with than your old teammates?" Berclaz held up his hands. "No pressure, of course."

Kurt had come to Vermont purposely without a bike in spite of everyone's insistence that it would be good for him to ride again. Until his full memory came back, if it would ever come back, he was afraid. They all said he wouldn't have lost the skill, and even he knew his superb conditioning wouldn't be completely gone after only a few months. But still, he didn't want to get on until he felt like he could handle it either way.

Maybe it was seeing Patterson that changed his mind. He saw in the Australian's eyes the same fear, the fear that after the injuries he had sustained there was a good chance he would never be the same again.

"Let's 'ave a go, mate. I reckon I'm game if you be." He gave a nervous smile, and Kurt sensed there was a certain pleading there too.

"I don't have any gear," Kurt said. He looked at the bike lying on the grass and knew that to ride it properly he would need shoes, tights, jersey, and a couple of thin layers for the slight chill in the air.

"No worries, mate." Patterson dropped a canvas bag in Kurt's lap. "It's all 'ere."

Berclaz winked. "C'mon, Kurt, it's a beautiful day and we can do a nice easy ride. The local bike shop guy says there's a nice loop from here to Tunbridge and over the South Strafford hill, an hour and a half, easy. We got a map." He held it toward Kurt as if offering proof that they had gone to great pains for this.

231

Dufour looked at the bike and then at the attentive faces of both Patterson and Berclaz. He zipped open the bag and pulled out the contents: his racing shoes, some leg warmers, and a pair of team shorts, undervest, and lastly, a long-sleeved *maillot jaune*. He looked at Patterson, quizzically.

The Australian shrugged. "Ya may not remember, mate, but it's yours. Besides, it's all we could come up with."

Rather than question the motives, Dufour stood and motioned the others up the hill to the guest cottage where he was staying. "We can change up there," he said.

Within fifteen minutes, they were on the road, the three teammates coasting gingerly down the dirt access road and then down the paved hill to Sharon where the ride would really start.

It was a beautiful New England fall afternoon. The air was warm and still, and the roads they pedaled had little traffic. They rode easily, spinning smoothly with a learned cadence that only men with thousands of miles in their legs could master. For Dufour and Patterson, even though they hadn't been in the saddle for months, the feeling was both natural and therapeutic. They pedaled side by side in silence, with Berclaz tucked behind, letting the physical act of being back on their bikes speak to them in ways that no words could.

Dufour's mind began to work, again probing the memories he still had from the bike.

"Hey, John, remember the first Rumorosa Cruise?" He smiled and turned to Patterson.

"Bloody 'ell, mate. We thought you was fuckin' crazy, takin' off like that. Reckon we 'ad to spank ya when we saw the scarecrow ya'd laid on the side a the road." He smiled and shook his head.

They rode on in silence, each recalling to themselves these and other experiences they had shared. After about an hour, Kurt's legs had begun to loosen up, to begin to feel like they had some power, even though it had been a long time and top form faded fast. They turned right and began the long climb out of Tunbridge toward Strafford. Berclaz moved easily in front of them, pedaling steadily but setting a

232

pace that was neither too easy nor too hard. Dufour and Patterson got into a rhythm, sitting back on their saddles, and spinning the low gears required to handle the hill's steepness. The sweat began to flow and it felt good. Soon they were over the top and picking up speed down the other side, shifting into bigger gears, and feeling the rush of the warm fall air.

Instinctively, they formed a single pace line when the road leveled and curved its undulating way through the Strafford Valley past open meadows and fenced horse paddocks. They were going faster now, spurred on by the day and their eagerness to feel the speed, and the need to put muscle into pedals again. Twenty-five smooth hard strokes and then a slight pause, letting the man behind come through to break the wind. It came back naturally.

Dufour knew the road and that they would take a right by the church to begin the three-mile climb up Strafford Hill. As they approached the intersection, Kurt spoke to them both. "Right turn up here then it's three miles to the summit. Road gets steeper near the top."

Berclaz smiled and put his hand on Dufour's shoulder as they rounded the turn. "I talked to that local bike shop guy. He said some hotshot around here has made it from the church to the summit in ten-thirty." He winked and pushed the timer button on his handlebar computer. "Let's go."

Instinct ruled. There was no protest, no hesitation, and no excuses. Berclaz easily took the lead and upped his gear despite the increasing slope. They were moving faster now, Dufour comfortably on Berclaz's wheel and Patterson, already starting to struggle, trying to hold Dufour.

Within a mile, Patterson was off the back. The road got steeper, and yet Berclaz increased the tempo. Dufour was beginning to hurt...the familiar pain was coming back and rather than surrender to it, he wanted it. He instinctively ran through the ingrained techniques: deep, steady breathing; slide back slightly on the saddle; hands on the tops; and drive the pedals around smoothly, from the hips, with every ounce of power. Concentrate on the wheel in front. Up and up. He watched Berclaz's hips, the familiar shape of his sculptured calves, the slight shudder of his shoulders as he, too, began to lay out everything he had. They climbed fast now, at a tempo few men in the world could match.

Suddenly, Dufour's mind snapped. There were people, thousands of people, lining the road and screaming his name. Chopper rotors thumped high above and he, Berclaz, and a brace of motorcycles were ripping through deafening walls of people and horns and shouting. He felt the power surge through him, and he knew this was the moment, the final all-out effort he was compelled to make. The road became steeper, only a few clicks to go. He shouted, desperately: *"Allez, Claude! Allez! Allez! Allez!"* and powered up to Berclaz, *coude à coude*, elbow to elbow, to where they could see each other's faces.

Berclaz was soaked with sweat and a white residue appeared at the corners of his mouth. It was a hot day in the Alps and the loyal teammate had done his job. He clenched his teeth and, with every bit of passion he could summon, looked into the face of his team leader, noting the wild eyes and the now recognizable expression of determination to lay it all out. *"You're a minute up! You've got the fuckin' jersey...now keep it!"* The words were all that was needed.

There, in the last five hundred meters of Stratford Hill, watched only by some cows and a lazily circling hawk, Kurt Dufour in the *maillot jaune* and driven by fresh memory, gradually pulled away from his teammate, powering his way up the steep slope to the summit...back, finally, from the darkness.

***

He rocked himself back and forth on the side of the road, his chest still heaving from the effort and his head in his hands. His bike, dropped at the summit, lay by his side in the tall grass. It had all come back in one overwhelming rush...the day on L'Alpe d'Huez, the deal with Garnier, the drugs, the time trial, the double cross, the Paris skyline, Otto, Ramos...Jennifer.... It felt like his head was exploding.

He was oblivious as his two teammates rolled up and now stood watching him. As his breathing slowed, he let his mind explore the locked room that suddenly, inexplicably opened, recalling deliberately and step by step, all the things that had happened from the day he arrived in France. It took quite a few minutes sitting numbly in the grass, his head in his hands. Without realizing it, he was mumbling to himself.

"Reckon 'e's gone postal on us, Claudie."

"Look at this...." Berclaz pointed to his handlebar computer. "Shattered the record by fifty seconds, took the jersey, and then *pfft!*" He made a circular motion around his ear as if Dufour was crazy.

The two stood over their leader, blocking the sun when he finally forced himself to look up. "Holy shit", he said as he finally collected himself enough to speak. "It's all come back. I remember everything...I think." He wiped his forehead and, eyes closed, flopped on his back next to his bike. Then, silently, a line of tears began its way down his face.

There was awkward silence from the two riders who stood over him. They shifted from one foot to another. Finally, Berclaz cleared his throat.

"You haven't forgotten how to climb," he said.

The two dropped their bikes and sat on the grass next to him.

Kurt lay there, eyes tightly closed, for several more minutes. Finally, he took a deep breath and sat up. The tears had stopped, and sweat from the fast climb soaked through his yellow jersey. He wiped his eyes.

"How did I crash in Paris? I don't remember the tunnel," he said without emotion.

Berclaz and Patterson exchanged looks. "Sure you're ready for this? Your doc says not too much all at once," Berclaz said.

"Fuck the doctor. How'd I crash in Paris? I still don't remember any of that. I don't remember going into the tunnel." He looked hard at each of them.

"Garnier copped a goon, put 'im on a security moto to take ya out." Patterson pulled a long piece of grass and put it in his mouth before continuing. This had not been revealed to Kurt as yet, and Patterson seemed to be the one designated to let it out. "Far as anyone knows, 'e kicked your bars when it got dark in the tunnel. Did the job, no worries." Patterson rubbed a nasty scar on his left knee.

"They found the moto driver later," Berclaz said, "with a bullet in his brain. An American, no less."

"An American?" Dufour was incredulous.

"Reckon ya'd met before...'is name was Donald Conway." Patterson watched closely for the reaction.

The news sunk in slowly. Conway, the sick father who's sinister, half-crazed threat still burned clear in his mind.

"How did...." Dufour stopped himself. He didn't want to know anymore. The bastard was gone. Chapter closed.

"Birds of a feather...somehow Conway and Garnier found each other...." Berclaz assumed Dufour wanted to hear more but stopped when Kurt held up his hand.

"What happened to Garnier?" He wasn't sure about the letter and what that had done. He suspected that many of the grisly details hadn't been revealed to him during his convalescence. There were still loops to close.

Patterson cleared his throat and looked skyward to find the right words. "Well, mate, it's like this. The driver, Conway, 'e was wasted."

"You just told me that. No loss."

"Yeah, right. Well, ya see, Leguerre, he didn't seem to be in on it, least not all of it. The payoff deal, now that was in your letter, so 'e was part of that, no worries. But the whole thing about the positive dope test on ya, now that was news to 'im...." He watched Kurt's face register confusion, then looked quickly at Berclaz.

Berclaz took over. "You saw the reports, the accusations that you had taken EPO, that your piss test was positive, and that eventually they proved that your sample had been switched with Poulain's?"

Kurt nodded. He'd been given some of the articles about the unbelievable aftermath to jog his memory, stories with him as a central character but, until now, seemingly about someone else. For the first time on his own, he recalled the most painful truth. "The bastard got DQ'd and the jersey eventually went to Chimello...and I was lying in the hospital."

"'at's right, mate. Most bizarre bloody Tour finish in 'istory…certain winner crunched with less than an hour to go, big-time French champion finally caught on chemistry after *his* DNA matched *your* sample. Finally fucked, fair an' square."

Berclaz continued, "Well, before anyone knew there'd been a switch, Leguerre must've suspected, or knew, or something, because he told Katherine Anderson to come to his hotel—and you know they found him dead of some sort of poison. Nobody knows who did it."

Kurt looked from one to the other, wondering if they knew more.

Patterson responded. "Some figure 'e did it 'isself. I reckon it was the Kraut, ya know the little bastard who was supplyin' the soigneurs with the latest juice from Comtec. 'e 'as a drug for everything…go fast…die slow, whatever suits the need."

Kurt nodded slowly. He was recalling the conversation he'd had with Patterson the morning of the time trial.

"Nobody knows for sure," Berclaz said. "It's still a big mystery. What Leguerre was doing in the hotel room before the race finished, why there was no evidence of a struggle…. Apparently, the TV lady got a call from him just before the race entered Paris."

Dufour held up his hand. Suddenly, he didn't want to hear any more of the sordid details. Again, he laid back in the grass, closing his eyes to the lowering sun and the lengthening shadows of the late-October afternoon. France and the Tour were part of his own memory now, a faraway distant memory that he could recall but that somehow still didn't seem real.

He wanted to see Jenny. He searched his mind for her, recalling their conversations now, remembering the first time he had met her in the hotel in Angers, and the stirring she had caused in him even then. And he remembered her by his side on L'Alpe d'Huez and their clinging, long-awaited embrace at Château de Vougeot. How it must have hurt her to see what happened to him, to be at his hospital bedside when he couldn't remember her, when he couldn't feel the emotion that now made him want her.

"What about Jenny? Where is she?" Kurt's eyes were still closed, and he offered the question to his silent friends as if it was merely part of the memory puzzle he was reconstructing.

Patterson sensed what was going through his mind and he wanted to say it right. "She was pretty busted up, mate. Came back to New York and quit the network, just like that." He glanced at Berclaz. "Rumor 'as it she took some other job and left the country."

"Where?" Kurt didn't move.

Berclaz stirred and cleared his throat. "I heard she met some guy after the Tour who offered her a job leading bike tours."

"Bike tours? You've got to be kidding." Dufour sat up and looked at them both. "Where?"

"It's one of those luxury tour groups. Bunch of wealthy people ride for a few miles and then stuff themselves with gourmet food and fine wines. Italy, Greece, France…who the hell knows?"

"She just left?" The returned memory made it painful.

"Ya didn't recognize 'er, mate. She's a sheila…she was so bonkers over ya that she couldn't deal with ya forgettin' 'er. Plus, the whole Tour was too much for 'er. I told 'er you'd probably someday remember again…."

"I can imagine what you told her."

"Yeah, well I told 'er if she'd give ya a root, ya'd probably get yer memory back, or at least pretend to." Patterson grinned. "I even told 'er I'd pretend I was you for a while, just to keep 'er around…."

"Thanks, pal. Obviously that didn't work."

They slowly got to their feet and picked their bikes off the ground. The sun was low and the air was rapidly getting chillier. It was time to ride the few miles back to the lake and the warmth of the cabin.

And for the first time in a long while, Kurt was thinking about what was next.

****

Chapter 20

The Show

"Well find him, for chrissake." Katherine Anderson slammed down the phone and reached for her pack of cigarettes. She started to take one then pushed them away. There was no smoking allowed anywhere in the network's New York building, including her small office on the thirty-fifth floor. It would take her ten minutes to get down to the street, time she didn't want to take right now.

"Fucking Australia." She muttered this to herself and then swung her chair sideways so she could look out the window. She gazed down on Sixth Avenue and noted the overcast November sky and wet pavement far below. There was a sea of traffic in the street and hundreds of umbrellas bobbing along the sidewalks. A miserable day that matched her mood.

The phone rang again and she swung back, pouncing on it before it could ring a second time.

"Who is it?"

"Jesus, Katherine, can't you say hello first?" It was the unmistakable voice of Arnie Campbell, calling from sports two floors below.

"Arnie, get your ass off the phone unless you can tell me how I can reach Otto Werner. What the hell is he doing in Australia anyway?"

There was a chuckle from the other end. "Don't you know that I would only call if it was to help you?"

Anderson softened somewhat. Arnie Campbell had gone to bat for her after her stories from Paris on the Tour. They were a good bet for a news Emmy and he would get credit as the producer, even though it was not the way he'd like to win one. He wanted to help her wrap it up.

"You know how I can reach him?" She leaned forward toward the phone, very interested in the response.

"Well, not exactly. But I did speak to Jeff Martin. Otto's recruiting some new riders down there."

At the mention of Martin's name, Anderson flushed. She was glad Campbell wasn't in her office. It was just a summer fling with a good-looking sports guy. She had her own show now and needed to be connected with more important men.

Campbell continued. "He's with an agent. Apparently they're traveling around to races."

"So, he must have a cell phone." Anderson was getting more exasperated. She couldn't wait a week. Her show outline was due in three days and she had to be sure she could line them all up. She had Phil Sterling and at least one of Dufour's teammates confirmed. Kurt himself had consented to appear on the show, although somewhat hesitantly. Otto was the missing link she needed, the one colorful person who could comment on every side.

"Hey, this is a favor," Campbell said. "I've got my own shows to prepare." In the winter season, he oversaw the network's weekly anthology shows on football, basketball, and hockey, offering little time for anything else. Even so, he had a special feeling for last summer's Tour de France assignment and had kept in touch with Jeff Martin and Phil Sterling. They had all stayed keenly interested in Dufour's recovery and the aftermath of the still unfolding story of drugs and payoffs.

He changed the subject. "So, do you have enough for your premiere?"

"I want the Tour piece to be the lead segment. We also have a great story on how the tennis players fix their exhibition matches and a fun one on the male groupies who follow the women's national soccer team around." She grinned into the phone, knowing that Campbell didn't approve of her formula for success...probing the dark side of the sports he loved to legitimately cover.

"Sorry I asked."

"Listen, if you can give me a good lead, I'll put a PA on it. We've got to track him down within the next thirty-six hours or I lose the biggest part of my story."

"Which is?" Campbell could only imagine what she had in mind to launch her new show. The network had named it *Controversy: Sports Behind the Lines,* a weekly half-hour tabloid show that was to be pure Anderson.

"American hero robbed of his victory and his memory. French hero DQ'd for drugs. Wonder boy gets his memory back and has to decide what's next. We connect them on the show and fill in all the amazing, sordid details, including incriminating Jérôme Garnier for drug trafficking and trying to buy the race."

"But the only witness to the payoff deal was Leguerre, and he's dead." The memory of the hotel room, the dead body, and Katherine's single-minded push to get a story flashed through Campbell's mind.

"Yeah, but I got the note he wrote just before he died. Found it on the floor in his room." She smiled in triumph into the phone, giving Campbell just enough to suck him in.

There was silence, then slowly from Campbell. "Sterling thought you'd picked something up, you know."

"Phil's no dummy." Anderson loved linking herself to the best in the business, especially when their story angles were considered accurate, straight reporting while hers always had a certain taint to them.

"What did it say?"

"Oh, just that Garnier was masterminding the drug thing, Poulain was a fraud, and how it all came down. We gave it to the French authorities in exchange for following the arrests." She had Arnie drooling for more.

"Did they get Garnier?"

"The gendarmes always get their man. Watch the show Arnie."

"You're killing me, Katherine. Leguerre's note crucifies Garnier and reveals Poulain as a doper, but did it say how they switched the blood samples? What slimeball made that happen? It certainly wasn't Leguerre."

Anderson drummed her fingers on the desk. "That's the missing piece right now. I'm betting Patterson has a handle on who did *that* dirty deed. Maybe I can squeeze it out of him on the show. From what I could dig up it was some sleazy German doctor who worked for Garnier and was seen sneaking around the team vehicles every day, a minor player in the scheme of things. Whatever."

"I'm surprised at you Katherine." He paused to change the subject, teasing her.

"About what?"

"Sex. Your story has to have sex, or at least romance. What about Jennifer? She's disappeared."

Katherine sighed. "Yeah. I really wanted to bring them together on the show. You know, she comes out from behind the curtain at just the right moment.... It doesn't work, Arnie. Besides, he didn't want any part of it."

"Dufour?"

"Right. Says he's lost touch with her and he won't do the interview if I bring it up." She leaned back in her chair and swung her feet onto the desk. She was satisfied that she had a great piece without the girl. Especially if she found Otto.

***

Kurt Dufour was nervous. He sat in the expanse of the limousine wondering if his agreement to appear on this kind of show was the right thing.

John Patterson sat opposite, leaning forward uncomfortably and looking out the window, probably thinking the same. His dark wool suit draped stiffly over his lean body, and the collar of his new dress shirt was at least one size too big, leaving a space at the neck that accentuated his look of discomfort. He wasn't used to wearing a suit and tie and it showed.

They were the only two on the ride from Greenwich to New York. Peter Dufour had declined the trip, making it obvious to Kurt that his father didn't think much of the show appearance.

242

Their instructions were to report to the network studio's green room where they would meet up with Otto Werner, just back from Australia, and Phil Sterling, the British commentator Kurt knew mostly by reputation and from a few brief interviews. There, they would be briefed on the show details before going on the air.

"How ya feelin, mate?" Patterson had turned from the window to his friend.

"Nervous." Kurt drummed his fingers on the armrest and continued looking out the window.

"Bloody should be. Sorry ya doin this?"

"Maybe."

They rode in silence for a few minutes, pretending to notice the early-winter landscape along the Hutchison River Parkway just over the New York line.

Patterson cleared his throat. "Maybe it's a good thing that ya go on TV. Ya know, make a clean breast of it. Folks need to see that ya all right, that ya 'aven't gone bonkers."

"Do you really think anybody cares?" Kurt stopped drumming his fingers and looked at his friend.

"Fucked if I know."

Patterson decided he better offer more. "You leadin' the Tour, then the crash. This is bloody fuckin' America, mate…it's a juicy story. Every bloke in America wants to 'ear this one out, no worries." He watched Kurt closely for reaction.

Kurt shook his head and said nothing. The whole thing reminded him of the trial about the girl six years earlier. Surely that would come up. And he recalled the story several years earlier about the Olympic skater who was attacked by her rival's hit man. He saw his life becoming a series of sensational headlines and he didn't like it. At least, Otto had made it back to New York and would appear on the show. There was some consolation in knowing that friends who believed in him would surround him.

They rode in silence again. Patterson watched his friend and thought about what had happened. At first, no one was sure he would recover his full memory and mental capacity and, once that had been assured, what would happen next.

Beyond that first ride back in Vermont, Kurt had shown little interest in getting back into cycling, despite frequent phone calls from Otto and visits from Patterson and other teammates. While at his parents' home in Greenwich, he had received thousands of cards, letters, and e-mails from cycling fans around the world encouraging his recovery, most with hopes that he would be back in the sport soon. And there were calls from a few agents, lesser known ones who would be willing to represent him, with the hope, of course, that he'd decide to race again.

But with little response from Kurt, the good wishes and the agents' calls had trailed off. The world marches to new news and Kurt's story would likely be relegated to periodic *where is he now* features.

He faced the first of these today. It was November and Katherine Anderson's new show about the scandal in sports was the perfect forum to air the conclusion of Kurt's unbelievable Tour de France saga. The world's biggest sporting event plagued by drug scandals, payoffs, and now even murder had people both shaking their heads and eagerly consuming the latest revelations. This would be Kurt's first public appearance since the crash in the tunnel and the first time the whole sordid mess would be fully revealed. The network had hyped the show unmercifully. Good ratings were guaranteed.

Anderson herself had convinced him to appear, assuring him that he needed this to put doubts about his recovery and nagging questions about his character to rest once and for all. She had promised that she would take the high road, at least with his role in the mess, and that his story would be straightforward and truthful, the best way to silence those who perhaps believed that he was somehow guilty of taking drugs and payoffs.

Kurt's decision to appear had not been easy. Since his memory had returned, he had felt an uneasiness about everything, especially his career as a cyclist and what he would do next. He had convinced himself that going on the show was a step toward closure…that his recovery was complete, that he was ready to move on.

But to what? He wasn't ready to answer that question, particularly in front of a national TV audience. To this point, he hadn't had any desire to race again. He hadn't been on a bike since that October ride in Vermont, and he didn't feel like saying maybe yes or maybe no. In fact, he suddenly didn't feel like talking about any of it. Not yet.

Patterson was watching him. He sensed the turmoil and leaned forward. This was his moment.

"Fuck 'er," he said.

"What?" Kurt blinked in amazement.

"I said, fuck 'er."

"Fuck who?"

"Fuck Katherine Anderson and fuck 'er bloody network, and fuck 'er new TV show." Patterson leaned back and, facing Kurt directly, started undoing his tie. He smiled wickedly.

"What are you doing?"

"Same thing you are, mate." He leaned over his shoulder and, without taking his eyes off Kurt, spoke to the driver. "Kennedy Airport, change in plans." He winked.

"Excuse me, sir?" The driver's eyes darted from his rearview mirror to the road in front of him.

"What...?" Kurt's question hung in the air. He wasn't sure how to finish it.

Patterson leaned to the driver and said something in his ear. The limo slowed, crossed into the right lane and then shot off at an exit marked *Whitestone Bridge, New York Airports.*

Patterson turned toward Kurt again. This time, his face was much closer to his. "Ya don't wanna be on that goddam show. Ya don't wanna sit there an' answer 'er goddam questions or tell 'er why ya agreed to accept a payoff then double-crossed the bloke...ya don't wanna try to explain why Leguerre's dead."

"You're goddam right I don't...." He started to smile. He knew Patterson too well. It was all planned out, down to the last detail. This would be good. Then he thought about the commitment.

"But we agreed to go on...I can't just bail out."

"No worries, mate. Otto's got it covered, and Berclaz is goin' on too...'e's more'n 'appy to stand for ya." He grinned and pulled two airline tickets out of his jacket pocket. He tossed one across.

Kurt opened the envelope and scanned the ticket, twice. He looked from it to his friend. "Melbourne?"

"'bout as far away as ya can get, mate. It's springtime there. We'll be stayin' on me old man's ranch."

"Jesus Christ, John." He thought for a moment. "I didn't pack anything...."

Of course Patterson expected this. "No worries. Got clothes and a toothbrush waitin' for ya. And a bike." He winked.

Kurt shook his head and said nothing. He knew he needed to get away, take some time to think. Being half way around the world was probably the best place to go and, with a trusted friend like Patterson, to sort things out. Besides, he liked the impulsiveness of it and the fact that he wouldn't have to put up with the probing questions.

He settled back in his seat and looked out the window at the depressing row houses packed along the Van Wyck Expressway. He wouldn't miss the States. Staying at home in Greenwich had become painful. Jennifer was as good as lost, and he wasn't ready to make decisions about his future. Not yet.

***

The studio set was sparse and dramatic. Katherine Anderson, the host, sat on a stool attached to a small table where she could place her notes and rest a hand-held microphone. A montage of huge floor-to-ceiling sports-action blow-ups formed the backdrop next to a giant TV screen over the host's shoulder that, when not showing video clips, displayed the *Sports Behind the Lines* logo. Four other stools, also with tables and microphones, were lined up next to her for her guests. Altogether, it had the look of part-media interview stage, part-sports bar, a paradox that was totally planned.

The show opening was her idea. They gave her rapid-fire cuts of dramatic moments set to fast tempo music: a slamming serve at Wimbledon, a dramatic goalkeeper save at the World Cup, and Kurt Dufour punching the sky as he crossed the line in Morzine. Freeze frame and the word *Controversy* stamped over the picture of Dufour, a change to ominous music and the rest of the title…*Sports Behind the Lines*. Then another montage, this time in grainy black and white of men conversing with their heads down, money changing hands, and athletes in locker rooms, arguing. The suggestion was clear and dramatic. Sport was not all great saves and glorious victories.

Katherine Anderson's hastily modified opening tease didn't reveal the anger she felt at being notified, just minutes before they were to go on, that Kurt Dufour was a no-show and that there were still missing pieces. The logo faded into a wide shot of her approaching the host position into a close-up as she began her delivery….

"Welcome to *Behind the Lines*, a sports show that pulls no punches and wades into the controversy and corruption that can be found in nearly every big-time sport. Tonight, we go inside soccer, tennis, and cycling to bring you some startling revelations. Our first guests are from this past summer's extremely controversial Tour de France, where French hero, Jacques Poulain, was a doper and the first Tour winner to be stripped of his title. British commentator, Phil Sterling, American team director Otto Werner, and cyclist Claude Berclaz will help me reveal the truth behind American Kurt Dufour's alleged drug-taking and payoff scandals that resulted in his near fatal crash on the race's last day and the bizarre deaths of two men connected with the event. And now, just revealed, Dufour's surprise disappearance.

We'll be right back….

THE END

247

The Author

David Chauner is recognized as one of America's most influential figures in the sport of professional cycling. As a cyclist, he competed nationally and internationally, medaled in the U.S. national championships six times and was a member of the 1968 and 1972 Olympic Teams. Since he retired from racing in 1975 he has remained actively engaged in the sport as a writer, commentator and professional event organizer. Chauner was inducted into the U.S. Bicycling Hall of Fame in 1998 for his many contributions to the sport and has published articles on cycling in all major cycling magazines as well as *Sports Illustrated* and the *New York Times*. Villard Books published his first book, the *Tour de France Complete Book of Cycling*, that he co-authored in 1990. He is currently the CEO of World Cycling League. High Road is his first novel.

For more information go to www.davidchauner.com

Made in the USA
Charleston, SC
07 February 2015